7-9-80

TURBO

by the same author

TURBO

Douglas Rutherford a Pseud.

James Douglas Rutherford McConnell

St. Martin's Press
New York

The events and characters in this story are entirely fictitious.

First published 1980 by
MACMILLAN LONDON LIMITED
4 Little Essex Street WC2R 3LF
and Basingstoke
Associated companies in Delhi, Dublin, Hong Kong,
Johannesburg, Lagos, Melbourne, New York, Singapore
and Tokyo

Library of Congress Cataloging in Publication Data

McConnell, James Douglas Rutherford, 1915-
   Turbo

   I. Title.
PZ3.M13495Tu   1980   [PR6025.A1697]   823'.914
ISBN 0-312-82332-0   80-14237

For the Russel family –
   Steve, Doris, Brian, Heather, Stephanie
   and Richard

2113917

The author wishes to thank those who gave help and advice in the preparation of this book:

SAAB (GB) Limited made their TURBO available for many thousands of miles of testing both in Britain and on the Continent.

The SAAB Centre, Middle Wallop, provided technical information and lent support in many other ways.

William Murray and the Clarendon Carriage Company advised on the Rolls-Royce Phantom II and Bob Vincent supplied details of the transponder.

CHAPTER 1

A hand shaking my shoulder broke the dream. I came awake still fighting to escape. The strap across my lap held me firmly in the seat. For a brief moment I was back in that Belfast cellar, waiting for the bucket of water that would waken me to another round of torment. Then I opened my eyes and the panic subsided.

'Adjust your seat to the upright position, please, sir,' the air hostess told me severely.

Tunis already! We'd been over the Alps when I nodded off, doped by the champagne I'd imbibed before and during lunch.

The passenger on my left was eyeing me curiously as I straightened my seat. Sunlight was slanting through the window beside me. The pilot was making his approach to El Aouina airport from the East. As he tipped his wing before levelling out for the run in he presented me with a marvellous view of the city of Tunis laid out below. The land-locked lagoon, bisected by the road leading to the port of La Goulette was dead calm. By contrast the sea beyond was flecked with white caps. The mountains behind Hammam Lif jutted purply-grey into the unbroken blue of the sky. The white villas of Carthage and Sidi-bou-Saïd slid past below. The aircraft made a sudden lurch earthwards. Moments later came the squishy bounce of the landing wheels hitting the runway – none too gently.

'Please remain in your seats till the aircraft has come to a complete standstill. And no smoking, please, till you are inside the airport buildings.'

As the Boeing slowed to taxiing speed I released myself from the seat belt, hauled my shoulder-bag from under the seat and stepped over the legs of the two passengers between me and the gangway. I was travelling light, for I intended to be on my way home again as soon as possible.

A glaring air hostess advanced on me as I tottered towards the exit. I sank into an empty seat just short of the doorway. When

7

it was opened I pushed past her and got down the steps ahead of the first-class passengers.

The heat of North Africa hit me at once and with it that strange acrid scent which pervades the whole Arab world. The suit which had seemed cool and light on a chilly May morning in England now felt far too hot.

In the long, austere airport building the immigration officer scanned the form I had filled out on the aircraft, and flicked over the pages of my passport.

'What is the nature of your business in Tunisia?'

'I've come to buy a car.'

'You have come from England to buy a car in Tunisia?'

He squinted at me suspiciously. As virtually all cars in Tunisia are of foreign manufacture his incredulity was not surprising.

'That's correct. It's a very old car. What we call vintage.'

'This I do not understand. Will you explain it more clearly, please?'

He had retained my passport and his eyes were registering my collar, tie, suit, shoes, shoulder-satchel. A small, self-important Frenchman who had been travelling first-class was jostling against my left elbow, breathing heavily to manifest his impatience.

I tried to explain as simply as possible. 'I am in the motor trade. Okay? But my company deals in used cars, not new ones. Some cars become more valuable as they get older. Right? Like antique furniture – or vintage wine.'

His fingers worried at the pages of my passport. He was young and slightly aggressive, a recent product of Tunisia's intensive educational programme. He probably regarded me as a prime example of the decadent West.

'You understand that you will need clearance from our customs authorities?'

'Yes.' I gratefully accepted my passport. 'I think that's all been taken care of.'

The Hertz desk was at the far end of the huge shed-like building. Within twenty minutes I was fixed up with a neat little Renault 17 TS. The delightful and very emancipated Tunisian girl who dealt with the hiring gave me expert directions on how to find my way through the capital and strike the road to Hammamet.

8

'Yes, we have an agency in Hammamet.' She answered my query with a smile and smoothed her dress against her hip with a well-manicured hand. 'You can return the car there if you desire and they will deal with the payments.'

The hour of the siesta had ended and traffic was thick as I navigated my way round the centre of the city, stopping now and again to check the two maps I'd bought before leaving the airport – one a street plan of Tunis, the other a road map of an area which included Cap Bon and Hammamet.

Traffic on the twenty-mile run was variegated and untidy. Gleaming Peugeots and chipper Berliet lorries mingled with rattletrap Citroen 2 CVs and delapidated trucks. Arabs swathed in off-white *cachabias* ambled on mules and donkeys along the soft verges under the irregular shade of dusty trees. Now and again I passed a family on the hoof, the lord and master at the head, his bowed wife trailing some distance behind, followed by a gaggle of children in brilliantly-coloured clothes.

The Rolls-Royce I had come to see was an unknown quantity. My instructions were to confirm that it was as good as described and get it back to London.

'If it's driveable, drive it,' Ritchie had told me. 'I'd rather you stayed with the car than trust it to a forwarding agent. We've had some unfortunate experiences freighting cars by sea. There's a boat runs regularly from Tunis to Naples which takes cars and passengers. From there you've only got about fifteen hundred miles of motorway.'

I'd been working for Ritchie nearly a year now. He ran a very profitable business in West Kensington. 'Automobiles of Quality' dealt almost exclusively with Rolls-Royce and Bentley. The advertisements in British and foreign motoring journals proclaimed: 'We will travel anywhere in the world to purchase a classic Rolls-Royce or Bentley.'

That 'we' was a little misleading. I was the one who did the travelling. When he had offered me the job Ritchie made it clear that I might be required to do a bit of trouble-shooting. He'd heard through a mutual friend that I'd had to get out of the Army and was looking around for a job. I'd had a good deal to do with helicopters and plenty of experience with armoured cars, so I knew my way round an engine. My main qualification,

9

however, was that I'd restored a Black Label Bentley with my own hands.

I took to Ritchie at once. He would have fitted better into the reign of Elizabeth I than of her namesake. At some time during a lurid career he had lost one eye. Rumour had it that he had served as a mercenary in the Congo and since then had been involved in a number of swashbuckling episodes.

'Yes, you might well wonder how I came to be a second-hand car dealer,' he'd said to me during that first interview. 'I admit it was a sort of retreat from active service but after I'd had some of my guts shot to hell my doctor advised a more sedentary life. I opted for this. There's good money in it, and as I am fascinated by these old cars I find the whole thing fairly convivial. Did you know that the auction record for an old Rolls is £80,000? I expect they'll be into six figures within a year.'

'Over £100,000?' I queried, not really believing a used car could fetch that amount.

He nodded, fixing his single blue eye on me. 'But make no mistake about it, this game can be quite rough. There aren't many old Rolls left to be discovered. The Indians have already banned the export of any more. Isn't it ironic that the symbol of the Raj has become a national heritage? That's why your Army background appealed to me more than experience in the motor trade. It's sometimes dicey going in and getting your Silver Ghost out of a country that's been turned upside down by a revolution.'

I'd had ample proof of how true that was during the ensuing year. It was extraordinary the places that Rolls-Royces had found their way to during the seventy-five years of the famous marque's existence. Ritchie had a mysterious intelligence which brought him information about limousines, open tourers, sedanca de villes lying forgotten in the stable blocks of abandoned palaces or in the garages of dispossessed millionaires.

The Tunisian assignment, however, looked a comparatively simple one. The information had reached us in the most banal way. Ritchie had spotted an advertisement in *The Observer*:

Rolls-Royce Phantom II 1929. Mileage 39,000.
Saab 900 1979. Mileage 3,274. At present in Tunisia.

Offers over £30,000 for the pair. Buyer to pay duties. Write to Mr Tenniel, Butt, Staveley & Butt, Lincoln's Inn Fields, London.

'Sounds like a firm of solicitors acting for executors.' Ritchie reached for the first volume of the London telephone directory. 'That mileage figure can't be genuine. God knows how many times the speedo's been round the clock. Still, it's worth a try.'

He found a number in the book and dialled it without hesitation. After a verbal passage at arms with some secretary he was soon talking to Mr Tenniel. When he put the 'phone down he grinned at me.

'You heard most of that. They're acting as executors for some old girl who's been living in Tunisia since the 1920's. He claims the mileage is genuine. That's why I offered him thirty-five grand sight unseen.'

'You're taking a chance, aren't you?'

'Can't lose.' Ritchie helped himself to one of the long thin cigars which he habitually smoked, lit up and leaned back in his spring-loaded desk chair. 'I made him a firm offer because I gather somebody else had been pussyfooting around.'

'What do you think it's worth?'

'Forty, fifty grand if it's as described. Maybe as much as sixty if there's more than one buyer who fancies it. The money is payable in the UK and he says they've got full clearance from the Tunisian authorities to export the car to England. I'm going to take a certified cheque round to him this afternoon just to clinch it. I want you, Patrick, to fly out to Tunis on the first available 'plane. Get your hands on that car before anyone else does.'

'What about the Saab? That's part of the deal, isn't it?'

'I'm not worried about the Saab. You may be able to flog it out there. Raise enough to pay for your trip. But if not, I don't mind writing it off.'

That had been thirty hours ago, and the cold drops of a rain storm had been beating against the office window. Long before I reached Hammamet I was sweating profusely and I knew that the back of my shirt was wet against the seat cushions.

The main street of the seaside town was dusty and littered with the droppings of creatures great and small. Some kind of market had taken place and the odour of animals hung in the air. Arabs wandered vaguely across the street, most of them cloaked in their long woollen robes, many of them barefoot. I noticed that the younger women went with uncovered faces in Western clothes, whilst most of the older ones clung to the all-enveloping traditional dress, holding their veils between their teeth. One Arab was driving three camels down the highway. Another was putting a pinioned goat into the boot of his car.

It took me a little time to find anyone who could understand my enquiry in French. In the end an oldish, bustling man wearing a dark blue suit and a red fez came to my rescue. It was hard to tell whether he was French or Arab.

'The Villa Céleste?' A blast of garlic hit me as he repeated the name, his face three inches from mine. There were deep wrinkles in his cheeks, where small colonies of bristles had survived the passage of a tired razor-blade. 'It is the Villa Céleste that you seek?'

I assured him that such was the case. He pointed towards the road leading south round the bay. 'It is between the road and the ˋsea. At three kilometres.'

'Thank you.'

He looked at me accusingly. 'But Madame de Sonis is dead, you know.'

'Yes, I did know. But there's somebody who's expecting me at the Villa.'

He stood in the roadway, watching me with narrowed eyes as I turned the Renault and headed in the direction he had indicated. All I knew about the person I was to meet at the Villa was her name, Mademoiselle Favel. She had been companion-secretary to the old lady and was staying on in the job long enough to wind up her employer's affairs. I pictured her as a middle-aged spinster with thick spectacles and wispy hair.

The sea was glinting on my left as I headed out into the country again. I had to sound my horn repeatedly at small carts which had got onto the wrong side of the road and at donkeys and mules which had wandered off the soft verges, unchecked by their dozing riders.

The entrance to the Villa Celeste was unmistakable. It broke

12

the line of a long, white-painted wall which bordered the road for several hundred yards. The heavy, iron gates were open, but as I turned in I had to brake. A furniture pantechnicon was just lumbering out. It bore French number-plates and the sign indicated a Paris firm of furniture removers.

When it had turned onto the road I drove in slowly. As I passed through the gates I glanced to left and right. A strip of twenty yards or so inside the wall had been cleared of undergrowth. Down the middle of the strip on either side ran a modern security fence about ten feet high. It was almost certainly electrified and to judge by its professional appearance probably comprised such sophisticated details as infra-red lighting, electronic sensors, micro-wave curtains and all the other features of a modern security system. I wondered what Madame de Sonis kept here that merited such defences.

Obviously the system was now inactive, for the wire-mesh gate in the inner fence was open and there was no one to check arrivals. I drove on up a sloping avenue bordered by a thick jungle of low, stunted trees. Then, after a couple of hundred yards, I emerged into an earthly paradise. The Villa had come into view, outlined against the sea and shaded by tall pine trees. Beyond it the ground dropped away steeply, but on this side it was surrounded by well-watered lawns, at the edges of which beds of dazzling flowers basked in the sun. There was no gardener in view, but in several places water sprinklers were showering moisture over the mown grass.

Gravel crunched under my tyres as a rove into a square space in front of what was obviously the main entrance to the Villa. The locked doors of the garage were on my left. In the centre of the forecourt stood the round structure of an ancient well, now covered by a circular wooden lid. Bougainvillaea tumbled from a verandah which ran round the outside of the low, dazzlingly white building.

As I got out of the car a faint breeze brought a scent of sea up from the beach. The only thing to break the silence was the swish of the gently rotating sprinklers. Despite its well-kept appearance the place had a deserted atmosphere, as if the pantechnicon had carried off the last of the occupants as well as the furniture. Curiosity took me to the garage doors. Somewhere behind them must be the Phantom II which I had come to collect, but they were firmly bolted and padlocked.

I rang the bell beside the front door at intervals for the next three minutes. Still nobody came. Standing there I had begun to catch the sound of dance music from the other side of the Villa. I moved round the corner of the house, keeping in the shade of the verandah. Now I could see the bay and the long beach curving round to the old fort of Hammamet. The white wall which surrounded the entire property, and the security fence inside it, separated the grounds from the beach. But within this defensive perimeter, in a hollow below the Villa, lay a kidney-shaped swimming pool. Its gently stirring waters were a brilliant blue. At one end of the pool a pergola of vines shaded a cluster of tables and chairs and a bar. The music was coming from in there somewhere.

Two women were lying on the warm paving-stones at the side of the pool letting the sun dry their gleaming bodies. One was dark and rather short, with a strong, well-emphasized body and dusky skin. The other was fair-haired, long-legged and slim but deliciously curved. Neither of them was wearing a bathing costume and they were both tanned all over, their bodies unmarked by disfiguring bikini-shaped white patches.

As I looked down the darker woman sat up and unscrewed the top of a bottle of suntan lotion. She began to massage it into the back of her reclining companion with a circular, finger-tip movement.

At that moment I heard the sound of a car engine at the other side of the house and the crunch of tyres on the gravel. Feeling at the same time frustrated and guilty, I spun round and moved back along the verandah. I came round the corner of the house just as a man slammed the door of a white Mercedes coupé and turned towards the front door.

He was slim and small, with a clipped black beard, a curved nose and the sharpest eyes I had seen for a long time. His light-grey suit was hand-tailored and he wore a tie even in this heat. I guessed his age to be in the early thirties, though the beard made it harder to tell. In one hand he carried a short cane, to the end of which was attached a tuft of long, black hair. I guessed it was a device for discouraging flies.

14

His eyes veered towards me and he gave me a quick, assessing inspection.

'Good evening, sir,' he said in English. 'Am I speaking to Mister Malone?'

'Yes.'

The registration number of my Renault had told him little. Presumably the garlic breather with the fez had wasted little time in putting the word about that a foreigner had been asking for the Villa Celeste.

We moved towards each other and he gave a stiff little bow. 'I am Aziz Cheloui. Lawyer of the late Madame de Sonis.'

I took the extended hand. The palm was hard and dry, the broad gold ring warm against my flesh. 'We've been dealing with Butt, Staveley & Butt in London. We understood that they were handling her estate.'

'That is correct, yes.' Cheloui smiled confidently, 'Most of Madame's bequests are to beneficiaries in England. I am in constant touch with Mr Tenniel.' He glanced towards the front door. 'Miss Favel should be here. You have sounded the bell?'

'Yes. There was no answer. I was just about to see if I could find anyone.'

'We were not sure when to expect you.' Cheloui put his finger on the bell-push and kept it there. We could hear the bell ringing somewhere inside the house. 'My wife is here somewhere. She stayed to help Miss Favel with the furniture-removal people from Paris. Perhaps they have gone down to the pool for a swim.'

I studied him furtively. It was difficult to match him with either of the sensuous figures I had seen beside the pool.

'Fatima has must go into town,' he muttered with ungrammatic disapproval. 'Since Madame is dead everything is at fours and fives.'

He walked to his car, reached inside and gave a series of long blasts on his horn. A stork took off from the roof in alarm and flapped towards the pine trees.

'Even Ahmed has disappeared. Come. Let us see if they are at the pool.'

We strolled round the house, our feet sinking into the lush Bermuda grass.

'You have come for the cars, is it not? Mr Tenniel has confirmed that payment is agreed. At this end we have arranged everything for their transhipment.'

'Is the Rolls driveable? If it is I may take it back myself.'

'Driveable?' Cheloui laughed. 'It is as a new car. Since Monsieur de Sonis is dead it is scarcely if it has been used. But the old Ahmed, he cherishes it as a child and exercises it as carefully as a stallion at stud.'

We came to the top of a flight of blancoed steps. The two women had heard the horn and were coming up them, breathless and laughing. Both had drawn bathing wraps round themselves and the material was clinging to their slightly moist bodies. At close range I could see that the dark woman was considerably older than the other. Her face was heavier and more lined. The younger woman seemed to be about twenty-two or -three. I had to command my eyes not to roam and to concentrate on her face. It was alive and intelligent rather than beautiful, but the mouth and eyes were very attractive.

I was still wondering where she fitted into the cast when Cheloui introduced her as Miss Favel. As we shook hands she gave me a veiled look and I felt that I was being very shrewdly summed up. I was trying hard not to let my expression betray me, but something about her smile made me wonder if she'd guessed that I had been looking down from the verandah.

Cheloui appeared to have the run of the house, even though most of the rooms had been stripped of their furniture. While the women went off to dress he took me into an air-conditioned sun-lounge where some garden chairs and tables still survived.

As we sipped non-alcoholic drinks he told me that Monsieur de Sonis had been a Frenchman who had made a fortune exporting olive oil and wine from North Africa to Europe. He had married an English girl in the 1920's and soon after that retired to Hammamet, where he bought five acres of land and built the Villa Celeste. He had died just before the Second World War. His widow sat it out at the Villa for another forty years, surviving the German Occupation of 1940–2 and the social upheaval which had followed the departure of the French in the 1950's.

'She was a woman of a personality – extraordinary!' Cheloui exclaimed. 'Very courageous. Very strong of will. That earned her the respect of the Arabs. In the later years, alas, she became obsessed with the idea that she was surrounded by enemies who wanted only to kill her. She brought in an English firm of security consultants and this propriety was surrounded by every protective device known to the science. An obsession!'

'Did she have no issue?'

'Please?'

'Were there any children? I mean, who are her heirs?'

'No.' Cheloui answered my first question. 'The marriage was childless. Her share of the estate is divided up between a number of cousins in England. The bulk of her husband's fortune is tied up – you say that? – here in Tunisia.'

'You don't think there will be any snags about getting the Rolls out of Tunisia?'

Cheloui shook his head. 'There is no problem. I have arranged all that. Monsieur de Sonis bequeathed the car to her at his death, so it is part of her personal estate.'

We turned as the women came into the room. Madame Cheloui had put on a white costume which could only have come from a Paris couturier. Mademoiselle Favel was wearing a light-blue dress pinched at the waist by a scarlet belt.

As Cheloui poured out two more glasses of the iced drink, I caught the secretary's eye. It was clear that she resented the way in which the lawyer had taken the duties of host upon himself. I moved over towards her, formulating a polite French phrase in my mind.

'*Vous êtes la secrétaire de Madame de Sonis depuis longtemps?*'

She smiled. '*Depuis cinq ans, monsieur.* But you don't have to talk to me in French. I speak English too.'

'Romy is a polyglot,' Cheloui said over his shoulder. 'She speaks not only French and English perfectly but also German and Arabic.'

'That's not bad,' I said, feeling very foolish about my attempt at French conversation. 'How did you – ?'

'It was easy for me.' The smile Romy Favel gave me transformed her rather studious expression. 'My mother was a Tunisian – an Arab – and my father was French.' She made the statement with a defiant kind of pride, and I wondered which of her parents she was secretly ashamed of. 'My father sent me to school in France, but I went to secretarial college in England. And for a time I was *au pair* in a German family.'

Despite Cheloui's boast on her behalf her English was not perfect. She spoke with a certain hesitation and a slight accent which I found charming. She may have guessed that I was wondering how an attractive young woman with such dazzling qualifications had buried herself away with an old woman of eighty.

'Madame de Sonis,' she explained, 'was a very successful novelist. She has begun to write soon after her husband's death. She has had more than twenty novels published in England and America.'

'I suppose I ought to have heard of her but I'm afraid – '

'Oh, she wrote under a nom de plume. Her pen name was Virginia Somerset.'

'Yes, that does vaguely ring a bell. Were they – er – romantic novels?'

'No. Crime,' Romy said, laughing. 'Usually of a very blood-thirsty nature.'

'Oh.' I took refuge in my glass of chilled lemon juice. 'I suppose she needed someone to type them for her.'

'Yes. But there was always much research to be done and I was travelling often for her.'

She looked over and saw me watching her lips. Her English was correct and pronounced very distinctly, with emphasis on syllables which in English are often slurred.

'I think that Madame de Sonis became a victim of her own imagination,' Cheloui remarked. 'She was in her old age surrounded by her own plots. The criminals whom she had invented became for her as real beings and came back to threaten her here.'

Madame Cheloui nodded agreement. She had not spoken since our introduction. I wondered whether she understood English. When she was not nodding approval of her husband's comments she was glancing secretively towards Mademoiselle Favel. There was a curious tenseness about these people and it was not due to the strange emptiness of the vast Villa.

'About the cars,' I said, turning to Romy. 'I was told that you were the person I had to contact. Is that correct?'

'Yes.' She shot a quick look towards Cheloui. 'I am occupying myself with all the things at the Villa of which we have to dispose. Aziz has very kindly been helping me with complicated things like exchange controls and export licences – '

Cheloui shrugged in self-deprecation. 'Is my job.' He flashed a smile, exposing brilliant white teeth. 'Mr Malone said he might drive the Rolls-Royce back to England himself – '

'What about the Saab?' Madesmoiselle Favel cut in. 'That's been bought as well. Hasn't it?'

'Well – ,' I hedged. 'There's not much doubt about the Rolls but I haven't actually had a chance to see the cars yet.'

There was a short silence. They had instantly picked up the dubious tone in my voice. Ritchie had entered a little *caveat*: 'On the understanding that the cars are as described.' I had reminded them that this deal still had to be clinched.

Cheloui finished his glass and put it down with controlled patience.

'Of course Mr Malone must see the cars, my dear. Where is Ahmed, do you know? There was no sign of him when I arrived.'

'He must be near. I have warned him somebody might be arriving this evening to collect the Rolls. Let us go and see if we can find him.'

We walked down a corridor and through the broad front hall.

'You have made arrangements for a hotel?' Cheloui asked me. 'It is very hard to secure a room for a single night. We have several excellent hotels here in Hammamet but they are booked up at this time of year by the packet tours.'

'Well, as a matter of fact I haven't actually – '

'Ahmed is back!' Romy had gone ahead to open the glass front door. 'The garage doors are open.'

As we walked across the gravelled space in front of the house I could see the proud frontal of a Rolls in the shadows of the garage. A diminutive man was gently polishing the stainless steel of the radiator with a soft cloth. At the sound of our footsteps he turned. He was wearing the full livery of a London chauffeur of the 1920's – leather leggings, breeches, high-buttoning jacket, peaked cap and gloves. In this heat he must have been sweltering, but there was not a drop of perspiration on his lined old face.

Cheloui spoke a few words of Arabic to him. In his own language the tone of his voice was quite different. It sounded harsh

19

and aggressive. I guessed he was explaining who I was and what I'd come for. The old man's eyes flickered towards me, then veered away, as if I was some unclean thing which it was forbidden to look on. He turned and slowly, with great dignity, went to the door on the driver's side, opened it and climbed into the driving seat. He switched on, and, as sometimes happens with a perfectly tuned Rolls of this age, the engine immediately fired. The faint murmur of the engine and the hiss of the air intake were scarcely audible. I heard the crisp snick of first gear going in – one of the most sensually satisfying noises in the world of machinery. The big car glided forward, its dark green paintwork gleaming in the sunlight.

Ahmed stopped the car when its rear was clear of the doors. I knew at once that Ritchie's instinct had been right. This one was going to break the auctioneers' records.

She was a short-chassis Phantom II Continental, fitted with a Sedanca de Ville body. The rear of the coachwork was adorned with hand-painted simulated canework. The massive front mudguards swept down to broad running-boards, recessed to carry the twin spare wheels mounted on them. A hinged glass sun-vizor projected out over the rather shallow windscreen and a chrome spot lamp by the driver's door also served as a rear-view mirror. Needless to say, there were no bumpers, though the springs projected aggressively at the forward end, swaddled in leather oil-retaining gaiters. The old man had slid back the front section of the roof, which had disappeared into its recess.

I moved round beside him to gaze at the controls. He looked diminutive behind the enormous steering wheel, which carried the levers for the hand throttle and the advance and retard mechanism. The dashboard and woodwork were of beautifully grained Circassian walnut. The main dials were enclosed in a heart-shaped panel in the centre. The gear and brake levers were at the driver's right side. Ahmed leant back and opened the door to the rear compartment. It was like a small drawing-room, very private and almost totally enclosed. The windows and doors were like those of a miniature railway train. The upholstery was of fawn moquette, the deep pile carpets matching in colour. In the recess on each side were an ashtray, twin scent bottles and a small mirror. A glass division separated the occupants of this princely chamber from the driver, and damask curtains screened them from the stare of common folk.

Ahmed left the engine running and with practised agility clambered out. He moved to the long bonnet, unfastened the catches and lifted one side.

'Fantastic,' I murmured. All I could do was stare at the immaculately clean engine with its brightly polished brass pipes and gleaming metalwork. The top of the cylinder head was level with my eyes. The sound of the gently turning engine was like distant music. It was impossible to imagine that the car had been in better condition on the day when it had been delivered.

'You want to check it over, give it a test drive?' Cheloui asked, with a callous practicality which I found revolting.

'There's no need. I'm perfectly satisfied.'

I turned towards Ahmed, wondering how I could find words to congratulate him on the way he had maintained this magnificent car in such perfect condition. Just for a second he met my eye and I realized that of all these people I was the only one who knew what was going on in the old man's mind. I sensed without being told that he had been this car's keeper since the day it had arrived. He must have been a young man then, smart enough to get the plum job as chauffeur at the Villa Celeste. Between him and the car there had grown up an extraordinary affinity. It had been literally his *raison d'être*. When Monsieur de Sonis had died that purpose had continued. Even when the old lady had gone the Rolls remained. Now a stranger had come to take it away and for Ahmed that was the ending of life.

It would have been less cruel if I'd put a cord round his neck and strangled him slowly.

Romy's voice broke into my thoughts.

'Come and look at the Saab. I can give you a demonstration.'

'I'm not sure that I —'

'Come,' she repeated, moving towards the second car in the garage, her eyes willing me to follow her.

'I have a feeling Mr Malone is not very interested in the other car, my dear,' Cheloui called out.

It was this officious intervention that decided me.

'I might as well have a look at it,' I told him, and followed Romy.

She had slid into the driver's seat before I reached the car. She leaned over to push open the door on my side. As I settled in my seat and slammed my door she started up the engine and, using the mirrors only, reversed out into the gravelled patio.

'Jesus,' I exclaimed. 'This is a Turbo!'

She stopped the car, turned to me and spoke very quickly and earnestly.

'Listen! Try to stay behind when they go. If that does not work come back to see me somehow. I have to talk to you alone.'

It was not easy to shake off the Chelouis, who seemed ready to take on the role of Romy's bodyguards, protecting her from the dangers of being left alone with a British car dealer. Cheloui wanted to conduct me personally to the Hotel Miramar, where the manager was a client of his. In the end I told them firmly that I had some private business that I must discuss with Mademoiselle Favel. Cheloui looked daggers. He had guessed that something had passed between Romy and me during the moment when we'd been alone in the car.

'Thank God for that,' Romy said, as the Mercedes departed down the avenue in a swirl of angry dust. 'They did not want to leave you here with me alone.'

'Why on earth not?'

'Come inside and I will explain it to you. I need a drink. Something stronger than Aziz gave to us.'

At the doorway she turned back. Ahmed was standing beside the Rolls, a hand resting on one of the massive front mudguards.

'*Ahmed. Tu peux garer les voitures.*'

Back in the sun-lounge with its gaudy garden chairs and tables she poured herself a Scotch on ice-cubes and, when I nodded in reply to her enquiring glance, did the same for me. She sat down in one of the chairs and crossed her brown legs. It was extraordinary how her manner and attitude had changed now that she was no longer in the presence of the Tunisian couple.

'You are wondering about what I said in the car.'

I nodded without comment.

'I need your help to get away from here.' She made the statement sound dramatic, tossing her long hair back with a shake of her head which I soon learned was a characteristic gesture. 'There

22

is nothing more for me to do. The cars are the last things to go. The new owner has agreed to purchase all the modern furniture that is left.'

'What's to stop you leaving?'

'The Chelouis. They will find some way to stop me. That is why I need someone to help me – an ally. When I saw you I thought at once that you were the sort of person who could – '

She broke off and bit her lip. It was a sign of returning tension. My instinct that I could easily be dragged into some complex problem of personalities had not been mistaken.

'I'm not sure that I'm the person to help you.' I watched the whisky swirl round the ice-cubes in my glass. 'It sounds more like a personal thing, something you've got to overcome in your own mind.'

'It is more than that!' she exclaimed angrily, irritated by a comment which might have sounded patronizing. She was holding my eyes, an intense expression on her face. 'Madame de Sonis's death was not natural.'

Startled, I put my glass down on the chair-side table.

'She was convinced that someone was trying to kill her.' Romy's deep blue eyes were still fixed on me. 'And I do not believe her fears were purely imaginary. That is why we bought the bullet-proof Saab. She was too frightened to go out in the Rolls-Royce.'

'It's bullet-proof? A bullet-proof Turbo?'

'Yes. It came direct from Sweden. You cannot tell that it is any different from an ordinary car unless you examine it closely. I doubt if even Aziz knows, and of course old Ahmed is only interested in the Rolls. It was always me who drove her in the Saab.'

I stood up and walked to the window which overlooked the slope on the seaward side of the house. The water of the swimming pool was still stirring gently, though the heat had already dried the marks of wet feet on the paving stones. Beyond the wall, on the beach, a cowled Arab was leading a pair of camels upon which a couple of dumpy female tourists swayed perilously.

'Have you told Cheloui about your suspicions?'

'My God, no! He is the last person whom I would trust. He is quite capable to have put pressure on the police doctor to sign

23

the death certificate. These professional people are as thick as thieves here in Hammamet.'

'He seems almost more French than Arab.'

'That is a pose. He was trained in France but he is very anti the West. If Gadaffi ever takes over Tunisia he would be one of the first to welcome him.'

I turned away from the window and moved round till I could see her face again.

'His wife's rather a mysterious person.' I suggested. 'She hardly spoke a word.'

'In Cheloui's presence she is submissive, silent. But when we are alone together it is quite different. She is a wonderful woman, very nice. It will be hard for me to break away from her, but I must.'

She reached for a packet of Gauloises Longues on the table and lit up with nervous movements. When she'd inhaled deeply she swivelled round in the chair and looked up at me. I sensed that some kind of appeal was coming and felt embarrassed in advance. It was a new experience to be talked to like this by a woman I'd only just met. I could only conclude that years of living alone with a slightly unbalanced and very old woman had begun to affect her. But her next question caught me by surprise.

'You will take the Saab, won't you?'

'The Saab?' This was an abrupt change of subject, but I welcomed the return to more practical matters. I knew Saab were marketing a bullet-proof car from an article I saw in their house magazine, but this was the first one I'd come across. 'Well, it is a more interesting proposition than I'd thought. What I expect I'll do is drive the Rolls back myself and have the Saab sent back by sea.'

She got up and went to stub out her partly-smoked cigarette. She spoke with her back still towards me.

'I have a better idea than that.'

'Oh?'

'Let me come with you. I am familiar with the Saab. And if you are going to drive the Rolls across Europe you might be glad to have another car in attendance.'

I covered my hesitation by reaching for the glass and drinking some more of Madame de Sonis's malt whisky. It was true that she had suggested a neat solution to the problem of getting the Saab back to England – there were strong arguments in favour of having an accompanying car just in case Ahmed had done more polishing than greasing. But I was not happy about having this brittle young woman in tow.

'I don't know,' I hedged. 'I'll have to contact my partner. We might decide to garage the car here in Tunisia until we find a buyer and ship it direct to the country concerned.'

I finished the glass and set it down. She had turned and was watching my face. Her expression was indictive not so much of disappointment as of despair. I had to tell myself not to be weak. More than once in the past I'd let the appeal in a woman's eyes get the better of my judgment and lived to regret it bitterly.

'Now, I really must go and see about a hotel. Cheloui mentioned the Miramar. Do you think – ?'

'You'll never get in,' she told me, with an impatient shake of her head. 'The package tour operators take every room.'

'Perhaps in Hammamet – '

'If you enjoy the company of fleas and bed-bugs there's a *hotel de passe* in the main street but I warn you there will be a continual *va-et-vient* during the night.'

'In that case I suppose I'll have to go back to – '

'You'd much better stay here,' she said with forced casualness. 'The removers only took away the antiques. The guest suite is still furnished and I can soon make up a bed for you.'

I needed no telling that this invitation owed nothing to my personal charms. She was quite simply afraid of being left alone in this empty, echoing house.

'All right,' I agreed. 'But strictly on the understanding that you let me take you out to dinner somewhere.'

'There is no need for that. Fatima has left plenty of food in the kitchen and there   still some very good wine to be drunk. And I am a not bad cook.'

She was suddenly quite different and I realized that I'd lifted an enormous weight from her mind. As I unpacked my few things in the luxurious guest suite I wondered if she knew more about the death of Madame de Sonis then she had told me. If so, I could sympathize with her nervousness. The perimeter of security defences was not exactly reassuring and the stripped reception rooms harboured suggestive echoes. It was all too easy to feel a shadow of menace hanging over the Villa Celeste.

I stood about in the kitchen, drinking the familiar Gordon's and Noilly Prat, while she expertly drummed up a meal. I didn't know whether she was putting on a deliberate display of provocativeness or whether the whole thing was unconscious. As she stooped to put plates in the oven, leaned over the wide table to smooth a cloth or stood on tiptoe to reach glasses down from a high shelf, the material of her dress rounded the form of her body. And yet I was not tempted to lay even a finger on her. That scene I had witnessed at the side of the swimming pool kept intruding itself into my mind.

Later, as I lay in the big double bed of the guest suite, full of succulent steak and vintage Burgundy, I listened to the chorus of cicadas in the trees outside and wondered what I'd let myself in for this time. For while I had been drinking the Fine de Thibar which she gave me after my coffee I had agreed to her suggestion that we should take the two cars back to England together. Only then did I become sure that she had planned it all in advance. There was a regular service between Tunis and Naples and she had already reserved space on the boat which sailed the following evening.

CHAPTER 2

'Look, there's Vesuvius.' I pointed across the bay at the chopped-off cone of the mountain rising behind the russet ruins of Pompeii and the white modern houses of Sorrento. 'And that island further to the right is Capri.'

'But it is a so small mountain!' Romy answered reproachfully. 'And I thought it had a plume of smoke trailing from the top.'

'You've been looking at old prints. The last time it erupted was during World War II and since then there has been no smoke.'

The crossing from Tunis had taken fifteen hours and now, at eight in the morning, we had come up on deck to find the ship steaming into the breath-taking bay of Naples, trailing a white wake. Already the Villa Celeste and its strangely disquieting atmosphere seemed a long way behind us.

Cheloui had not seemed unduly surprised when he had arrived at the Villa the morning after my arrival to find Romy and me just finishing the breakfast which Fatima had served for us on the verandah. He contented himself with giving me a dry, worldly-wise look.

Romy told him that I had agreed to take both cars back to England and that she was going to come with me and drive the Saab. She stood beside me to make the announcement as if she wanted to convey to Cheloui that she was no longer alone, that now she had an ally.

'There's nothing more I can do here,' she told him rather defiantly. 'I can get all my things into the Saab. Fatima can have any food that's left and it'll be easier for you to dispose of the remaining furniture if I'm not living here.'

Cheloui took it equably, though I could tell from his sharp little eyes that his brain was adjusting rapidly to the new situation.

'That seems to be an excellent solution.' He nodded, his gaze moving from Romy's face to mine and back again. 'If there are some loose ends I can tie them. I am sure that if Madame were able to communicate she would want to thank you for your devotion and loyalty, my dear.'

Had there been irony in that remark? I thought I had detected an undeclared hostility in the look that flashed between them, but before Romy could say anything Fatima came waddling along the corridor from the direction of the tradesmen's entrance. She was gabbling hysterically in Arabic.

Cheloui listened, then calmed her and sent her back to the kitchen.

'What was all that about?' All I'd been able to make out was the name of Ahmed which had been used about twenty times in Fatima's recital.

'It seems that Ahmed has vanished,' Cheloui said thoughtfully. 'He is not in his hut. She says he has left everything folded and tidy as if he was going away for a long time, with his chauffeur's livery laid out ceremonially on the bed.'

'It does not surprise me.' Romy shook her head. 'It would have broken his heart to see someone else drive the Rolls away. Think of it. Fifty years he has cared for that car. Nearly double my lifetime.'

Now that Romy had broken the news of her departure to Cheloui and seen him accept the situation with such good humour she did not seem to mind being left alone with him. When they went into what had been the office to make their final arrangements I went out to the garage to check that the cars were fully fuelled and ready for the drive across Europe. The Rolls only needed a few gallons of petrol and when I drove it into Hammamet to fill the tank her behaviour on the road convinced me that the mechanical side of the vehicle was in as good condition as the bodywork. According to Romy it had hardly been used these last five years. A run across Europe on well-surfaced roads could do it nothing but good.

The Saab was a most unusual vehicle. I'd had some experience of the turbocharged version of the fuel injected engine and knew that it boosted performance quite dramatically. What I wanted to find out was how much weight the bullet-proofing added and how this would affect performance. The first difference from a standard car which I noticed was that the windows were fixed and could not be wound down. Closer inspection revealed that, in common with the windscreen and rear window, they were fitted with inch-thick panels of glass or transparent plastic.

I found the instruction book and service record in the glove pocket and with it a specification in English of the conversion which had been carried out to make the car bullet-resistant. The thickness of armour plating supplied was sufficient to resist fire from powerful hand-guns such as the .9 mm Browning Parabellum and the .9 mm Luger, rather than the higher velocity rifles like the 7.62 NATO rifle or the 5.56 Armalite. Armour steel of 2 mm thickness had been fitted to the sides, roof, rear seat-backs and front bulkhead. The floor area was similarly protected against blast from grenades or small bombs. As the windows would not open, an intercommunicating system linked an unobtrusive microphone on the window panel with an interior speaker. An air-conditioning system, powered by the heavy-duty battery, compensated for the lack of fresh air. The springs had been uprated to carry the extra weight and the tyres were fitted with Tyron run-flat safety bands, so that a driver could power out of trouble if his tyres were burst by fire. An added refinement was the Explosafe fuel tank, which could not blow up.

I reflected that Madame de Sonis's persecution complex must have been very strong indeed to make her seek the kind of protection which could only be needed by targets for terrorists. It had cost her a cool £50,000, and had added over fifty per cent to the weight of the car. Ritchie was getting a double bargain here. Obviously Mr Tenniel was not aware of the special features of his late client's 'second' car. In fact, to a casual observer it looked like a normal car, for the trimming had been skillfully replaced to conceal the modifications and a vinyl roof had been added as an additional cosmetic.

Rather than trust the local filling station I decided to run in to Tunis with it and have all the levels checked at a competent garage. I was surprised at how little the performance was affected by the extra weight. Acceleration, of course, was not so fierce as with the standard model but once the car was rolling the turbocharger quickly came in to punch the heavy vehicle from pottering speeds to really high speeds.

The morning had ended by the time I returned. Cheloui had made his farewells and departed. I never found out whether

Romy had seen Madame Cheloui again. As the larder had already been cleared by the eager Fatima, I took Romy to lunch at the nearby Miramar Hotel and then, after sending off a cable to tell Ritchie what I was doing, I helped her to pack her belongings into the Saab.

When at last we moved off in procession down the avenue there was only the weeping Fatima to wave us goodbye.

The drive to Tunis and through the city to La Goulette was hair-raising. I let Romy go ahead of me in the Saab to open a passage for the Rolls and was thankful that I was not having to do this alone. The population rushed to the roadside to watch the great car pass and our progress was accompanied by a hubbub of shouting, cheering and laughing Arabs. Small boys ran along beside the Rolls and, whenever it was checked, tried to climb onto the running-boards. One driver of a Citroën coming the other way was so astonished by the sight of the Phantom II that he crashed his car into a tree.

The atmosphere of a ship, even on a one-night crossing, favours confidences, and I had learned a little more about Romy that night as we walked round the deck before going down to our respective cabins. Though she was as much a Tunisian Arab as French her outlook was predominantly what she called 'Westernized'. She was an only child and had suffered the instability of a constantly changing home background.

'I was studying for my *Baccalauréat* at a *Lycée* in Paris when both my parents were killed in an air accident. Of course, that affected my examinations and as a result I never went to University, where I wanted to study English. But perhaps it was a good thing, because I decided to do a year's secretarial course at Winkfield Place in England instead.'

'What did you do about a home with both your parents dead?'

'Well, Winkfield was residential and I had an aunt in Paris who looked after me in the holidays. But we did not get on and as soon as I had completed my course I took a job as a sort of *au pair* secretary in Germany. It was the only way I could get my independence. But I've always had secret literary ambitions and when I was appointed to the post with Madame de Sonis I just could not believe my good luck.'

Her fluency in English was returning. She was still talking rather formally but with less hesitation. I hoped she would not lose that slight suggestion of a French accent which matched her chic style of dressing so well.

'But it is of me we have been talking all the time. What about you? What is your life story?'

I went to the rail and leaned on it, looking out over the calm sea through which the ship was swishing. She came and put her elbows on the rail beside me.

'A series of episodes more than a story. Usually ending pretty disastrously.'

'Are you married?'

'That was one of the disasters.'

She turned her head to look at my profile.

'I can't believe that it was your fault.' Her voice sounded sincere but when she spoke again I had an uncomfortable feeling that she was reciting a prepared speech. I went on staring at the dark water. 'You don't realize how grateful I am to you for letting me come with you. It was asking a lot, I know, but the moment I saw you I knew you were a strong as well as a kind person – and that is what I needed to free myself from the trap I was in.'

This kind of conversation was threatening my resolve to regard her as no more than a second driver and keep her at a distance from the emotional point of view. I pretended to shiver and turned away from the rail.

'That's quite a chilly wind. I think I'm going to get some sleep. We have a long drive ahead of us tomorrow.'

She had put a hand on my arm to stop me going.

'There is something I must tell you. I was not speaking the truth last night – about the death of Madame de Sonis.'

She was looking at me in an irresistibly appealing way, with a curious blend of trustfulness and guilt. I was sure she was going to unload some particularly intimate confidence onto me, but there was no way I could dodge it.

'Not telling the truth?'

'No. It was I who killed her. No, please do not say anything till you have heard me. I did not tell you that a month ago she learnt that she had terminal cancer. She took it very badly. That was one thing all her security fences and armour-plated cars could not keep out. She could not endure to face the prospect of pain, or hospitalization in Tunis. She begged me to get her something which would enable her to end her own life when she could stand it no longer. In Tunisia that is not difficult. Now you understand why I had to get away. If Cheloui found out about it he could have me convicted of murder.'

'But no court would – '

Her hand tightened on my arm. 'I knew you would understand. But please – . Never speak of it again. It is something I have to forget.'

Now, as we stood at the rail watching the coast come closer, the problems ahead of us were purely practical. I hoped we would be cleared through customs quickly and in the north of Italy by nightfall.

A loudspeaker behind us crackled out an announcement in French and Italian.

'We'd better get down to the cars.' Romy was having to hold her hair back to stop the off-shore wind from blowing it across her face. I wanted to say something to make up for the curt way I had finished off our conversation the night before, but I could not think of the right words.

'You'll be off before me,' I said. 'You've got all the documents for the Saab, haven't you? We'll rendezvous just beyond the customs area.'

We had to wait in our cars for a long time before the crew, with much activity and shouting, released all the heavy vehicles from the chains which had been holding them to the deck and got the drawbridge into position at the front of the vessel. The Rolls and Saab were in the first line to be signalled forward, but as I approached the ramp an impatient Italian driver cut in front of me. Rather than challenge him with the precious Phantom, I gave way and then, of course, I lost my place in the queue. In the end I was half a dozen cars behind Romy as we all waited our turn to move into the customs shed.

The sun was shining out of a blue Neapolitan sky and I had pulled back the sliding panel over the front seats. By contrast, the interior of the shed seemed dark and it took me a moment to

32

readjust my eyes. The long bonnet stretching ahead of me nearly bumped the stomach of a customs officer who was standing in my path, holding up a clipboard. I halted, while he stood back from the Rolls, and made a show of checking a list on his board.

Then he signalled me to pull out of the queue and drive towards a separate bay at the extreme edge of the shed. It was equipped with a special ramp, onto which a car could be driven so that its underside was exposed. Alongside was a small cabin, presumably for body searches. A team of four uniformed men stood waiting. All of them wore belts carrying holstered automatics. One was holding the leash of a large Alsatian which sat obediently at his feet.

Obviously the Rolls had been singled out for the full treatment. I hoped it was because of the Italians' passionate interest in cars. I was soon disenchanted.

The senior officer, who flaunted a cut-throat moustache, stepped forward and indicated the spot on the ramp where I was to stop. I turned the master switch to the OFF position and then some instinct made me remove the Yale key from its slot. The Rolls was, of course, fitted with Sir Henry Royce's ingenious switch. If the key was removed the master switch was turned off and the car was effectively immobilised. I slid the key into the fob pocket under my belt, pulled back the long hand-brake lever and tried to put on my most co-operative expression.

The officer came round beside me and nodded curtly.

'*Il passaporte, per favore.*'

I had laid my passport ready on the seat beside me. I picked it up and handed it to him. He examined it carefully, slowly turning the pages and comparing me with the photograph.

'You are British?' he asked in English.

'*Si* – I mean, yes.'

'This – very old car.'

'Yes,' I said proudly. 'Fifty years, in fact.'

'Fifty years?' He whistled and stepped back to survey the Rolls again. Just for the moment his officious hostility had softened. '*Come mai*? She is like a new! But Rolls-Royce is English manufacture. This car is plated from Tunisia.'

'It has been in Tunisia since it was new. The owner has died and my company have bought the car. I'm taking it back to

England by road. It's only in transit through Italy. All the papers are here.'

I handed him the folder of documents which Romy had procured for the car's transportation. He took them to a high desk and began to check them with the help of one of his aides. The man holding the Alsatian stooped to tickle its ears and it looked up directly into his eyes. The fourth officer was prowling round the rear of the car. He caught sight of his own reflection in the gleaming paintwork, took his cap off and pushed a tuft of hair back under it.

The officer was coming back with the folder. He handed it to me with a nod and I breathed a sigh of relief. Ritchie had warned me that if I came back through southern Italy I might have to pay a handsome bribe, most of which would probably find its way into the hands of the Camorra, the Calabrian version of the Mafia.

'All in order?' I took the folder and replaced it in the briefcase beside me.

'The papers are in order, yes. You have anything to declare?'

I had been waiting for that question. As I was in charge of such a valuable property as the Phantom II I was certainly not going to fool about with contraband, even on the smallest scale.

'No. I shall buy my allowance of drink and cigarettes on the cross-channel ferry. All I have is my personal things in that small bag.'

'You have nothing else to declare?'

'No.'

'You are carrying no merchandise of any kind?'

'Merchandise? No, definitely not.'

He nodded again and I was about to reach for the switch when he said: 'Will you please to come out of the car. Leave the keys.'

'You don't need a key,' I lied. 'There's no lock on the boot and the self-starter is operated by a push-button.'

He nodded curtly, pretending to understand what I was talking about. Taking care not to stuff the gear lever up my trouser leg I climbed out of the car. Across the shed I could see other vehicles passing through comparatively quickly. There was no sign of the

34

Saab but it could have been screened by a long articulated lorry which blocked my view.

The other three members of the team, including the dog-handler, were converging on the Rolls. The senior officer directed me towards the cabin.

'Please wait in here, *signore*.'

He showed me inside, closed the door and turned a key on the outside. Through the window I was able to watch the search. It did not worry me because I knew there was nothing for them to find. I had heard that there was a thriving traffic in contraband cannabis resin from North Africa to Europe and I assumed that was what they were looking for.

My small shoulder satchel was taken out and carefully placed beside the car. The Alsatian strained towards it and sniffed inquisitively. One man had vaulted into the long pit which the car straddled and had begun to examine the underside, tapping it here and there with a small hammer. The senior officer beckoned the dog handler forward. He went straight to the near-side rear door and opened it. The Alsatian stepped delicately into the plushy interior with its buttoned upholstery, mirrors, hanging tassels and cushions. It sniffed the carpet, then turned its attention to the seat. 2113917

At once its excitement increased. It uttered a series of excited whimperings and high-pitched barks and began to scratch at the seats. Already I was rapping on the window. The material on those seats was irreplaceable. Nobody took any notice of me. The handler, restraining his dog by the leash, turned round and nodded to his colleagues. He pulled the dog out of the car, reached in his pocket and gave it a sweet.

Two of the customs men had taken hold of the lower part of the back seat, one at either end. They expected it to lift up like the rear seat of a modern car. By this time I was pounding the window, shouting at them to treat the car with more respect. Realizing that the seat base was fixed they turned their attention to the back rest. I had supposed that this also was fixed but to my surprise I saw that they had managed to work it loose. As they lifted it away and placed it on the ground beside the car, I could see a small triangular space between the seat back and the curving rear of the car.

The customs men were talking very excitably now, peering into that dark space. I stopped beating on the window. A couple of Carabinieri, resplendent in blue uniforms, had strutted over from the other side of the shed with the instinct of vultures homing on a kill. The dog was straining again at his leash and the whole of the search team were now concentrating on the exposed compartment. Their bodies blocked my view and I could only tell that they were struggling to pull out some long and heavy object.

The Alsatian had begun to whimper and bark as they lifted what they had found out of the car and laid it on the ground. Then I saw. It was a human form, not much bigger than a child's, clad only in an old shirt and a pair of denim trousers. One of the customs men carefully cushioned the head and laid it so that the face, with its closed eyes, was pointing towards me. It took me a few moments to recognize him. The neat grey livery, the polished black boots, the gloves and the cap had seemed to be as much a part of Ahmed as his own skin. Without them he looked just like one of the hundreds of shrunken, wizened Arabs I had seen trudging along the verges of the Tunisian roads.

The cell where I was to be held pending investigation and further interrogation was already over-crowded before I was pushed in. The heat and the stench hit me even before the door clanged shut behind me. The five occupants looked up with more resentment than curiosity. I could see why. The furniture of the cell consisted of four mattresses and one bucket. There was a small barred window high up on the outer wall.

I leaned my back against the door and met the stare of five pairs of shrewd eyes. 'Jesus Christ!' I breathed.

'Another Brit! Thank God for that!'

A small man, sitting cross-legged on the floor beneath the window, beckoned me towards him.

'Come over here, son, but mind how you tread.'

I picked my way over the recumbent bodies and squatted down beside him. He held out a hard, creased and grubby hand.

'The name's McQueen. Am I glad to see you! None of these wops can speak McQueen's English. What have the buggers nabbed you for?'

McQueen had a broken set of teeth, shifty eyes and the stature of a professional jockey. His eyes were red and watered continuously so that he frequently had to wipe the beads of moisture from his cheeks.

'I'm not too sure what the charge is going to be. It depends how good the Italian medical service is.'

Ahmed had not been quite dead when he was taken out of the secret compartment which had been constructed behind the rear seat of the Rolls. I had seen the customs men bring out an almost empty bottle of water and some remains of bread and fruit. The old chauffeur must have resorted to this final, desperate plan to avoid being separated from his beloved Rolls-Royce. The last I'd seen of him was when the stretcher on which his tiny body lay was pushed into an ambulance and driven away.

The procedure for formal charging and commitment to custody took hours. As a criminal who had been caught red-handed, I was subjected to summary treatment. The plain-clothes man who questioned me had a very limited command of English. All I could gather was that the charges made against me would depend on whether Ahmed lived or died. I had certainly been booked for resisting arrest. When the customs officer started to put the handcuffs on me I did not exactly cooperate. In the end the two Carabinieri had to hold me. The officer got even by fastening my hands behind my back and clamping the cuffs viciously tight. I half expected to be subjected to the beating which I'd heard was a usual feature of commitment to an Italian prison. Perhaps because of my foreign nationality I was treated with a certain cold respect. But my demands to communicate with the British Consul met only with the unhelpful reply of '*Dopo, dopo*'. Amid the scenes of vociferous and wild excitement which had accompanied the discovery of Ahmed, there had been no way of finding out what was going to be done with the Rolls, nor what had become of Romy.

As I was marched away to the cells I experienced a chilling sense that I was entering a frightening, bleak and hostile world. I was glad to talk to someone who spoke my own language, but when he heard my story McQueen picked thoughtfully at the few good teeth which he had left.

'If he lives I'll be charged with smuggling an illegal immigrant

37

into the country. If he dies I don't know what they'll do. They could even charge me with manslaughter. What can one do to get in touch with the Consul?'

'Sure, there's no hurry,' McQueen assured me. 'They take their time here. Do you know how long I've been awaiting trial? Ten months.'

'Ten months? You've been in here ten months?'

I stared round the wretched cell. The prospect of spending even a week in these conditions was appalling.

'But that's nothing. The legal system is in a shambles in this country. There's nothing unusual about being in prison for three or four years before your trial comes up. Someone told me they have law-suits in Italy which have been going on for over a hundred years.'

'What were you arrested for?'

'Running cannabis resin. There's a lot of money in it – if you're lucky. There's hundreds of tons of the stuff in Algeria and they'll pay well to get it shipped. I made three good runs, but they caught me on the fourth. I still think it was worth the risk. I've got a tidy bit of cash stacked away for when I come out.'

I was rubbing my wrists, which were still feeling the bite of the handcuffs, and flexing my arms to work the stiffness out of them. McQueen noticed the movement.

'They put the cuffs on too tight? The bastards. They gave me three days on *la balilla*.'

'*La balilla*? That was the name of a pre-war Fiat, surely?'

McQueen laughed without humour. 'Not in prison, it isn't. It's an iron bed they strap you to by the ankles and wrists and just leave you there. You're on a hard mattress with a hole cut in the middle. I don't have to tell you what that's for.'

I studied his face and decided that he was not pulling my leg.

'I just hope they'll count the time I've served already as part of my sentence. I'll be lucky to get away with ten years.'

'Ten years for smuggling pot?'

McQueen shook his head pityingly. 'You've got some nasty shocks coming, son. Did you say you didn't know you had this stowaway on the car?'

'No, I had no idea he was there. I was more surprised than they were when they found him.'

38

'Do you think you can stick to that story through a tough interrogation?'

'Certainly I can. It's the absolute truth.'

McQueen laughed again. 'I can see you're new to all this. After about twenty-four hours in the interrogation cell you'll be happy to settle for a dozen years in jug just to get away from them.'

I learned from McQueen that the other occupants of the cell had all been caught smuggling, in most cases cannabis resin, and like him were awaiting trial. There was only one Italian – a pale young man who lay stretched on his mattress, staring at the roof, his lips moving in silent prayer. Our other companions were an enormous German who slept continuously and two Frenchmen who played a non-stop game which involved holding up a flat palm, a clenched fist or two fingers.

The afternoon and evening passed with desperate slowness. I sank into my own thoughts and tried to avoid further conversation with McQueen. The man seemed to delight in being excessively depressing. At about six o'clock two guards came to remove the Italian, who was shaking with fear as they led him out.

'I'm glad I'm not in his shoes,' McQueen observed lugubriously, as the door was locked again. 'They're worst with their own people.'

A couple of hours later McQueen himself was taken away.

'Best of luck, son,' were his parting words. 'You stick to that story if you can, but I expect we'll be seeing each other quite a bit in the next few years.'

Gloomy though he was I missed him when I was left alone with the somnolent German and the two Frenchmen. All three of them had given me a cursory inspection and dismissed me as a foreigner and a bourgeois. I tried to find relief from boredom and apprehension in contemplation but my thoughts kept running away with me. At first I had just not been able to realize that this was actually happening, that I, Patrick Malone, was incarcerated in an Italian prison with a strong chance of being sentenced to a long term of imprisonment. The uncertainty and the lack of information was beginning to work on my nerves. I would have given my eye-teeth to know the answers to the questions which kept chasing themselves round in my mind. How long was I going to be kept in this comfortless cell? Was Ahmed dead or might he still recover to tell them that he had stowed away in the car of his own accord? Had Romy realized what had happened to me and was she doing something to get proper legal representation, or had she been identified as my companion and arrested also? When I questioned the guards who brought the evening meal they simply shrugged their shoulders.

It was very late in the evening, getting on for midnight by my watch, when a guard came and quietly unlocked the door. I was stretched out on my pallet fully dressed and still very wide awake. The other three men appeared to be asleep.

'*Venga, signore,*' the guard said in a low voice, beckoning to me.

Trying to suppress thoughts of midnight interrogation in underground torture chambers I followed him out into the corridor. I could not tell why, but I somehow felt that my status as a prisoner had changed in some subtle way.

I was led the full length of the long corridor with the doors of cells on either side. From beyond them came the sound of quarrelling voices, snores and sleep-calls. There was a strong smell of disinfectant in the air, almost powerful enough to overcome the more acrid odours of confined humanity.

'*Avanti, signore.*'

My guide had opened a door beyond the end of the prisoners' corridor and was signalling me to go in. I entered, mentally bracing myself for whatever was to come.

To my surprise I found myself in a small and reasonably pleasant waiting-room. It was furnished with half a dozen easy chairs and a couple of low tables. I didn't observe the furniture with much interest because my whole attention was riveted by the squat figure standing under the hanging light in the centre of the room. He stood not more than four and a half feet in height. The upper half of his body had the proportions of a six-footer, with strong shoulders and arms. His legs were short stumps, either because of some deformity or terrible injury. The lack of height had no effect on the power of his personality. Intensely black eyes fixed themselves on my face. Heavily tufted brows meeting above the nose accentuated the fierceness of his gaze. His chin was bearded and his long moustache curled upward at either end. He wore a faded suit of blue denim with baggy trousers and a plain shirt open at the neck, but despite this simple attire I could tell that this was a man who cast a very strong shadow.

The voice, when he turned to give a brief order to the guard, was deep but muted, like a bass whisper. The guard nodded respectfully, moved to the door and let himself out.

The man in the centre of the room waited until the door was firmly closed before gesturing me to a chair. He himself remained standing, which meant that he had the advantage of looking down on me.

'Mister Malonay. That is the correct pronunciation?'

'No,' I said wearily. I'd made this same correction ten times already that day. 'The name is Malone.'

'As you wish.' The man shrugged as if he was making a big concession. 'My name is Varzi. How do you?'

Not sure how to respond to the stilted greeting I merely nodded and waited to hear the reason for this midnight summons.

'This situation in which you find yourself.' Varzi took a turn up and down the room with a peculiar rocking walk. 'It is very unfortunate.'

'Yes,' I said, cheering up a little at the friendly, almost sympathetic tone. 'I'm still suffering from the shock of it. I was taken completely by surprise when they found the body. I had – '

'To participate in bringing an illegal Arab immigrant into the country is a very serious offence,' Varzi interrupted, abruptly changing his tone, halting to face me. His sentences, phrased with exaggerated emphasis on certain syllables, came out slowly as he composed them in his mind. 'And if the man died the charges will be much more serious – possibly even murder.'

'But I had absolutely no idea he was there,' I protested. 'He must have – '

'The authorities have ordered strict measures to stop this traffic. They consider your arrest to be a major capture. They are sure to press for the maximum penalty.'

'Excuse me.' I was bewildered by the sudden switch from sympathy to severity. 'May I ask what your position is? You're not a lawyer, by any chance?'

'No, I am not a lawyer. But your case interests me.'

He took a case of short cigars from his pocket, selected one and lit it. His hands were very large but some of his fingers were slightly distorted and swollen round the knuckles.

'You appreciate that you may face not only a very heavy fine but also a long term of imprisonment.'

'All you people seem to assume that I am guilty. No one has given me a chance yet to make a statement. But I am completely innocent and intend to prove it – '

'That could be very expensive. Perhaps as much as the fine itself. And in our country the legal processes can be extremely slow. The criminals who bombed the bank in Milan were not tried till ten years later.'

The man's eyes were so intense that it required an effort to meet his gaze steadily.

'Did you have me brought in here to put the wind up me, persuade me to plead guilty maybe?'

'No.' Varzi took the cigar from his mouth and pointed it at me. 'It is because I believe I can help you. You see, I am quite convinced that you are an innoce.at victim and that the Arab secreted himself in the car without your knowledge.'

'Well – ' I smiled for the first time since my arrest. 'It makes a change to hear that. But what makes you so sure? You don't know me from Adam.'

'Adam?'

'You don't know anything about me.'

'Perhaps more than you think, Mr Malone.'

Varzi half closed his eyes and gazed over my head as if he was a TV newscaster reading from a back screen behind my head. 'You were born in Slough, Buckinghamshire. Your age is 34. You left school before you had finished your education and unsuccessfully tried your hand at several employments before joining the British Army at the age of 26. You were assigned to special duties in Northern Ireland and were discharged from the Army a year ago after an incident in which three civilians were killed. You have been convicted of a number of traffic offences and were once disbarred from driving for a year for repeatedly breaking speed limits. You now work for a car dealer. You travelled to

42

Tunisia to purchase two motor cars and are now on your way back to London.'

'You are a detective of some kind,' I said, assuming that the Italians had been more efficient than I'd given them credit for and had got my dossier through Interpol.

'No. I am not a detective.'

'You have been talking to Miss Favel.'

'No, the young lady who is accompanying you is not the source of my information. By the way, you need have no concern about her. I have taken the liberty of informing the hotel where she is staying that I will be responsible for all her expenses while she is in Naples. If our discussion is as satisfactory as I hope, that will not be for very long.'

I sat back in my chair, studying the man with a new interest. His last remark had made it obvious that some kind of a deal was going to be suggested. I could not believe that Varzi was in this because of a quixotic love for the British. Behind his bland manner there was a core of ruthlessness. I was becoming more and more sure that I was in the presence of someone who wielded a great deal of power. And I knew from what Ritchie had told me that in Southern Italy true power resided with the Mafia.

'It is very good of you to take such an interest in my case.' I was now choosing my words carefully. 'Do you think there is any hope of these charges being dropped?'

Varzi nodded seriously, his dark eyes watching me. 'Yes. That can be arranged.'

It was a little like a chess game, each of us making his move and then waiting for a reaction from the other.

'I don't know how I could ever repay you.'

'If you accept my help there is a favour that I will ask of you.'

An important piece had been moved on the chess board. I was beginning to understand why this strange interview had to take place at midnight.

'It may not be easy.' I suggested, 'to prove that I knew nothing about the stowaway.'

'That will be no problem.' Varzi dismissed the suggestion with an impatient wave of his hand. 'Information can be laid before the police which will prove to them that you are innocent.'

'And you have that information?'

43

'I can provide witnesses, yes.'

Varzi moved towards one of the chairs, turned his back to it and placed his strong hands on the arms. Then, with an expert tilting movement, he got himself seated. His stubby legs stuck out straight in front of him.

'You mentioned a favour,' I said carefully.

Again Varzi nodded approval. 'I see that you are the kind of man with whom one can do business.'

'I only hope that your conditions will not be beyond me. I'm not a very rich man.'

'The cost to you will be nil. Just a small service. You desire me to help you?'

'Yes, but before I commit myself I'd like to know what this small service is.'

Varzi's eyes flashed and his head jutted forward. 'I am surprised that you hesitate. A promise to do one small favour against a prison sentence of perhaps a dozen years.'

Even half a day in that prison cell had made me ready to grab any chance to escape a long sentence. My commonsense told me to beware of entering into an agreement with this mysterious and alarming personality. But my capacity to make balanced judgments had been weakened by the shock of my arrest, McQueen's lugubrious predictions and the long, uncomfortable vigil with my cell-mates. My Army training had conditioned me for that kind of treatment, but here there were two factors that made all the difference. Firstly, there was the thought of that beautiful Phantom II abandoned to the tender mercies of the Italian customs authorities. Secondly, there was Romy. Varzi's concern for her well-being and solicitude in paying for her hotel had more the sound of a threat than reassurance. Given the circumstances in which I found myself, I can perhaps be forgiven for accepting what seemed to be a way out.

'This small favour – does it involve only me?'

Varzi instantly guessed the reason for my hesitation. 'I assure you that the favour I will ask does not involve the person of the *signorina*. You hesitate because you are a man of your word?'

'I like to think I am.'

'That is good. Because if you make a deal with me it will be binding. As from this moment. You are willing to discuss it?'

Varzi's intense gaze was almost hypnotic. I knew that I was gradually being drawn into something unknown but the alternative to acceptance was even more unattractive.

'It's a deal. Tell me what I have to do.'

Varzi's features relaxed. Another man might have smiled, but it was impossible to imagine a smile on the Italian's face.

'You will take a diamond to England, a very valuable diamond, and deliver it to a member of my family.'

I was surprised as much as relieved and Varzi saw it.

'Yes, Mr Malone, it involves for me both trust and risk. But circumstances may make it necessary for me to leave Italy soon and when I do I will not be able to take the funds I need with me. I would never get them past the Italian customs. As you see, it would not be easy for me to disguise myself.'

Certainly Varzi was a person who would be very easy to recognize from a physical description. I was bemused enough to wonder if he might be a fellow inmate of the prison who was planning an escape. A Mafia boss would surely have no difficulty in getting funds to any country he chose.

'So I take the risk for you.'

'For you it is less of a risk. When this present charge has been dropped you will have a clean record.'

'You really think you can clear me?'

'Yes. If Ahmed survives he will tell the truth under interrogation. But if he is to survive he will require better medical attention than he is receiving at the moment. I will arrange for him to be put under intensive care in a private clinic. When he recovers consciousness he will talk and you will be cleared.'

'And how long before I am released? You yourself said the process of law can be very slow.'

'In your case they will be rapid. I am in a position to guarantee that.'

I decided not to pursue that question. I stood up and began to pace thoughtfully up and down the small room. The favour was such a straightforward one that I began to suspect some catch. It did not make sense that Varzi should be willing to entrust such a valuable diamond to a complete stranger. However, that was not my problem.

'What about the Rolls?'

45

'The Rolls-Royce? It may be more difficult to obtain clearance of the car.'

I stopped walking and faced him. 'That car is a very valuable property. I couldn't go back to England and just leave it here.'

'You can return and collect it later. With the Saab you can make the journey more quickly – and speed is important to me.'

'The Rolls can cruise as fast as any long-distance lorry and they make the journey in a couple of days, despite enforced rest stops. No, the Rolls has got to be part of the deal.'

'A few minutes ago I told you that the deal would be binding.' The husky voice had become a growl. 'When you asked me what the favour was I took that to be acceptance. Now you hesitate. I said that I could produce evidence that would lead to your release. I can equally easily produce evidence that will lead to your conviction – and the conviction of the *signorina* also.'

So the Rolls was to be retained as a guarantee that I carried out the mission. I found it hard to accept that condition, but if he was going to demand a hostage it was marginally preferable that he should choose the Phantom rather than Romy. One piece of good luck was that the *maresciallo* who had relieved me of my possessions had failed to find the small key under my trouser belt. And another factor which had to be considered was the fate of poor old Ahmed. The knowledge that his survival might depend on my decision put a little extra pressure on me to accept Varzi's proposition.

'Okay,' I said. 'It's a deal.'

'And you will not renegate on it?'

'No. You have my word. And can I have yours that the Rolls will be kept safely till someone can come back and collect it?'

'Yes. It will remain in the customs area in a bonded warehouse. Access to that is very carefully controlled. You need have no fears. Please sit down again.'

I did as he asked. He studied me thoughtfully.

'You have given me your word and I am sure that you mean it – now. But there may be a temptation when you are far away from this prison and back in England to forget that you have made this deal with me. My family would not like that and I assume that you – and the *signorina* – will wish to go on living in England without fear. You know already that I am well informed and have influence.'

'There is no need to threaten,' I told him. Now that I had taken the plunge my confidence was coming back. After the hours of waiting and uncertainty, knowing that I was powerless to influence my own fate, I now had an assignment. That put me back on familiar ground. 'If I make a deal I honour it.'

'I hope that you will,' he said with great emphasis. 'And it is a condition of our agreement that you speak of it to nobody. Before you leave this room you will know exactly what to do, but after that you must forget that this interview ever took place.'

'All right. I get the message. What about this diamond? Where do I collect it from and who do I deliver it to?'

'You will be released tomorrow.' Varzi was now speaking with the brisk authority of a superior officer giving orders to a subordinate. 'You will go without delay to a *trattoria* called Bella Napoli in the Via dei Buggiardi and ask if Signor Varzi has left a package for you. When you have collected it you will leave Naples immediately and return to England as quickly as possible.'

Varzi heaved himself out of his chair, and pointed the stub of his cigar at me like a pistol.

'Now, this is very important. For the handing over of the diamond you will proceed by car. My family will be informed of the registration number of the Saab which the *signorina* was driving. That will be your identification. So long as you are in that car they can always locate you. That is clear?'

'It would have been easier to identify me by the Rolls. No one could mistake that.'

'The Rolls is too – what can I say? – flamboyant. It will always be surrounded by a crowd.'

'Mm. So I take the diamond back to England and just wait. I suppose the rendezvous will be on the road or in a street somewhere?'

'That is correct. You take the diamond back. You wait for instructions – and you go to the rendezvous in the Saab with the Tunisian number-plates. When you hand over the diamond it is finished. Just a simple favour, as I said.'

'Suppose I am searched and the diamond is found?'

'That is a risk which we both have to face,' Varzi said seriously.

47

'But your chances of getting the diamond into England are a hundred times greater than mine.'

'Well, *signore*.' I stood up and offered him my hand. There was every reason for keeping this thing on a friendly basis. 'I must thank you for getting me out of this mess.'

'No thanks are necessary, Mister Malone.' He took my hand in his strong grip. His palm was dry and very hard. 'This is a business deal in which there are advantages for both of us. Within a few hours you will know that I have kept my part of the bargain. Then it will be for you to keep yours.'

CHAPTER 3

During the next sixteen hours I had a taste of what it must be like to suffer solitary confinement. Presumably owing to the influence of Varzi I was not taken back to the crowded cell but was locked in a smaller single cell with a bed, table, chair and toilet vessel. They had brought me my shoulder satchel, so I was able to shave and wash. I wished I'd had the foresight to pack a book. That would have prevented my thoughts from chasing each other round in meaningless circles. I kept going over my interview with Varzi, wondering who the hell he was and trying to fathom what lay behind the proposition he had put to me. I'd had to make a snap decision in there, choose the lesser of two considerable evils and I could only hope I'd made the right one. The cell was eight feet long and I must have paced it a thousand times.

By four o'clock the following day I was beginning to wonder if Varzi was really as influential as he had claimed.

I was standing on my chair looking morosely down at a small stretch of street which was visible from the window when the door of my cell was unlocked. This time my visitor was unmistakeably English. He had a studious, well-meaning face and wore steel-rimmed spectacles. The trousers and coat-style shirt with sawn-off sleeves were vintage Marks & Spencer. Though still young, he was beginning to go bald on the top of his head.

'Mr Malone? I'm from the Consulate. My name's Dempster. How do you do? Sorry not to have been able to get along sooner but we've been up to our eyes. I say, they've done you proud! This looks like a VIP cell. I suppose the place is so full that – '

'Mr Dempster,' I interrupted the flow. 'Have you any news of Miss Favel?'

'Miss Favel?' Dempster averted his eyes from the toilet facilities. 'Oh, she's fine. As a matter of fact she is waiting outside for you.'

'Waiting for me? Does that mean I am going to be released?'

'Yes, I'm glad to say we have been able to secure your release.' Dempster was a little nettled at my anticipation of what was to be a surprise announcement. 'You have Miss Favel to thank for that. Things looked very black for you. The Italians have been very tough lately on illegal immigration and until today it seemed more than likely that you would also face a much more serious charge.'

'Has Ahmed recovered?'

'Yes, and he has made a statement which confirms what Miss Favel told us.'

'So he admitted to stowing away in the car?'

'Yes. It appears so. Mind you, that would not have led to your release without the energetic representations of the Consulate. So, we'd like you to remain in Naples until the loose ends have been tied up.'

'How long is that likely to take?'

'Two or three days. Maybe longer. You can never tell with these legal complications. Now, if you can get your things together I will arrange for your discharge.'

I had to admire Dempster's persistence as he dealt in his heavily anglicised Italian with the complexities of a prisoner's discharge. There was no way of telling from the attitude of the officials whether this change in my fortunes was due to the activities of the Consulate or the influence of Varzi. For the moment I could see no way of reconciling Dempster's request that I should remain in Naples with Varzi's command to leave for England without delay. The first thing was to get out of this prison, where it was so difficult to think straight.

'Your car is still down in the customs pound at the docks,' Dempster explained, when finally the last form had been completed and we emerged into the evening sunlight. 'I'm afraid we cannot get it released just yet. Romy – Miss Favel has been staying at the Hotel Verona. I expect you'll put up there too?'

Romy had been sitting patiently in the Consulate car for the last hour and a half. When she saw us coming she swung her legs out and came running to meet us. I was surprised by the genuine expression of concern on her face.

'How wonderful! I have been waiting and waiting and when you did not come out I thought that something had gone wrong. Lionel has been just marvellous.'

Her eyes were shining as she turned from me to Dempster.

The man from the Consulate was blushing modestly. It was evident that she had done a lot of good work on him and put him under the spell of her attraction.

'Just routine,' he said. 'It comes with experience.'

'Are you all right, Patrick?' She studied my face anxiously. 'Did they treat you properly? I was so worried when you did not come through customs. Nobody would tell me nothing except that you had been arrested.'

'You should have come to us without delay,' Lionel said. 'Even if we hadn't been able to secure Mr Malone's release it would have saved you a lot of worry.'

'So what happens now? Will they let you have the Rolls back?'

'Not right away. In any case Lionel wants us to stay in Naples for a few days. Just till the case is sorted out.'

'That is good! I like this place, and I found a very nice hotel, thanks to a kind man who came to my rescue when I was all alone at the docks.'

'Was he – ?' I began, then bit off my words.

'What?'

'Nothing. Lionel said you were at the Hotel Verona.'

'Yes, that's the name. It was the manager there who advised me to go to the Consulate.'

'I'm glad you did. I tried to get them to let me contact the Consulate but nobody took the slightest bit of notice. Well, I suppose we'd better find a taxi. You left the Saab at the hotel?'

'Yes. There's an underground garage. It's quite safe.'

'I'll run you back,' Lionel said, moving protectively to Romy's side and leading her to the car. 'It's not much out of my way.'

At the hotel he seemed reluctant to surrender Romy to me. He opened the door for her, blushing again as he held out his hand.

'Well, I must be getting back to the office, but I'll be seeing you again, of course.'

Romy did not take his hand. Instead she went up to him and gave him a really good kiss. He drove off looking very pleased with himself.

'When I heard they were going to release you I booked a room for you, just in case,' she said when Lionel's car had disappeared into the traffic. 'It's on the same corridor as mine.'

Humping my shoulder-bag I followed her through the automatic glass doors into the air-conditioned coolness of the foyer. As we walked towards the reception desk she put her arm in mine.

'Thank God, they released you. You can't imagine how worried I've been.'

I looked down at her in some surprise. She gave my arm a squeeze and glanced up shyly.

'I was worried about you too but there was no way I could communicate with you, or find out what was happening.'

'I was making a thorough nuisance of myself,' she said, laughing. 'I think the Consulate realized they'd have no peace till they did something about you.'

'I'm very grateful to you. I could only hope that you'd go to the Consulate. You had disappeared from the customs shed before they arrested me.'

'Thank goodness I got through without a search. I was carrying a bottle of Tunisian perfume. You know that the most exotic perfumes are made in Tunis? The recipes are family secrets which are passed on from generation to generation.'

At the reception desk I booked in and collected a room key. As we rode up in the lift to the seventh floor I gave Romy a brief account of what had happened, omitting any reference to Varzi.

'It was very wicked of old Ahmed,' she commented. 'But he has been punished enough. He very nearly died, you know.'

'Have you seen him?'

'No. They took him to some special clinic where he recovered enough to tell them that he had made the secret compartment and planned the whole thing.'

'What'll they do to him?'

'Send him back to Tunisia, I expect. I tried to telephone to Aziz but I could not get through to him – neither at his home nor at the Villa.'

The lift doors opened automatically and we stepped out onto the thick carpeting of the landing. A pert little chambermaid was waiting to ride down with a trolley loaded with used sheets and towels.

'Do you mind if I come in?' Romy asked as I unlocked the

door of my room. 'I've been feeling very lonely and abandoned these last two days, and it's so nice to have you back.'

'Come on in,' I said. There was something different about her now. She seemed less brittle, more feminine. 'I'm going to have a bath and a change of clothing. God knows what bugs I may have picked up in that gaol, and I slept in my clothes last night.'

She sat in the easy chair while I unpacked and waited patiently while I had a long, cleansing shower. I had just got a shirt and trousers on when the telephone in the bedroom rang. I went through in bare feet to pick up the receiver.

'Room 718.'

'Mr Malone?'

'Yes,' I said. The husky, almost whispering voice had been recognizable from the first syllable.

'I just want to be sure that you understand. It was not due to your Consulate that you were released.'

Before I could answer the caller had disconnected.

As I put the receiver back Romy commented: 'That was short. Who was it?'

'Oh, it was only — ' . hesitated. My mind was busy adjusting to the realization that w.thin fifteen minutes of my arriving at the Hotel Verona Varzi had been informed of my whereabouts. 'It was the manager, wishing me a pleasant stay in the hotel.'

'He didn't do that to me,' she said drily.

By the time I'd finished dressing and emerged from the bathroom I had decided tha: I would be wise to stick to the deal I'd made with Varzi, even though I had no actual proof that I owed my release to his efforts.

'I have to go out for a bit,' I told Romy. 'But we'll meet up for dinner. You deserve to be taken somewhere really good, after all your efforts.'

'Let me come with you. Please! I have been stuck here for two days. I tried going out for a walk but the men here just will not leave a girl in peace. I suppose it's my blonde hair.'

More than that, I thought to myself. It's your nicely rounded figure, your lovely long legs and the way you walk, not to mention your disturbingly blue eyes and something about your mouth which sets the imagination racing.

Aloud, I said: 'There's a particular bar I want to visit. It may not be the kind of place a young woman would want to go.'

'You mean the sort of place where men go to pick up tarts? That is why you don't want me to come?'

'No. Nothing like that. It's just that – . Well, someone I met in prison asked me to do him a favour and pass a message to some friends of his there.'

'Then why cannot I come too? I am the girl who got you released from prison – or have you forgotten?'

'All right, then,' I agreed. I was beginning to feel rather touched by Romy's unconcealed pleasure at being reunited with me again.

I left the Saab in its underground garage and asked a taxi driver to take us to the Bella Napoli in the Via dei Buggiardi. He gave me a sharp look and glanced with curiosity at Romy before switching on his meter.

The drive took us away from the plush quarter where the Hotel Verona stood into the noisy, crowded area down by the port. The Via dei Buggiardi was one of those streets given over almost entirely to cafés, restaurants and trattorias. The taxi driver stopped in front of a café-bar which seemed more prosperous than the others. It had a row of small evergreen trees in boxes at the front and a canopy over the entrance which looked like one half of an enormous shell-fish. When I asked the driver to wait, he shook his head vehemently and demanded immediate payment. As soon as he had the money, he did a U-turn and headed back in the direction from which we had come.

I took Romy's arm, wishing now that I'd made her stay behind. Neapolitans were staring at us, not all with friendliness. The interior of the bar was gloomy and at first it was hard to tell whether there were other people there or not. The thump of a loudspeaker playing jazz music filled the place with sound. On the left was a long bar with the inevitable Gaggia coffee machine behind it. Opposite, against the wall, were a number of tables. The seats behind them were upholstered in shiny mock leather. As my eyes accustomed themselves. I saw that about half the tables were empty. Four men were standing at the bar, talking to the white-aproned barman. Everyone in the place stopped talking to look at us when we came in. The barman, a splendid figure with a magnificent black moustache waxed and curled to a point at either side, came down the far side of the bar to meet us, his sharp eyes measuring us up and putting us into the appropriate slot – *stranieri*.

'*Desiderate, signori?*' he enquired.

'You speak English?'

'A leetle.'

I moved closer so that I would not have to raise my voice too much.

'Did Signor Varzi leave a package here for me?'

His expression did not change. He just gazed steadily at me for perhaps five seconds. Then he came round from behind the bar and gestured us to follow him to the far end of the room.

'*Accomodatevi a questa tavola.*' He pointed to the last table in the far corner of the long room. We seated ourselves side by side with our backs to the end wall, looking down the length of the narrow room. '*Cosa prendete da bere?* What you like for dreenk?'

'Romy?'

'Oh, a Cinzano, I suppose.'

'Two Cinzanos, please.'

'*Due Cinzani. Va bene.*'

He moved back behind the bar to prepare the drinks, managing to make the performance as eloquent as if he were conducting an orchestra. In the bar conversation was gradually picking up. The four men at the counter had moved into a closer huddle and were arguing in low voices. Every now and then one of them would glance in our direction. I thought that there was not one among them who did not seem capable of cutting his grandmother's throat.

A waiter who had been in the back part of the premises appeared in time to collect our drinks from the barman and put them in front of us. He was tall and thin with an unbelievably pallid face. The warm air was already condensing on the outside of the glasses. The Cinzano had been well chilled and spiced with a chip of lemon peel.

'I bring your cigarettes in a moment, sir,' the waiter said, as he put the pay-slip under the ash-tray.

'But I didn't ask for – ' I began, and then stopped.

The waiter nodded and smiled reassuringly.

We nibbled the olives which had been provided and drank the Cinzano slowly.

'Are we waiting for your prison friend?' Romy asked me in a low voice.

'No. I don't think he'll be here.'

'Then what on earth is the point of all this? I've never been in such a sinister place in my life.'

'Just wait,' I told her. 'You didn't have to come, you know.'

After that we didn't talk, just drank slowly and watched. We could see the pedestrians and traffic moving beyond the big front windows. Two of the couples paid their bill and left. The place was emptying slowly but the men at the bar were still engrossed in their long, intense argument.

The next time he passed our table the waiter laid a packet of cigarettes before me. The outer cellophane wrapping had been removed.

'With Signor Varzi's compliments,' he said, bending so that his mouth was near my ear. His English was very much better than the barman's. Like so many Italian waiters he'd probably had a job in London at one time.

I nodded, picked up the cigarettes and casually put them in my pocket. Now the thing to do was to get out of here as soon as we could do so without indecent haste.

'Finish your drink up,' I told Romy. 'Then we'll have to see if we can get a taxi back to the Verona.'

She gave me a curious look. She had wit enough to realize that there was something going on here which I had not told her about.

A few minutes later I was trying to attract someone's attention to pay the bill. The barman had moved down and had joined in the conversation of the four cut-throats. The tall, thin waiter had gone to a glass cabinet at the end of the bar nearest the entrance and was lifting slices of pizza onto plates for a pair of young lovers who had been kissing in the furthest, darkest corner.

I had subconsciously noticed the black Mercedes which drew up at the kerb outside. When four men got out I wondered why they found it necessary to wear waterproof coats on such a fine day. As they strode across the pavement towards the Bella Napoli they glanced searchingly to left and right. They were beginning to unfasten the buttons of their overcoats. As the first man pushed the glass door open I suddenly realized what the purpose of their visit was.

I acted on reflex. There was no time for explanation. I gave the table in front of us a violent push. It crashed onto its side. scattering the fragments of the broken glasses across the floor. I grabbed Romy and dragged her with me down onto the floor. If the tiled surface had been bare earth I would have tried to burrow into it. I knew with absolute certainty what was about to happen. My mouth was dry and the electric shocks of fear were running across my tongue. I rammed Romy's head down and pressed my own cheek against the ground, squirming to become as flat an object as possible. The overturned table prevented me from seeing what was happening in the bar, but I did not want to look.

There was not long to wait. The extended burst of automatic gunfire sounded deafening in that confined space. It was accompanied by a few brief screams and the crash and thud of bullets hitting walls, furniture, human bodies.

In panic, Romy tried to rise and run. I thumped her back into a prone position. A series of shorter bursts followed the first long one. Chips of glass from the mirror on the wall behind where we had been sitting showered down on our backs. Then the terrifying concussion of the guns was succeeded by silence. I kept my hand pressed down on Romy.

'Lie still,' I hissed. 'Pretend you're dead.'

I felt her shiver but she lay still. In my mind's eye I pictured one of the killers prowling down the room, searching in case there was anyone who had survived to describe the incident. The only sounds were the dripping of liquid and from somewhere a terrible gargling noise. Then I distinctly heard the sigh of the entrance door closing on its pneumatic spring, and a moment later the sound of a car accelerating away.

I rolled over and raised myself on one elbow till I could look over the edge of the fallen table. There was nobody else in the bar, as far as I could see. Nobody vertical, that is. I got onto my knees, still searching and ready to dive again. I felt detached and cool, strangely dissociated from it all. The four men who had been standing at the bar lay in an untidy heap on the floor, their arms and legs flung into grotesque or obscene attitudes. The tall

waiter who had brought me cigarettes was sprawled near the
door, his body slammed against the base of the bar by the punch
of bullets. The lovers were still locked in each other's arms,
linked as irrevocably now as a sculpture by Rodin.

All over my body my flesh prickled and the skin over my
temples and scalp contracted. Romy stared up at me wildly,
began to scramble to her feet. Her eyes tried to focus me for a
moment, her mouth hung wide open. I helped her upright.

'Don't look,' I told her urgently, twisting her away from the
apocalyptic scene in the long room.

Then she saw the long line of bullet holes traversing the wall
at chest height just behind where we had been sitting. She turned
towards me and began to laugh, that terrible half laugh, half wail
of total hysteria. She started to run towards the street. I grabbed
her by the arm, swung her back, slapped her on the cheek so
hard that her head rocked. But her mouth closed, her eyes focussed
and the laughing stopped.

Still gripping her by the wrist and pulling her after me, I
took her down the short narrow corridor from which the tall
waiter had appeared. We passed the doors of the toilets and came
to a back room where crates of bottles and cartons of cigarettes
were stored. On a line of hooks were hanging the street clothes
of the two waiters. A guitar lay on top of a case of Punt e Mes
and someone's motor-cycle helmet had rolled onto the floor. At
the far side of this storeroom was a strong door, bolted on the
inside.

Still dragging Romy I went to it and drew back the bolts,
praying that it was not locked as well. I turned the handle and it
opened. Outside was a small back-yard, littered with empty
crates, cartons and refuse. We picked our way through it and
emerged into a narrow alley where half a dozen grubby children
were playing. They stared at us as we hurried by. After a hundred
yards we were able to turn right when the alley joined a side
street which ran into the Via dei Buggiardi.

By the time we reached the street onto which the Bella Napoli
fronted people were beginning to run in that direction. Glancing
along the pavement I saw that a crowd had already gathered
round the entrance. We turned and walked the other way.

The reaction did not hit Romy till we were back at the Hotel

Verona. We had walked a good mile before picking up a taxi to take us back to the hotel. During the whole journey she had remained dumb with shock and she still did not speak as we rode up in the lift. I decided to take her to my room because I still had the unfinished bottle of whisky I'd bought on the flight from London to Tunis, and I knew she needed a stiffener.

She assented silently to anything I suggested and seemed a thousand miles away as I unlocked my door and showed her in. She stood at the window with her back to me as I found the whisky and poured a generous tot into the bathroom tumbler. I did not add much water.

'Here. This will make you feel better.'

When she turned I saw the mark of my hand still flaming red on her cheek. She took the glass and sipped the whisky, her blue eyes watching me over the rim.

'I'm sorry I had to slap you like that. It was the only way of getting you under control.'

When you've been close to death the life forces flow more strongly. We were a man and a woman who had been within a few inches of death and had walked away from it. That can be one of the strongest aphrodisiacs.

Her eyes moistened, this time with genuine tears. She put the glass down carefully, just in time before her control broke. Then she gave way and the next moment she was in my arms, her face against my chest, pressing herself to me with all the strength in her supple, golden body.

CHAPTER 4

'I'd like to stay here like this for ever but we've got to start moving.'

Romy had pulled the sheet up over our sweat-dampened bodies. The smooth white material moulded the curve of her hips and emphasized the deep tan of her shoulders and breasts. In the last half hour all the reserves and restraints I had felt had vanished. There was no part of her now which my hands would not dare to caress. It cost me a great effort to release her, roll over and swing my legs to the floor.

She sat up, her expression changing as the memory returned of what had happened at the Bella Napoli.

'Because of the shooting. But that had nothing to do with us – had it, Patrick?'

'No.' I began to pick my clothes off the floor and put them on. 'That was some Mafia type vendetta. It was just a coincidence that we happened to be there. But somebody might report that a foreign couple were in the place, and if that taxi driver informs on us they could trace us back here.'

'My God, it was terrifying! I have never been so frightened in my life. I did not know that guns could make so much noise.'

The horror was coming back. I did not want to give her the chance to dwell on it.

'You'd better get dressed,' I told her briskly. 'I want to be on the road within the next half hour.'

'Within the next half hour?' she echoed incredulously. 'But I thought we had a whole night ahead of us. If I'd known we were only going to have so short a time I would have shown you – '

'Don't tempt me.' I pulled my trousers on, tucked my shirt in and firmly fastened the belt. 'And don't do that. I'm serious, Romy. It may be dangerous for us to stay here.'

Romy stopped her acrobatics and let her legs fall back on the bed. 'But where are we going?'

'Back to England. If we drive through the night we can be at the Channel some time tomorrow morning.'

She shook her head in bewilderment, got out of bed and began to hunt for her underwear.

'But what about the Rolls? And we promised Lionel that we would stay here till things were cleared up.'

'Someone can come back and collect the Rolls. If not me, then Ritchie. And I'll leave Lionel a message, telling him that unexpected developments have forced me to leave Naples.'

'This message you had to deliver for the person you met in the prison, Patrick. Did you ever get a chance to deliver it? And why did the waiter bring you a packet of cigarettes when you'd never ordered any?'

'I'll explain in the car. You said it was in the car-park underneath the hotel?'

'Yes. You can go straight down in the lift. It's in bay number 36. I haven't used it since the middle of yesterday.'

When she had dressed and combed her hair with my comb I sent her along to her room to collect her own things.

'When you're ready come back here. Meantime I'll 'phone down and ask them to get our bill ready.'

Alone in the room I finished the glass of whisky which she had only half drunk, then picked my jacket off the floor where I had flung it. The packet of cigarettes which the pallid waiter had put on the table at the Bella Napoli was still intact. Though the outer wrapping had been removed, the folded end of the paper packet had been stuck up again. Using the tip of a biro I carefully unfastened it and withdrew the silver-gilt paper which enclosed the twenty cigarettes. The middle sections of four cigarettes had been removed to form a neat chamber in the heart of the package. As the cigarettes rolled apart they revealed a small parcel of tissue paper. In it was the diamond.

It was about the size of a sugar-lump and as it lay in the palm of my hand its fifty-seven facets glittered with a thousand lights. I gazed at it with fascination, but it did not answer any of the questions which crowded my mind. What was its history and how much was it worth? Had it once adorned the bosom of a Sultana or Czarina? What desperate circumstances had forced Varzi to entrust it to a stranger? Why had I, a foreigner, been

61

selected to carry it to England? Only one thing was certain: there was no better way in which a fortune of perhaps £100,000 could be encapsulated in a space of one cubic centimetre.

I carefully reassembled the package, which provided as good a hiding-place as any, and placed it in the breast pocket of my shirt.

It was tempting to slip away from the hotel without notifying the management, but I knew that modern hotels have their own detectives and use sophisticated methods of catching people who abscond without paying. I sat down on the edge of the bed to dial the reception desk.

'It's Mr Malone. Room 718. I'm afraid I've had an urgent message and I've got to return home without delay. Could you have my bill ready for me in five minutes? And the bill for room 714 as well.'

'Just wait one moment, please, Mr Malone.'

I waited impatiently, fuming at the self-important officiousness of the modern breed of hotel clerk. A couple of minutes passed before the man came back on the line.

'Your bill is taken care of, Meester Malone.'

'How do you mean?'

'*Il signor Varzi* will pick it up. He has leave instructions with us. Your room and the one of the *signorina Favel*.'

'That's very kind of them. So there's nothing to stop us departing whenever it suits us?'

'No, *signore*. You leave the keys in the rooms, please.'

I hung up thoughtfully, then put my things into my shoulder satchel. I put on the jacket of my light-weight suit. When I buttoned it I could feel the packet of cigarettes pressing against my left tit.

Why does it always take a woman so long to put a few things into a suitcase? Twenty valuable minutes had been lost before Romy was ready to join me. As we rode down in the lift to the basement she sensed my irritation.

'I'm sorry if I kept you waiting. I think I'm still rather dazed by what happened. I found myself just standing there staring into space.'

'Mm.'

It was well after nine o'clock by the time we had won clear of the Naples traffic and were heading north towards Rome on the Autostrada del Sole. I settled myself more comfortably behind the wheel, getting the feel of the Saab before moving over into the fast lane. A gentle pressure on the accelerator was accompanied by a muted and not unpleasant whine as the booster came in. Even with the extra weight of the bullet-proofing, the two-litre engine pushed the car up to a hundred and twenty miles an hour in an exhilarating burst of power. During those first few miles I was checking the instruments to determine what the car's safe cruising speed would be. I noticed that the speedometer needle moved round to the maximum speed recorded on the dial before the engine revolutions had gone into the red area. I concluded that car could cruise indefinitely at 200 kph so I settled down to maintain an average as near two miles a minute as possible.

Light was fading from the sky and the double ribbon of road stretched endlessly northwards. Fifteen hundred miles of motorway lay ahead and it was exciting to think that by morning we would be near to the English Channel.

My monosyllabic replies to Romy's observations made her realize that I wanted to concentrate on my driving. Fortunately the Italians are accustomed to cars moving really fast on their motorways and are prepared to move over. If I was momentarily checked to slow below 100 m.p.h. the Turbo rapidly thrust me up to my maximum speed. By Italian standards that was not really fast. I was passed by one Ferrari which must have been doing 170 mph.

As Naples dropped behind and the distance separating us from the Bella Napoli increased, I felt myself beginning to relax. The signs indicating the interchanges at Cassino, Frosinone and Colleferro loomed up and vanished. I even began to feel hungry and remembered my unfulfilled promise to stand Romy a really good dinner.

We were on the *raccordo annulare* skirting Rome by half-past ten. I pulled into an *Aereo di Servizio* and we collected a couple of plates of hot food from a self-service counter. Till I started eating I did not realize how hungry I was. The meals I had been given in the prison had not been intolerable, but I had been too keyed-up at the time to eat much.

We drank three large cups of coffee each with our meal. When I'd pushed my plate away and was starting on the third, Romy leaned forward with her elbows on the table.

'It wasn't just coincidence, was it, Patrick?'

'What?'

'That the shooting happened when we were in that café. Was that what the message was about? To warn them?'

'No. The message had nothing to do with it. Christ, if I'd known there was going to be a massacre like that I'd never have gone near the place.'

'But you seemed to be ready for it. I mean, even before those men came in you had us down on the floor.'

'That was pure reflex. I've been in situations like that before. You develop a kind of extra sense. When I saw the Mercedes stop and the way those men came across the pavement unbuttoning their coats I guessed what was going to happen.'

'Anyway, you saved both our lives. That line of bullet holes just where we had been sitting! I can't get it out of my mind.'

'Yes. It was just a touch close. I think they were after the four who were standing at the bar. They just killed the rest so as to eliminate any possible witnesses.'

Romy unwrapped a couple of lumps of sugar and put them into her coffee. She began to stir it, then looked up at me with a puzzled expression.

'If you're so sure it had nothing to do with us, why were you in such a hurry to get away from Naples? And there must have been some very big reason for you leaving the Rolls behind.'

Her questions were making me face reality, which I'd not really had a chance to do before now. I would have liked to confide in her, discuss the very quick decisions which I had been forced to make, perhaps even get some reassurance that I'd done the right thing. But I did not want her to know about the diamond I was carrying. It would make her nervous when we were entering France and England and I knew that customs officers can pick up such nervousness as a hound scents the trail of a hare.

'I'm afraid I panicked,' I told her. 'After the bar massacre I just wanted to get away from the place. By the time we'd got back to the hotel I realized that we were material witnesses to a gang killing, probably involving the Mafia or the Camorra. As

64

soon as we were identified the police would be wanting to know why we had not come forward and we would also have become targets for the gang who did the killing. They hadn't meant anyone to survive who could identify them.'

She nodded but did not comment. I was not sure that she believed I meant what I said.

'Well, I cannot say I am sorry that we have got ourselves away from Naples. Without Lionel I do not know what I would have done. He told me that if Ahmed died you could be charged with manslaughter and it might be months and months before your case came up. It was lucky Ahmed recovered enough to talk.'

'Yes,' I agreed, thinking of Varzi and the special clinic to which the old chauffeur had been transferred. In fact, it had all turned out very conveniently – for Signor Varzi. What convoluted intrigue he was involved in I could not fathom. All I knew was that I somehow fitted into his scheme of things. If I hadn't known that such people trust nobody I might have been flattered at the thought that he had chosen me to smuggle his diamond into England for him. Though the Phantom II, with its potential market value of over £50,000, was quite an effective hostage.

'Time to go,' I told Romy, checking my watch. 'We've had our half hour.'

As we moved out of the service area I found myself checking the road behind me in my driving mirror to see if anything pulled out to follow us. I did not doubt that Varzi had been instantly informed of our departure from the Hotel Verona, and I was jumpy enough to wonder if he was somewhere on the Autostrada del Sole, perhaps in that Ferrari which had passed us at 170 m.p.h.

'Why not put your seat back and get some sleep?' I suggested to Romy. 'I might want you to take a spell later on.'

'I'll lie back and relax for a bit. But I couldn't possibly sleep.'

She tilted her seat back and folded her hands. A few minutes later when I glanced round I saw that she had fallen fast asleep.

We were past Florence by half-past midnight. Rather thrn take the route over the Appenines and through the Alps via the Mont Blanc Tunnel, I decided to swing left and follow the coast along the Italian Riviera. Romy slept on as we passed La Spezia,

Genova, Savona and San Remo. She only stirred as I slowed down for the Italian frontier post at Ventimiglia.

'I must have fallen asleep.' She rubbed her eyes and tilted her seat upright. 'What time is it?'

'Ten minutes to three.'

'Where are we?'

'Just coming to the frontier. Where did you put that bottle of perfume?'

'It's in my handbag. But the French won't search us. It's the British customs I'm more worried about.'

It was the slackest hour of the night and very little traffic was moving across the frontier in either direction. I stopped the car level with the guard on the road, opened the door and stepped out. I did not want him to notice that the windows did not wind down in the normal way. The Tunisian registration number with its Arabic lettering could be explained easily enough but the fact that the car had been bullet-proofed was certain to arouse unhealthy interest. I wondered whether my nervousness communicated itself to him. He took the car documents and our two passports into the office to check them with a colleague seated at a desk. Through the window I could see them going through the inevitable list. If the Naples police had got a description of us and traced us back to the Verona Hotel, they would have had plenty of time to warn airports, sea-ports and frontier-posts to be on the look-out for us.

It was a relief when the officer came back, handed me the passports and with a curt nod indicated that we were cleared.

Romy was nonchalant as we cruised into the French customs area. I could feel the cigarette packet pressing against my chest. I knew that the bulge was clearly visible but I was working on the principle that the best place to hide anything is under the light.

Entering France was almost an anti-climax. The blue-uniformed *douanier* standing in the roadway outside the customs post seemed completely disinterested. He looked at me in slight surprise when I again stepped out of the car, and gave the documents and passports the most cursory examination.

'*Vous avez quelquechose à déclarer?*'

'*Non,*' I answered firmly.

'Mademoiselle non plus?'

'Seulement des articles personnels.'

His eyes flicked up in momentary interest when he heard her impeccable French. He handed the passports and papers back to me and saluted her.

'C'est bien.'

'We can go on?' I asked rather foolishly. I found it hard to believe that an armoured Saab with Tunisian plates had been admitted to France so easily.

'Oui, oui, oui.'

I got back into the car and drove gently away, switching on my headlights to illuminate the dark road ahead.

The halt at the frontier had banished the drowsiness and eye-fatigue which had begun to affect me after four hours of motor-way driving. I carried on for another hour before handing over to Romy at one of our stops for petrol.

'I shan't be able to go as fast as you,' she said, as she adjusted the seat and driving mirror. 'A hundred is about my limit.'

'That's all right. We're making good time. I only need a short nap. Wake me up when we get to Lyon.'

We were at Lyon by six o'clock and the sun had come up when I once more took the wheel, refreshed by two hours of deep sleep. We were skirting Paris on the Boulevard Périphérique soon after eight and rolled into Calais a couple of hours later.

The smiling, red-uniformed hostess at the Hovercraft terminal booked us onto the first ferry to Ramsgate. We had time for a wash and a quick Continental breakfast in the restaurant before boarding. During the forty-minute crossing I took a second cat-nap and was wakened by Romy, who had slept for the last three hours of our run through France. The hovercraft was already heaving itself up onto the concrete landing-ramp.

'You can put your watch back an hour,' I told her, as we sat in the Saab waiting to disembark. 'It's only ten-thirty by English time.'

'That's a bonus. I'd forgotten there was an hour's difference.'

Either because of her conversation with me or because the majority of our fellow-passengers were British Romy's English had become more fluent and less stilted, though she still had a trace of foreign accent.

67

'What about that perfume?' I asked as I watched her readjust the hands of her watch. 'Is it still in your handbag?'

'No.' She gave me a mischievous smile. 'I've put it in a safer place than that.'

'Where?'

She patted the space between her breasts. She had pulled them together with a tight, front-fastening bra to form a deep cleavage.

I laughed. 'That's the oldest trick in the game. If they search you properly that's the first place they'll look. Why don't you declare it? I don't mind paying the duty for you.'

I was becoming very conscious of the diamond in my pocket once more. I thought that if we declared the perfume they would be most unlikely to subject us to a thorough search.

'I've no intention of declaring it,' Romy said obstinately. 'If I can get this through without paying I'll have made a profit of about fifty pounds.'

As we bumped down the ramp and followed the line of cars to the customs shed I was thinking about the last time I had driven off a ferry at a port of disembarkation. It was hard to believe that only two days had passed.

I was prepared for a slow and difficult passage through British customs and I was not mistaken. The officer who stepped forward when I stopped beside the usual little desk was very young, very smart and very British, but his manner was one of icy formality.

Romy and I were both asked to get out of the car. She shivered and reached into the back seat for a cardigan. The sky was overcast and a chill wind was blowing in from the Channel. She came round the car to stand beside me, pushing her arms into the sleeves. I could only hope that the clip on her bra was a strong one.

After he had examined our passports and subjected Romy to a searching interrogation about the purpose of her visit to the United Kingdom, he turned his attention to the car. The documents were subjected to the closest scrutiny they had received so far. This time the fact that the Saab had been armour-plated did not escape attention. I had to go into long explanations and bring Romy in for corroboration before he was satisfied. When the search began I soon became convinced that he was putting into practice a procedure he had learned at some school where they train customs officers. All six of Romy's suitcases were hauled out and neatly lined up on the concrete floor. Then he went to work on the interior. The seat cushions were extracted and probed, the door trimmings were removed, revealing the 2 mm steel panels behind them. The spare tyre had to be deflated, the floor was tapped with a small hammer, the trim under the instrument panel was explored, the roof lining prodded. When he tried to insert a probe into the petrol tank I had to explain that it contained not only petrol but a honeycomb of expanded metal cells which would prevent an explosion in there.

He stared at me suspiciously. I was trying not to show resentment. Forty-five minutes had passed and every other car had been cleared except a mini-bus which was receiving the same treatment. We'd had the bad luck to hit a super-conscientious officer. There seemed to be an odds-on chance that when he had finished with the car he would subject us both to a body search.

'I can have a look at the tank when I inspect the underside, sir. Would you drive the car onto that ramp, please?'

I exchanged a glance with Romy and resignedly slipped in behind the wheel. I had already started the engine when I saw an older and more senior man come out of the customs office. He came towards our bay and spoke to the younger man. They turned their backs on us and walked away, talking in low voices. Then the young man came back, while his superior hurried towards the office without a further glance.

'What about the luggage?' I asked our own man. 'Shall I just leave it there?'

'No, you can put it back in the car, sir,' he said, very tight-lipped and angry. It looked as if, for some reason or other, he had received a dressing-down from his superior officer.

'Do you not want me to take her up onto the ramp?'

'No, sir.'

I switched off the engine and got out again. 'You don't want to search the suitcases?'

He shook his head. 'No, sir. But you'll need a customs clearance certificate for the car. What is your estimate of its value?'

We haggled briefly about the value of a bullet-resistant Saab Turbo, which was certainly not listed in Glass's Guide, and compromised on a reasonable figure. The officer asked me to open the bonnet so that he could check the engine, chassis and series number. Finally, he wrote out a certificate which I received in exchange for a cheque to the value of seven hundred and fifty pounds and an undertaking not to sell the car before the statutory ten days had passed. He handed me back the documents and passports and had the grace to help Romy and me load the suitcases back into the car.

'Thank you very much,' I said, as I slammed the lid of the hatchback and locked it.

Even now he found it impossible to smile. As I drove away I looked in the mirror and saw him staring after us, still frowning.

'You see!' Romy swivelled round towards me as we swung out onto the narrow road from Pegwell Bay. 'I did it!' She reached in and withdrew the bottle of Tunisian perfume. 'I've never been caught yet.'

I turned to smile back into her alive, eager face. She was so different now from the morose, frightened and introspective person I had found at the Villa Celeste. I felt very tempted to tell her about the diamond and the deal I had made with Varzi, but I couldn't bring myself to do so. Fatigue and reaction were beginning to get to me and I was afraid that with her analytic and penetrating mind she would put into words some of the questions which had begun to nag at me during the long drive across Europe.

CHAPTER 5

We were in London in time to have lunch at Le Coq Hardi before going on to my flat in West Kensington. We had done the journey from Naples in seventeen hours, and I still had not stood her the slap-up meal I had promised for her efforts to get me released from prison. She had made her decision to return to the United Kingdom on the spur of the moment and I had rather reluctantly agreed to let her use my flat as a base until she could get herself fixed up with accommodation. That half hour in the Hotel Verona had warned me how easily our relationship might go over the brink. If that ever happened I foresaw that it would be very difficult to disentangle.

I parked the Saab in the residents' space at the back of the block in Elton Square. We took out our hand luggage and I locked the car up carefully. It would be ironic if the Turbo was stolen by one of London's car thieves after I had safely got it back from North Africa.

A very hirsute young man was painting the railings alongside the parking space. He gave us a sheepish grin and a nod as we walked past him. He was wearing stained overalls, and slopping paint onto the railings with gay abandon. I noticed that he had not even bothered to clean down the old paint.

The main entrance to the block where I lived was always kept locked as a precaution against intruders. I selected a key from my bunch to open the door. We rode up in the lift to the third floor, Romy's nostrils tightening at the acrid tang of stale cigarette smoke in the small cabin. Our feet echoed in the corridor as I led her to the door of number 72.

She watched me as I used three different keys to unlock the door.

'The previous owners were comprehensively burgled,' I explained. 'They had these special Banham locks fitted and I always use all three when I'm away for any length of time.'

'Do you think it really stops them?'

'Not if they're professionals, but this at least makes it more difficult for them.'

I pushed at the door gingerly, expecting it to be checked by the usual pile of correspondence heaped up under the letter-box. It opened freely, the strip of draught-excluder swishing over the carpet inside.

'What's the matter?' Romy asked. I'd left her suitcase in the corridor and was staring down at the heap of letters and circulars which had been pushed back against the wall.

'These letters had been pushed back before I opened the door. They're usually in a pile under the letter-box.'

'Does that mean the door's been opened?'

I nodded, stooping to pick up the top envelope. 'Here's an envelope post-marked the day before yesterday, so it must have been recently.'

I picked up our two bags and held the door back for her to come in.

'Has anyone else got keys? One of your girl-friends, perhaps?'

'My ex-wife still has a set. But she never comes here now.'

Romy walked into the sitting-room, which had an open view across the District Line track towards Earl's Court. 'Perhaps you've been burgled.'

'Burglars would hardly bother to lock up so tidily after they'd left.'

I made a quick inspection of the four rooms. Everything was apparently as I had left it. All the window catches were securely fastened and intact.

'Perhaps Juliet came in for some reason. I'll give her a ring later on.'

It was strange to have a woman in the flat again. Contrary to Romy's suggestion, I had no girl-friend permanent enough to have been entrusted with the keys of my flat.

'You can be in here.' I told her, picking up her suitcase and taking it into the double bedroom which I had not used since Juliet's departure.

'What about you?'

'I sleep in the other bedroom. It used to be my dressing-room.'

She looked round the room and then gave me a shy and uncertain glance.

'It's a lovely room. Are you sure you – '

There was an odd feeling of constraint between us, almost as if the half-hour in the Hotel Verona had never happened. The reaction to our escape from sudden violent death had thrown us together before we were ready for it, and during the long drive back across Europe we had drawn apart again. Perhaps she had sensed my determination not to become committed to any new emotional involvement for she made no move to bridge the unseen barrier which had come between us. There had been none of the small gestures and caresses which lovers give each other, no hand resting on my thigh during the hours of driving, no shared reminiscences of our love-making, no expectation of a sensuous kiss as soon as we were alone.

'Don't worry,' I reassured her. 'This room has been unused for over a year. The bathroom's through there, if you want it, and there's permanent hot water.'

'Yes, I would like a bath. I just hope I don't fall asleep in it. I loved that drive back during the night but I suddenly feel very sleepy.'

'You go ahead with your bath. Have a siesta if you like. I just want to whip quickly through my mail and make a few 'phone calls.'

I closed the door on her, went back to the sitting-room and took the cigarette packet from my shirt pocket. I shook the cigarettes out and undid the little package which contained the diamond. In the sunlight streaming through the window it sparkled with even greater brilliance. I was sure that a diamond of this size must be worth at least a hundred thousand pounds. Naples and its prison were over a thousand miles away now, even as the crow flies. Back here in the familiar and commonsense atmosphere of my own flat it was harder than ever to believe the explanation that Varzi had given for entrusting me with his precious stone. There must be a great deal more behind this than he had told me, but if a possible explanation had suggested itself I'd pushed it back into the subconscious part of my mind. I did not want to know too much. As far as I was concerned the contact from his 'family' could not come too soon. I badly wanted to be rid of the stone and to feel that I had discharged my part of the bargain we had made.

Meantime, so long as it was in my possession I really would be worth burgling. I tossed it gently on my palm, trying to think of a good place to hide it. Romy had gone into the bathroom and I could hear the water rushing from the taps. I went into the kitchen, found the sugar-bowl on its usual shelf. I emptied out all the lumps, put the diamond on the bottom of the bowl and replaced the lumps. Then I put the bowl back in its place.

Through the bathroom door I could hear her humming to herself. She'd had time to strip naked. Only a thin panel of wood separated me from the golden body which I'd possessed in Naples. I tried not to think about it.

I went to the front door, scooped up the heap of letters and carried them to my desk. Through the window I could see a Jumbo planing down towards Heathrow Airport. I pulled the telephone towards me and dialled Juliet's number.

It rang for a long time before she answered.

'7485734, who is it?'

'Hello, Juliet, it's – Patrick.'

A pause. 'Patrick? You haven't called me for a long time.' Then, brisk and horribly cheerful: 'What's the problem?'

She'd always had the gift of wrong-footing me. The fact that she had ceased to care long before me had given her an advantage over me. Even now she could make me feel that I was importuning her. Perhaps she thought I had telephoned to ask her to come back.

'I've been abroad and I've just returned to the flat. You didn't by any chance come in while I was away?'

'Certainly not. Why would I want to go to the flat?'

'Just checking. I have a feeling someone's been in while I was away.'

'Not me, I can promise you. How do you mean you had a feeling? Was this just an excuse to – '

'You've still got a set of keys, Juliet,' I cut in on her. 'I asked you for them back but you never returned them.'

'You had no right to ask for them back at that time. Half the flat still belonged to me.'

'I know,' I said, controlling my voice. 'That's not the point. Do you still have those keys?'

'Yes, I think I've got them somewhere.'

'Well, will you have a look and see if they're still there? I'm not asking for them back, I just want to be sure – '

'Oh well, all right, if you don't mind holding on.'

She clattered the receiver down. I waited and reflected bitterly on what the legal processes of divorce can do to a relationship. But her voice still had the capacity to set up an ache in me, and I found that I was trembling slightly as I waited for her to come back on the line.

She was gone five minutes but she had the grace to apologize. 'Sorry to keep you waiting. I can't lay hands on them at the moment. I thought they were in the drawer of my desk but they seem to have walked.'

'Oh, well, it doesn't matter. How are you, Juliet? Everything all right with you?'

'Never better,' she assured me, and hung up.

I paced up and down the length of the flat for a few moments, trying to relieve tension. Juliet had always been careless with keys and maddeningly casual about locking up.

'Bath okay?' I called to Romy through the door.

'Heavenly,' she answered, and I heard the water swish as she moved. 'I hope you don't mind me using somebody's bath foam.'

'Help yourself.'

My pulses had slowed down and I'd got over the raw feeling which my words with Juliet had given me. I went back to my desk and braced myself to talk to Ritchie. I knew he would not like what I was going to tell him.

The telephone gave only three sets of rings before it was answered.

'Automobiles of Quality. Can I help you?' I recognized the voice of Anthea Dixon, Ritchie's secretary.

'Anthea, it's Patrick. Is Ritchie in?'

'Patrick! You're back. Did you have a good trip?'

'Yes and no. Is the great man in?'

'Yes, but he's with a customer at the moment.'

'Well, tell him I need to speak to him urgently. You can look after the customer, that'll keep him happy.'

'The customer's a woman – wearing a sari and a diamond in her nose.'

'Oh. Well, ask him to ring me as soon as he's free.'

75

While I waited I went through the letters which had arrived during my four days' absence. Among them was a reminder that my TV licence was about to expire, a Final Notice from the Inland Revenue and a curt note from Juliet's solicitors.

The 'phone rang as I was frowning over the latest shot in Moate, Sproate & English's inexhaustible locker.

'Hi, Pat! You're back home on schedule. You haven't been caning that Rolls up the autoroute, have you?' Ritchie's voice was strong and confident, with something of the quarter-deck about it.

'No, Ritchie, I haven't. As a matter of fact I wasn't able to bring the Rolls with me.'

I gave him a brief and carefully edited account of what had happened in Naples, including the finding of Ahmed stowed away in the Rolls and the successful efforts of the British Consulate to get me released. I did not mention Varzi. If I'd told Ritchie about the deal I'd made with the Italian he'd have shot it full of holes. Either that or he'd try to take charge of the situation, tell me what I ought to do, grab a slice of the action for himself. He may have opted for a sedentary occupation on doctor's advice but I'd noticed frequent signs of a craving for the life of intense and dramatic action which he had left behind him. If he came in on this I was sure it would escalate.

He listened without comment till I'd told him about the journey back to London. 'So the Rolls is still held by the customs at Naples?'

'Yes. They weren't prepared to release it just yet. But I managed to get away with the key to the master switch. So no one's going to drive the car anywhere without it.'

'I think you should have stayed with it, Pat,' Ritchie said quietly. 'I don't think you should have come back without the Rolls.'

Even though he spoke so quietly his words stung. Ritchie had the power to issue a rebuke in the politest possible terms and still make you feel like a worm. I'd known how he would feel and had already decided to give him some of the background to my decision to get out of Naples without delay.

'I had a good reason for getting out of Naples, Ritchie. Was there anything in your paper this morning about a massacre in the port area there?'

'Yes. It was headline stuff.'

'What did the report say?'

'As I remember it, three gunmen burst into this bar in broad daylight and shot everyone there. The report said it was the latest incident in a power struggle between two rival gangs. The bar was a meeting-place for one of the gangs and the other lot intended to liquidate as many of the opposition as they could. They probably shot anyone else who was there to prevent subsequent identification. That's standard practice.'

'Not everyone, they didn't.'

Ritchie paused, warned by my tone that I was going to surprise him. 'Meaning?'

'Romy and I were in that bar at the time.'

'Jesus! Who's Romy?'

'She came back with me to drive the Saab. Madame de Sonis's secretary. I told you about her in the cable.'

'Yes, yes. You say you were in the bar when this happened?'

'Yes. I saw it coming and we took cover in time. It was quite a happening. We baled out the back entrance to avoid involvement.'

'Wise move. No one saw you?'

'No. But we could have been traced back to our hotel and then awkward questions might have been asked.'

'What kind of awkward questions?' Ritchie asked shrewdly.

'Well, I'd just been cleared of a serious charge and there I was slap in the middle of a gang battle.'

'Yes. It does indicate a remarkable capacity to get into trouble. Rather an odd coincidence, wouldn't you say?'

I was glad we were having this conversation on the telephone and not face to face. Ritchie had a very practical and probing mind and there had been more than a hint of scepticism in his tone.

'You know what the south of Italy can be like, Ritchie. You warned me about it yourself.'

'Mm. We'll have to do something about the Rolls, but it might not be a good idea for you to go back there. I may have to go out myself.'

'There's a very good chap at the Consulate called Lionel Dempster – '

'We can go into that later. Meantime, I've got a buyer for the Turbo.'

'You realize it's the bullet-proof version?'

'That's just the point. Spot of luck, really. I've as good as sold it to a gentleman from the Gulf who desires protection without ostentation.'

'That's quick work. Actually, Ritchie, I'd very much appreciate it if you could let me hold onto the Turbo for a few days. My Alfa's gone in for a respray and she won't be ready for a day or two, so I'm without transport.'

'I'm not sure about that, Pat. My oriental gentleman may want to see it before he flies off home. Still, we can discuss that. What about having dinner together?'

'That sounds a good idea – '

'Fine. I'll book a table at the Mitre. Shall we say nine o'clock?'

'If you're booking a table, make it for three. I'd like to bring Romy along.'

'That's the secretary-companion person?' Ritchie's voice sounded doubtful.

'Yes. She's a bit shook up after that shooting incident. I feel kind of responsible for her.'

'Steer clear of lame ducks, my friend,' Ritchie warned me. 'They can trample all over you.'

When I'd rung off I opened the side drawer of my desk where I keep my personal book of telephone numbers. It wasn't in its usual place. I checked all the other drawers and the top of my desk. There was no sign of it. In the end I had to look up the number-plate manufacturer in Yellow Pages. After the usual objections about having too much work on hand and the problem of reproducing a Tunisian number-plate, he agreed to have a pair of plates done to my specification by midday the next day. If Varzi's family contacted me I was sure I could stall them till then, but there was still the chance that Ritchie's Gulf customer would not turn up or would decline the offer and then I might be able to get the Turbo back.

I was replacing the receiver when Romy came into the sitting-room. She had swathed her head turban-style in a small towel and had wrapped a bigger one tightly round the essential parts of her body. It looked as if it might fall off at any moment. I remained safely seated behind my desk. She must have known perfectly well that she looked and smelt like something out of the Thousand and One Nights. Probably the thousandth.

'My suitcases are still in the Saab, Patrick. I've got nothing to change into.'

'I'll go down and get them. Any special one you want?'

'I'm not sure where anything is, I packed in such a hurry.'

'I'd better bring them all up,' I said with resignation.

'That's very sweet of you. I'm sorry to be such a nuisance.'

'My pleasure,' I lied and sat watching as she walked out through the door on bare feet, the white material of the towel offering a running commentary on the movement of the body it concealed.

Down in the street I noticed that the railing painter had knocked off and gone away, leaving the job unfinished and a spatter of paint-drops on the pavement as a souvenir of his personality. A Jamaican traffic warden was working her way down the pavement, checking the residents' permits on the parked cars and sticking cellophane-wrapped forms under the windscreen wipers of any that were not showing the permit. I explained to her that my own permit was on the Alfa and asked her not to book the Saab. She asked for proof that I lived in Edith Villas and I showed her an envelope addressed to me which I'd shoved in my pocket. She nodded and with a flash of white teeth in her dark face moved on down the line. Nice legs. She made the hateful uniform look almost seductive.

It took me two trips to hump Romy's luggage up to the flat, and by the time I had finished she had enough possessions gathered round her for a long-drawn-out siege.

She looked genuinely apologetic when she saw me glance round what had once been Juliet's and my bed-chamber. It had not been in such a mess since the departure of my ex-wife.

'I can repack as soon as I've found the things I really need. Then we can put a lot of this back in the car.'

'The car's as good as sold already,' I told her. 'And you'd better look out something to wear this evening. You're going to be taken out to dinner.'

I closed the door on her and went back for that missing book of addresses and telephone numbers. I didn't find it, but by the time I had finished the search I had a strong feeling that someone else had recently conducted a similar search. Nothing was missing but, unless I was imagining it, everything was just a bit tidier than usual, as if a meticulous cleaner had been around, dusting and tidying.

The buzzer announcing that someone was ringing my bell down at the front entrance interrupted me while I was staring at the sugar bowl, wondering whether it really was the best place to hide the diamond.

I went to the hall and picked up the receiver of the intercom. 'Who is it?'

'You the gen'l'man owns the Saab I jus' spoke to?'

'Yes.'

'Well, someone jus' got in and drove that car away – '

'What?'

'They jus' got in and drove it away. Someone you know?'

'I'll be right down.'

The lift was occupied. I ran down the stairs three at a time, rushed out into the street and found my Jamaican friend staring at the empty space where the Saab had been standing five minutes before.

'Did you see who it was?' I asked her.

'Not good. I was jus' writing out a form for that white Jaguar when I see this man jus' walk up˙and drive your car away.'

'But how did he get in? The car was locked.'

'Man, he jus' put a key in the lock and open the door and then he drive away.'

I stared down the street at the unbroken line of vehicles passing at the intersection with the North End Road. It was building up to rush hour and the Saab must already be lost amidst the hustle of cars homeward bound. Then my eyes came back to the partially painted railings and the splodges of black on the paving-stones which the unskilful painter had left behind as a souvenir of his presence.

CHAPTER 6

The 'Automobiles of Quality' showroom was situated in a converted warehouse off the North End Road. Contrary to the lie I had told Ritchie, my Alfa was ready and I'd been able to collect it from the paint shop just before they closed. As I parked it in the nearest space I could find I was not looking forward to the interview. I had decided that it would be better to tell Ritchie what had happened face to face rather than try and explain it on the telephone.

It was hard to tell from the exterior of the showroom that it contained a quarter of a million pounds worth of stock, though the sign hanging above the doorway had been hand-painted in a style more suitable to Mayfair than West Kensington. I pushed open the small door at the side of the big black-painted doors through which the cars were moved. This led into the outer office, through which all visitors had to pass before they were admitted to the showroom. Here they came under the scrutiny of Anthea, enthroned behind the desk where she did all her typing.

Ritchie's secretary was a rather severe-looking young woman. She favoured very plain clothes, had her dark hair pulled back into a tight bun at the back of her head and wore spectacles with very large but thin lenses. I had once bumped into her at a pub and at first had failed to recognize her. She was wearing jeans and a summer shirt on a bare torso, her spectacles had been discarded and her hair tumbled down on either side of her face. She looked devastatingly sexy and I came to the conclusion that she affected her rather severe working disguise to discourage customers from chatting her up and trying to date her. From then on I had often wondered if she and Ritchie also had an off-duty relationship.

She was just putting the cover on her typewriter and turned with a frown, ready to tell me that the showroom had closed. When she saw who it was she smiled. We shared a secret, because I had never referred to that chance meeting in the pub.

'It's you, Pat. Good to see you. Ritchie said you wouldn't be coming in.'

'Something cropped up. I haven't missed him, have I?'

'No. He's still signing letters.' Anthea was shrewd enough to see that I was keyed up. 'We've had a hectic day. Sounds as if you've had your problems too.'

'You can say that again. Did the princess make a purchase?'

'The princess?'

'Lady wearing a sari with a diamond in her nose.'

Anthea laughed. 'Oh, her. I think she's going to buy the Mercedes 280 SL we took in part exchange for the Flying Spur.'

I found Ritchie in his very snazzy office with its large plate-glass window overlooking the showroom. He was sitting behind his Herman Miller desk wielding a gold Shaeffer fountain-pen with a flourish.

'Pat!' he exclaimed as he saw who it was. He had a special gift of always making you feel you were the one person in the world whom he most wanted to see. 'I thought you said you couldn't make it.'

'I thought I'd better come over, Ritchie. Something's – '

'Just let me sign these letters. Then I can let Anthea go. This is her evening for amateur theatricals.'

As I waited I stared through the window at the display of cars in the thousand-foot square showroom. It was a sight that always gave me pleasure. Ritchie only allowed Rolls-Royce and Bentley models in here. Other classic cars which we took in part exchange were housed in a separate garage at the back. In this front show-room there were examples of the coach-builder's craft from an early Silver Ghost to a Silver Cloud III. They had all been highly polished by old John Thornton, who had once been foot-man in the household of a belted earl.

Ritchie finished signing his letters. He took them through to Anthea's office. I heard him saying goodnight to her before he came back into his own sanctum.

Broad-shouldered and tall, he still held himself as erect as if he were about to go onto the barrack square. His clothes were formal but he managed to achieve a very individual style. The tweed jacket of bold check and the fawn twill trousers were made to measure. He wore hand-built buckskin shoes and a silk shirt that had come through some personal contact in Hong Kong. His slightly wavy flaxen hair was of civilian rather than military length and his soft blond moustache was luxuriant enough to be brushed up at the corners of his mouth. His cheeks had never lost the weatherbeaten look which was a legacy of the years he had spent under hot suns. He had startlingly blue eyes and it was not easy to spot that one of them was made of glass. The remaining eye was constantly on the prowl, searching for an answering glance from some attractive female. The quest was often successful for Ritchie had a look of carefree unscrupulousness which some women found irresistible.

He was a shrewd enough judge of character to tell that some unforeseen event had brought me round to see him and he knew me well enough to see that I was feeling very ill at ease.

'I guess the sun's under the yard-arm.' He grinned at me as he headed for the small fridge where he kept his drinks. 'You'll have your usual?'

'Yes, please. Make it a strong one.'

He cocked his eye at me. 'More trouble?'

I nodded. 'The Turbo's been nicked.'

He reached into the fridge, found two glasses and set them on top of it. Then he got out the ice-tray and put a cube in each before pouring a large measure of Gordon's. He added a touch of Noilly Prat and handed me my glass.

'Nicked? Since we spoke?'

'Yes. Must have been very shortly after.'

'Saabs are not an easy car to steal. And I suppose that one has Tunisian plates. It was well locked up, I suppose?'

'Yes. No question about that.'

'You're sure it hasn't been towed away by the police?'

'I've checked with them. They haven't taken it to their pound. In any case, it was in the residents parking space and that's Traffic Warden territory.'

'Did the police take down the particulars? I mean, they've got it on their list of stolen vehicles?'

'Oh, yes. I notified it as stolen, but they didn't seem specially surprised or interested. It seems that today's been a good day for car thieves.'

'Every day is a good day for car thieves. This can't have been a joy-rider, but I'm surprised that even a professional could have fiddled the lock of your Saab so quickly. Some intelligence work must have been done beforehand. You can get a key for a Saab if you know the chassis number.'

'There was a very suspicious character painting the railings outside my block when we arrived. I'm sure now that he was a spotter for whoever stole the car. But I can't see how he could have found out the chassis number; the bonnet locks from inside the car. At least I was able to give the Stolen Car Squad a description. And the unusual number-plates should give them another lead.'

Ritchie sipped at his drink and eyed me thoughtfully. It was typical of him to take this new blow so equably. This was a characteristic he had in common with men who have frequently been in tight and dangerous situations.

'It may turn up,' he reassured me. 'When they find it's a bullet-proof model they'll probably dump it. It wouldn't be easy for a crook dealer to sell a car like that. But I must say, Pat, you do seem to be what the insurance companies call a bad risk, just at the moment.'

'I do, don't I?' I took refuge in my gin and French and wondered what he would have to say if he knew about Varzi.

Ritchie sat down in one of his comfortable armchairs under a photograph of the team of Bentleys which had triumphed in the 1928 Le Mans 24-hour race.

'What I can't quite understand is what possessed you to take this companion-secretary person to a low-dive bar in the port quarter of Naples.'

'It wasn't such a low dive as all that,' I protested. 'I only went because I met another Brit. while I was being held in prison. A northern Irishman by the name of McQueen. He was certain he was going to get a long prison sentence and he asked me to deliver a message to this bar in the Via dei Buggiardi. Romy didn't want to be left alone, so I took her along.'

'And the gunmen chose that precise moment to make their hit. What happened exactly?'

I gave him a detailed account of the whole incident from the moment that I had seen the Mercedes draw up outside the Bella Napoli. He listened very intently, nodding from time to time. I knew that he could appreciate how I'd felt because he'd been through a dozen similar experiences himself.

'You were lucky to walk away from it, Pat. Sounds like Mafia gang warfare, with one faction trying to rub out the other and gain control of the port rackets in Naples. The only thing that worries me is that if you are identified it won't look too good coming on top of the stowaway episode. It may be asked why you didn't come forward to give information to the police, and suspicious minds might find it odd that someone who had just been let out of prison happened to find himself in that café when the shooting happened.'

I'd thought that it was a strange coincidence myself. The tall, thin waiter had been gunned down a few moments after handing me the diamond. Yet I'd told myself a hundred times already that if the gunmen had come because they knew that we were in the bar we would never have come out of it alive.

'I made a snap decision,' I said. 'It may have been the wrong one but last night in Naples things looked a bit different from now. You have to remember that I'd been arrested once already, and though the charges had been dropped it would have looked a little suspicious if it had then been found that I was at the scene of a gang massacre.'

Ritchie gave me a steady stare and I knew he thought my explanation was thin. But he did not push it. Instead he returned to the subject of the Rolls.

'I've telexed the British Consulate in Naples, asking them to look after our interests until one of us can get out there. You may have to go back, Pat, if they insist on you being there.'

'That's all right,' I said casually. 'I'm quite prepared to go back, but I don't think anything will happen for some time. What's bugging me is that I intended to bring two cars back for you and now I haven't got either of them.'

Ritchie finished his drink and stood up.

'It happens to the best,' he said, and then relapsed into ham Scottish. 'Dinna fash yersel', Pat. I expect we can sort it all out. What you need is a good booze-up. Can't you shake off this secretary-companion and we'll go the rounds?'

'I can't really. She doesn't know anyone in London and I feel kind of responsible for her.' I knew my explanation sounded weak, but I hesitated to tell Ritchie the truth, which was that I did not want to leave her alone in case the intruder who had entered my flat returned and surprised her there.

We found Ritchie in the cocktail bar of the Mitre, half-way through a double gin and French and engaged in earnest argument with a group of young men and their girl-friends. As we came up behind him I gathered from what I overheard that he was on his old hobby-horse about the danger inherent in the seventy mile an hour speed limit.

He realized that the eyes of his male listeners were focussed on something interesting behind him. With his instinct for sensing the arrival of an attractive woman in any room where he happened to be, he turned round. When he saw me he raised a hand in greeting, nodded to his new-found friends and came towards us.

'Hullo, Pat,' he greeted me. 'Where's the – '

'Ritchie,' I cut in quickly, before he could drop a clanger. 'I want you to meet Romy Favel.'

I was amused at his double-take and very gratified to have for once caught him off-balance. Romy had put on a dark-green dress which showed plenty of her sun-tanned chest and shoulders. Her long hair was now arranged in complicated sweeps and plaits on the crown of her head, which explained why she had spent a good hour in the bedroom after her bath. As I introduced them, Ritchie transferred his drink from his right to his left hand and I saw his expert eye make a quick appraisal of her person. He had brightened visibly and soon had taken her under his wing in that protective and solicitous way he had with women.

The evening went off well. During dinner he gave her his full atttention and for once his single eye was not roving round the room. Before we reached the coffee stage he had found out a good many things about her which I had failed to discover during our five-day acquaintance. For instance, that she'd been born on St Valentine's Day, had won medals for springboard diving, adored the poetry of Kahlil Gilbran, had written several short stories and wanted to find a job in a publishing house in London.

His eyes followed her appreciatively as she departed to the

ladies' room while he was settling the bill with one of his sheaf of credit cards.

'She's got it all,' he informed me. 'Amazing how much more attractive a good-looking woman is when she can talk as intelligently as that.'

'You really brought her out of her shell, Ritchie. I haven't heard her talk about herself like that before. She's always been somehow reserved with me.'

Ritchie gave me a slightly pitying look. 'You know why that is, don't you, old son? She obviously thinks the sun rises and sets out of your backside. Did you see the way she looked at you when she was telling me how you swept her to the floor and saved her life when those gunmen came into the bar? You've done yourself a bit of good there, old Pat. I can see why you're feeling responsible, as you call it. Is she shacking down with you?'

'I told her she could stay in the flat till she's found somewhere to live.'

Ritchie made a quick calculation, added something to the credit slip for the tip and signed it. The waiter took his card and the bill and the slip away to the cashier.

'You keep her there, my friend. If you don't snap her up someone else will – and p.d.q. too.'

We were waiting in the corridor for Romy when she came out of the ladies' room. I noticed that she had a three-stemmed orchid pinned to the green dress. She touched it with her hand as she came over to join us.

'Which of you do I have to thank for this?' she asked, smiling.

It would have been very much in character for Ritchie to have laid this on, but when I looked at him he was raising an eyebrow at me.

'I'm afraid I can't claim the credit for that. Nice timing, Pat.'

I shook my head. 'Nothing to do with me. Where did you get it from?'

Romy's smile vanished. 'Oh dear, it must have been meant for someone else. I assumed it was from one of you.'

I could tell that, like me, she thought that this was Ritchie's style more than mine.

'What happened?' I asked her.

'When I came out of the dining-room one of the waiters

stopped me and gave me this. He was gone before I had time to react. So I accepted it and borrowed a pin from a woman in the ladies.'

'What did he say? Did he ask you your name?'

'No, he seemed sure he had the right person. He muttered something which I couldn't make sense of – . I think I ought to try and find him and give it back.'

'You stick to it, my dear.' Ritchie took her by the elbow and steered her towards the door. 'There's no one else in this place who could carry off such a magnificent orchid as that.'

'I like your partner,' Romy said, as we headed back towards Kensington in the Alfa. 'You didn't warn me that he had a glass eye. How did that happen?'

'I'm not sure. He doesn't talk much about his past. He was in the Army at one time and when he left it he became a mercenary. I think I once heard that he lost his eye in the Congo.'

'And he is missing one finger from his right hand. I didn't notice it till he was tasting the wine. What did he mean when he said he had a plastic gut?'

'That was something which happened in Greece. He told me he'd been hit in the stomach by a soft-nosed bullet, and had to go through a very big operation.'

'Ugh! He must be very brave. I mean morally as well as physically. I bet his life-story would make an interesting book.'

'If you could get him to tell it.'

'Oh, I think I could,' Romy said confidently.

I could hear the telephone ringing in my flat as soon as we stepped out of the lift. I wondered who could be calling me at twenty minutes past midnight but I did not hurry. So often I had rushed into the flat and grabbed the 'phone only to find that the caller had rung off at that very moment. As I closed and locked the door from the inside, the bell was still patiently ringing.

'Someone must want to talk to you very badly,' Romy said, laying the suede coat she had been wearing over the back of the sofa.

I went to my desk and picked up the telephone.

'Hello?' There was no response. I whistled into the mouth-

88

piece and said, 'Hello' more loudly. I heard the clatter of the instrument being picked up. The caller must have laid his receiver down, determined to wait for someone to answer. Then a thick voice spoke.

'Who is that speaking?'

'What number do you want?'

'I want to speak to Meester Maloné.' Once again a stress had been put on the last syllable.

'Who are you?'

'Is not matter. You are Meester Maloné?'

'Malone. Yes, speaking.'

A throat was cleared gruffly. 'I am relative of Signor Varzi. Signor Varzi you meet in Naples, no?'

'Yes,' I said wearily. The man's accent was so strong that he sounded like one of those television actors who specialize in foreign waiters. 'And may I ask who you are?'

'Now you do as I say, please,' the foreign voice continued, ignoring my question. 'You go out to public telephone in Elton Street and in five minutes exactly you telephone to me at this number. You have pencil?'

'Yes.' I reached for the pad on my desk and jotted down the number as it was dictated slowly. 'Right. I've got that.'

'Bring pencil and paper. And you tell nobody. Is important for you – and the *signorina*. You understand?'

'Okay. There may be a delay if someone else is using the – '

The dialling tone cut in before my sentence was finished. I replaced the receiver and checked my watch. The time was 12.22.

'I've got to go out and make a call from the kiosk in Elton Street,' I explained to Romy, who had listened to my end of this conversation with some astonishment. I tore the top sheet off the pad. 'Double lock the door and don't open it till you hear me call through the letter-box.'

'Patrick, what's all this about – ?'

'I've no time to explain now. Just do as I say, please.'

I waited outside in the corridor for long enough to hear her lock the door, then ran to the lift. The indicator showed that it was at the fourth floor and going up. Rather than wait for it I raced down the stairs. By the time I had let myself out through the locked doors and run the couple of hundred yards to the call-box the hands of my watch had moved round to 12.27.

Fortunately the booth was empty. I checked the number I had scribbled down, placed a coin in the slot and dialled. By the time the coin had dropped the receiver at the other end had been lifted and the same voice was answering. ' 'Allo. 'Allo. 'Allo.'

'It's Malone again,' I announced, my voice slightly breathless after the dash down three flights of stairs. 'Who am I speaking to?'

'My name Sagrano. Meester Maloné – '

'Yes.'

'You have kindly brought for me a gift from my cousin.'

'Yes. That's right.'

'Now we arrange for you to transfer it to me.'

'How do I know you really are Signor Varzi's cousin?'

'Because I know number of your car. Is Tunis 30 4392. Yes? Also I identify you when we meet by number of car. My cousin explain this?'

'Yes.'

'Where you have put the car?'

The question was loaded. It made me wonder whether this Mr Sagrano had some way of knowing that the Saab was no longer outside Edith Villas. I decided to lie.

'It's safely locked up in a garage.'

'What garage is this?'

'It's a private garage I use sometimes.'

'Then tomorrow we meet and make transfer.'

'That's too short notice. I can't do it tomorrow. You'll have to give me time to make arrangements.'

'Must be tomorrow, Meester Maloné. *La signorina*, she is well?'

'She's well, yes.'

'She pleased by the orchids I send?'

'What? What's that?'

'The orchids. She not receive them?'

'Yes,' I said, recovering myself. 'They were from you, were they?'

'Of course. She pleased?'

'Yes, very pleased. You have excellent taste in orchids.'

'Then, tomorrow Meester Maloné.'

'All right. I'll manage it somehow. Where do we meet?'

'You have pen ready?'

'Yes.'

'M3 motorway. You know?'

'Yes.'

'You take M3 motorway for 65 miles then main road 303 for 15 miles. At 15 miles is sign for village of Monxton. In $2\frac{1}{4}$ miles – you write this?'

'Yes. I'm writing it all down.'

'In $2\frac{1}{4}$ miles is lane on right, just before village. You turn up lane, drive slowly along grass track. Three o'clock exactly. I see you. I see car number. I contact you. We make transfer.'

'Okay. I've got that.'

'You come alone. Be certain nobody follow. Tell nobody. The *signorina* stay in London. Perhaps I send fresh orchid.'

'Yes, I get the message. I'll be there at three o'clock.'

'With Tunis car. Is very important.'

The connection was broken. I replaced my own instrument. The stink of stale cigarette smoke and another smell that was probably urine was very strong. I opened the door of the booth and jammed it with my foot to let in some fresher air while I recopied the instructions more neatly on a second sheet of the note-pad.

Back at the street door to the flat I found I had rushed out in such a hurry that I had forgotten my keys. I had to press the buzzer for flat number 72 and ask Romy to let me in. She was already waiting behind the door as I came along the corridor. She unlocked it as soon as she heard my voice.

'Why do you have to go and telephone from a public call-box when you have a perfectly good 'phone in your flat?' she asked as soon as I had closed the door behind me.

'Let's get ourselves a drink and I'll tell you.'

'I think I've had enough to drink.'

'You may be glad of a drink when you hear what I have to say. We'll open this brandy I bought on the hovercraft.'

On my way back from the call-box I had decided that I must tell Romy about Varzi and the deal I had made. I had hoped that the whole thing could be finished and closed without her becoming involved, but that disquieting incident of the orchid

91

changed everything. It had achieved its desired effect of making me realize that Varzi's people had a method of monitoring our movements. If Romy was going to be used as a lever to ensure my good behaviour, she needed to be warned. As I was pouring the brandy into two pear-shaped glasses I was trying to work out how much I ought to tell her.

We sat on the sofa and lit up cigarettes. Through the double-glazed windows we could hear the distant rumble of the traffic on the Cromwell Road and the siren of a police car in pursuit of some speeding driver.

'I know you did a very good job on Lionel Dempster,' I began. 'but it was not really because of him that the charges against me were dropped.'

She listened without comment as I told her about the midnight interview with Varzi and the bargain we had struck.

'I thought it better not to tell you,' I finished. 'If you didn't know about the diamond and weren't involved, no one could pin any blame on you. But that orchid business made me change my mind.'

'What does the orchid have to do with it?' She touched the flower which was still pinned to her breast.

'It was sent by Varzi's people. That means they knew exactly where we were and what we were doing and they wanted us to realize it.'

Romy drew on her cigarette. The ash fell unheeded onto her dress. Her eyes caught mine for a moment, then dropped. I could not quite measure her reaction. I had expected her to be surprised and frightened by my last statement. Instead she seemed to be pondering in her own mind, as if she was trying to link it up with something she knew already.

She noticed the fallen ash and brushed it off her knee. 'They chose a very complicated way of making their point.'

'It had the desired effect on me anyway. It showed an attention to detail and a delicacy of touch which was far more effective than crude threats of violence.'

She turned to the low table to stub out her cigarette. 'Yes, I think I see what you mean. How big is this diamond?'

'About the size of a sugar lump.'

'Can I see it?'

92

'Why not? You stay here and I'll fetch it.'

I went into the kitchen, retrieved the diamond from the sugar bowl and brought it back into the sitting-room. She took it and laid it on the palm of her hand, just as I had done.

'What would you say it's worth?'

She tilted it, studying it at different angles. 'At least a hundred thousand pounds. Madame de Sonis had one of about this size and she had it valued for insurance. But why couldn't Varzi have smuggled it into the country himself, or got someone he knew and could trust? Why did he have to ask you to do it?'

'I've asked myself those questions a few times already. Perhaps there was no one in his entourage that he could trust. Perhaps he thought that someone like me could get past customs more easily. You know,' I added, with hearty jocularity, 'clean-cut, clean-living Englishman with an honest face – '

'The sort of man who can be trusted never to pinch a diamond – or a woman.'

'Thanks for the compliment.'

She gazed at me with a perfectly straight face. 'You're welcome.'

She handed me back the diamond, picked up her glass and took a sip of brandy. I wondered what had caused her barbed remark. The awkward pause was punctuated by the squeal of a heavy lorry's brakes down on the Cromwell Road, followed by an ominous thud.

'Don't you feel that all this elaborate ritual for handing over the diamond is unnecessary? I mean, to me it doesn't ring quite true.'

As I had anticipated she had given expression to the doubts which had arisen in my own mind and started up a train of thought which I did not wish to follow.

'That's not my problem. I intend to do exactly as I'm told, hand over the diamond at the time and place of their choosing. That 'phone call was to fix the rendezvous. By three o'clock tomorrow I'll be shot of the whole thing.'

'Where do you have to go?'

'Better for you not to know. Somewhere west of London.'

'Can't I come with you?'

'Definitely not.'

'You may be going into danger. Remember the Bella Napoli. I can't believe that was coincidence. Not now.'

'It may not have been entirely coincidence. If that bar was a meeting place for Varzi's faction the shooting-up proves that he's under pressure – enough to be forced to make a deal with a foreigner like me.'

Romy took her shoes off and tucked her legs up under her as she settled into the corner of the sofa. The last person I had seen do that was Juliet. It made me uncomfortable to see Romy unconsciously adopt my ex-wife's favourite posture. The raw wound which Juliet had left still hurt but it was now a more distant ache. She had been very beautiful in a technical kind of way – like those fashion models you see in the pages of *Woman's Journal*. Romy's sexuality was more overt and the very sensuous way she had wriggled into a comfortable position and leaned back against the cushions had been completely natural and unconscious.

'Has it struck you that your arrest came at a very convenient moment to fit in with Signor Varzi's plans? I've wondered several times about the kind man who directed me to the Hotel Verona. I was so worried at the time that it did not occur to me to wonder how he came to be there so conveniently.'

'Yes, that did strike me.' I nodded, took my eyes off her legs and tried to suppress memories of my bedroom in the Hotel Verona. 'But how could anyone have foreseen that Ahmed would stow himself away in the Rolls?'

'No one could foresee it, but it is easy to understand. Without his beloved Rolls he had nothing to live for. I find it rather touching that he would not be separated from it. He was like a little foetus curled up in the womb of its mother.'

'The little foetus gave me a nasty moment when he was hauled out in Naples. I was certain he was dead.'

Romy nodded at the diamond, which I had placed on the arm of the sofa. 'Why did you not tell me about the diamond when we were in Naples? I would not have tried to smuggle my bottle of perfume. That might have spoilt everything.'

'The bottle of perfume suited me. It was small beer. I thought that if you knew about the diamond you would be nervous and your nervousness would communicate itself to the customs men.'

'I was very nervous at Ramsgate. That was a nasty moment.'

She laughed as she remembered. 'When I put on my cardigan the *flacon* nearly popped out. I thought he was sure to see me pushing it back into place.'

She looked down at the place where the Tunisian perfume had been concealed. I also looked. She was wearing one of those brassières which support the breasts from underneath, pushing them up into firm, emphatic mounds.

'I'm wearing it this evening. Do you like it?'

'I did think there was a nice smell. I wasn't sure whether it was your perfume or the orchid.'

'It's the perfume.'

She withdrew the pin which was holding the orchid in place. She held it in her long slim fingers, turning it slowly to admire its colours. I remembered what it had been like to feel those fingers caressing my body, to feel those nails spurring my flesh. 'It's hard to believe this was intended as some kind of threat. It's so beautiful. I must put it in water or it will wither. Do you have a small vase anywhere?'

She looked up and surprised the expression in my eyes.

I said: 'Yes. I think so. In the kitchen somewhere.'

She unfolded her legs and stood up, still watching me. I put the diamond in the fob pocket of my trousers and followed her as she walked on bare feet through to the kitchen. The green dress was slightly shiny and it rippled as she moved.

She found a small vase and went to the sink to fill it with water. I was standing behind her as she put the orchid into it. Now I was near enough to smell the perfume strongly and mingled with it a much more exciting human scent. From behind I put my arms round her, clasping her softness. She put the vase down on the draining-board, laid her hands on top of mine, pressing them closer. She tilted her head back against my shoulder to look up into my face, lips parting.

We stood like that for half a minute whilst heart-beats quickened and blood began to course. Then I turned her round, put my hands on her temples to tilt her head back.

She twisted her head sideways, turning her lips away and pushed herself gently away from me.

'No, Patrick. Don't kiss me. Please.'

She was breathing quickly, her voice not much more than a whisper.

'But why? What's wrong?'

'What happened in Naples – . I had not intended it. You must not think I am like that.'

I let my arms fall to my sides. 'But you were wonderful. It was the best – '

'I behaved like a woman of the street. I have been so ashamed of myself since then.'

I tried not to let anger and frustration creep into my voice.

'It was a perfectly natural thing to do. We'd just had a narrow escape from death. Heavens, you don't believe I'd think any the less of you because – '

'We were both under stress. I would never have let it happen otherwise.' She put out a hand to touch my cheek. 'Please try to understand, Patrick.'

CHAPTER 7

Next morning, over the boiled eggs and toast and coffee, we discussed Romy's plans in a realistic way for the first time. She told me that she intended to go round the flat-sharing agencies and see if she could rent a bed-sitter until she was well enough established to get a flat of her own. Then she planned to visit Madame de Sonis's publishers to see if there was any chance of them offering her a job or putting her on to some other house which had a vacancy.

'I'll need to get some clothes too.' She looked out of the window at the steady rain. 'Especially a raincoat and some stronger shoes.'

'You're all right for money?' I asked, careful not to show too much concern. The previous night's rebuff still rankled.

'I am for the moment. I bought some American Express cheques in Tunisia.'

While she was getting ready to go out I 'phoned the showroom and left a message for Ritchie, telling him that I wouldn't be able to get in that day. I did not explain that I was going to spend the morning trying to hire the nearest thing I could find to a Saab Turbo and fitting a set of false number-plates to it.

By ten o'clock I had located and booked a black Saab 900 GL and hoped that with a faked set of number-plates this would be sufficiently good identification to satisfy Varzi's gruff-voiced 'relative'. I was just about to telephone the number-plate manufacturer, who had done rush jobs for me in the past, when Romy came to tell me that she was ready to go. She had put on a light-fawn suit with dark brown edging and lapels.

'Do I look all right? I mean, the sort of person a reputable publisher would want to employ?'

I looked at her dispassionately before I nodded. 'You look all right. Very nice, in fact. Yes, I think I'd employ you if I were a publisher.'

'How do I get to Leicester Square? It's so long since I've been in London I've forgotten how the Metro works.'

'The Underground.' I left the telephone directory lying open and stood up. 'You take the District Line from West Kensington and change to the Piccadilly Line at Earl's Court.

'Piccadilly Line at Earl's Court,' Romy repeated, concentrating hard. 'I'll try and remember that.'

'You've got that key I gave you? Don't lose it or you won't be able to get in. And if you get back before I do, lock up securely and don't answer the door-bell. If you get into trouble ring Anthea or Ritchie at the showroom. You've got the number?'

'Yes. I wrote it down.' We had reached the front door. She put a hand behind my neck and kissed me on the cheek. 'Please take care of yourself. I wish I was coming with you.'

'It'll be okay. By the time I see you again we shall be out of the wood.'

I was just about to open the door when the street buzzer sounded. I picked up the intercom.

'Who is it?'

'Mr Malone?'

'Yes.'

'Police, sir. About the car you reported stolen.'

'Oh.' I was surprised. The clerk I had reported the theft to had seemed totally disinterested and here I was being given a personal service. 'You'd better come on up. It's the third floor.'

I pressed the button which released the lock on the street door, then opened my flat door to let Romy out.

'It's someone from the police,' I explained. 'He's come about the Saab. You'll probably meet him coming out of the lift.'

I watched her hurry off down the corridor, then went back into the flat. I just had time to close the door of the chaotic double bedroom and take the breakfast things from the sitting-room into the kitchen before the bell rang.

The moment I saw the two men standing outside I guessed that they had not come about a simple case of car theft. I even wondered if they were police officers at all. One was short and tubby, with a balding head and chubby, sunburnt cheeks. He wore a grey suit. The other was clad in a shiny, brown leather jacket and flared trousers. He had ginger hair grown rather long around the ears and neck and a full moustache of Edwardian style.

'Mr Malone?' the younger man enquired.

'That's right.'

'May we come in, sir? We'd like to have a few words with you.'

'Yes. Come on in.'

I held the door for them as they walked past me, very self-possessed, alert and observant. I closed the door and followed them into my sitting-room. The older, tubby man had drifted unobtrusively towards the cabinet which contained my collection of vintage radiator mascots. The ginger man moved into the middle of the room and turned, waiting for me. He was so confident and sure of himself that I almost had the feeling that I was a visitor in my own house.

'Now, sir. You reported a car stolen yesterday afternoon.'

Slightly riled by the way in which they helped themselves to my living space, I said: 'I hope you'll forgive me, but you haven't introduced yourselves yet.'

'I beg your pardon, sir?'

'You've come without an appointment and I only have your word that you are police. How do I know that you really are?'

The two men exchanged a glance. I thought the older one nodded imperceptibly. Trying to conceal his resentment the other produced his card and handed it to me. I glanced at it, nodded and looked enquiringly at the tubby one.

'You've seen my I.D. card, sir, and I can vouch for my colleague.'

I knew from the brisk tone that it would not pay me to push this point any further. At least I now knew that the man who was doing the talking was a Detective-Inspector Bannerman of the Metropolitan Police. It was a little disquieting that an officer of that rank was interested in the disappearance of the Saab.

'Why don't you take a seat?'

I indicated a couple of chairs. Bannerman accepted the invitation but the senior man remained aloof. His tour of inspection had now taken him to the bookcase. I shrugged my shoulders and sat down opposite Bannerman. I expected the usual notebook to be produced but the detective had folded empty hands on his knees.

'This car you reported stolen, sir. I understand it was a Saab with a Tunisian registration number. Can you tell me how it came to be in your possession?'

'I'd just imported it – on behalf of the company I work for. That's "Automobiles of Quality" in the North End Road. We specialize in Rolls-Royce and Bentley, all second-hand stuff but of any age.'

'Yes, I understand that, sir, but this was a Saab.'

'I know. It was part of a package. The car we really wanted was a 1929 Phantom II Rolls, but the vendor wanted to dispose of both cars at the same time. They were in Hammamet in Tunisia. I flew out with the intention of bringing the Rolls back myself, but in the end I was able to make arrangements to collect them both.'

'You brought them by road?'

'By ship to Naples and then by road – at least, that's what we intended – '

'So you needed a driver for the second car?'

'That was no problem. The secretary of the owner of the cars, who was deceased, was coming back to England and I arranged for her to drive the Saab while I drove the Rolls.'

Bannerman nodded. 'So you returned to this country in a convoy of two cars.'

The remark had been put on the line in such a way that it could be taken as a statement or an implied question. I was already wondering how much they knew. It was obvious that the mere fact of my having reported a stolen car would not have brought two detectives to see me – if indeed the older man was a detective. For an awful moment I wondered if Ahmed had suffered a relapse and died, and the Italian police had requested my extradition. It was unnerving to feel that I could no longer think of the British police as a friendly organization to whom I could turn for help if I was in trouble.

'We certainly did not,' I said with some force, taking Bannerman's remark as a question. It was an advantage to me now that I had not told Ritchie the whole truth. My brain did not have to work so hard on the heavily edited story I was going to tell these policemen. 'I only got the Rolls as far as Naples.'

'Oh! How was that, sir?'

In a mirror I could see Bannerman's colleague still moving

behind me. He had now got round to examining a framed reproduction of one of Gordon Crosby's pictures of the Ulster TT. He wasn't really interested in the pictures. He was using the glass as a mirror and just for an instant our reflected gazes met. I was not too sure what I would do if he disappeared into the kitchen. One thing was certain: I would not be offering them mid-morning coffee, with cream and sugar.

'It's quite a story,' I said. 'You really want to hear it?'

'I always appreciate a story, sir – if it's a good one.'

I looked hard at Bannerman but he had kept his face absolutely straight.

'The Rolls-Royce I was buying had been in the same ownership since 1929 and had been looked after by the same chauffeur. He was an old Arab named Ahmed, and he was totally devoted to the car. I realized when I saw him that it was breaking his heart to part with it. Anyway, the long and the short of it is that he decided not to be parted from it. He stowed away in a special compartment he'd made behind the back seat. I'd no idea he was there until the customs people searched the car at Naples and found him.'

'I see.' Bannerman had listened impassively, moving his shoulders restlessly inside his shiny leather jacket. As I'd told the story I'd realized how improbable it sounded. How could one expect an unemotional Englishman like Bannerman to understand what went on in the head of a simple Arab like Ahmed? 'What did the Italian police do about it?'

'They arrested me, of course. I was put in gaol.'

'What day would that have been, sir?'

'Let's see. Today's Tuesday. That must have been Saturday. Saturday morning.'

'And you reported the car stolen on Monday evening. When did you arrive back in this country?'

'Lunchtime yesterday.'

The Inspector glanced towards his colleague as if offering him the opportunity to intervene, but the other man had found my copy of *A Pride of Bentleys* on a side table and was studying the photographs with interest.

'Let me sort this out, Mr Malone.' Bannerman had at last brought out a notebook and was jotting down some facts. 'You landed in Naples on Saturday morning and were arrested by the Italian authorities because they had found an illegal immigrant concealed in your car.'

'Yes,' I agreed. Bannerman had grasped the situation remarkably quickly.

'They must have felt they'd made what one could call a fair cop, sir. Yet according to what you have just told me you were back in London on Monday.'

'That's right. I was released on Sunday evening and we drove back through the night. I wanted to get out of Italy before they changed their minds.'

'So you were not detained for more than one day. How do you account for that?'

'A day and a half, to be accurate. Miss Favel – that's the former secretary who was driving the Saab – she got in touch with the British Consulate and they got busy. Luckily for me Ahmed had recovered enough to make a statement – he'd been unconscious when they took him from the car – and he confirmed that I knew nothing about him being there.'

Bannerman permitted himself a faint smile. 'Yes. It was lucky for you, sir. Now, this Miss Favel whom you mention. She had no difficulty in clearing customs?'

'No.'

'So you were released on Sunday. You must have been in Naples when those ten people were killed in the café there.'

'Yes. Though we didn't realize it at the time. We only found out it had happened when we got back to England and read the papers.'

I stood up and went to open a window. Perhaps the room was becoming stuffy, perhaps I simply wanted to confirm my freedom of action and my right to do what I wanted in my own flat. I had not anticipated that my reporting the theft of a car would result in my having to answer so many awkward questions. Had we after all been linked with the bar massacre and had the Italian police asked their British colleagues to check me over?

'Inspector, do you mind my asking?' I said, as I went to my desk to get a cigarette. 'Are you investigating the theft of a car from outside these premises or my adventures while I was abroad? I would just like to know so that I can be of more help to you.'

'There may be a connection, sir,' Bannerman said equably. 'I'd be grateful if you would answer a few more questions.'

I did not respond, but snapped the desk lighter and lit my cigarette. He took that to indicate consent.

'You arrived in Naples on Saturday morning and left on Sunday evening.' His eyes were down on his notebook and his next question was asked in an almost conversational tone. 'Apart from the intervention of the British Consulate, did you have contact in Naples with any other party?'

This was the crunch question. The fact that it had been asked at all made it certain that one or other of the risks I had taken to get back to England was catching up with me. The quiet way Bannerman had put his finger on the sensitive spot had caught me off balance.

'I'm not quite sure what you mean by that.' I exhaled smoke and appeared to be searching my memory. 'I met some rough characters in gaol, including an Irishman named McQueen who knew a good deal more about Italian prisons than I did. He gave me some idea of what I'd have to face unless the charges were dropped. That was another reason why I wanted to get out of Italy as quickly as possible.'

Concealing the truth from my own police was putting a lot of strain on me. I could only hope that it did not show. The temptation to blurt out the whole story was very strong, but would they be able to understand what it had felt like to be locked in an Italian prison with the prospect of having to stay there for the best years of my life? And if I came clean and told them about the diamond and the deal I had made with Varzi, would they be able to give Romy and me the protection which we would most certainly need?

I glanced at my watch. The time was coming up to eleven o'clock, and I still had preparations to make before I set off for the rendezvous with Sagrano. I did not think that I was about to be arrested, but if this questioning went on for much longer I was going to have to think of some way to get rid of them. In four hours, if all went well, I would have delivered the diamond and would have honoured my deal with Varzi. When that was done it would be easier to decide how to resolve my worries about the risks I had accepted in order to get back to England. Meanwhile, I could see no way in which the British police could have found out about the midnight meeting in the Naples gaol.

'And you made no other contacts in Naples, sir?' Bannerman repeated his original question, slightly rephrased, making sure that if I was lying it was not by mistake.

'No,' I said. 'As I say, I was only too happy to get out of the place.' Then, deciding that a little aggression from my side would not be amiss: 'So now that you've got the story of my life these past few days, what progress have you to report on the theft of the Saab?'

Behind me I heard the balding, older man shut the book with a snap and put it back on the table. Then, for the first time, I heard his quiet, placatory voice.

'As a matter of fact, Mr Malone, we have recovered your Saab. It is in the Stolen Car Squad's garage in Acton and if you like we can give you a lift up there now so that you can reclaim it.'

CHAPTER 8

It was midday by the time I had collected the Turbo from the police underground garage and returned to the flat. According to the report, it had been found intact in one of the car-parks at Heathrow Airport. Luckily I had remembered to bring my own set of keys so I was able to start it up. I would have liked to ask the Stolen Car Squad how they solve the problem of keys for difficult cars like the Saab, but by then I was too pushed for time to waste any.

After ringing up the car-hire firm to cancel the Saab 900 GL I had ordered I reached for the A-D volume of the London telephone directory. There was a possibility that Bannerman and his uncommunicative colleague would try to locate Romy and question her to see whether she corroborated my story. I wanted to tell her exactly what to say. I found the number of Madame de Sonis's publishers and asked to be put through to the receptionist's desk.

'Can you tell me,' I asked the girl, 'whether a Miss Favel has been in this morning?'

'Miss Favel? We have no one of that name on the staff.'

'No. She's a visitor.'

'Who was she coming to see?'

'I don't know. She was going to call in about getting a job.'

'There has been no one of that name this morning,' the girl told me in dismissive tones.

I pressed the cradle down and dialled the number of the showroom.

'Automobiles of Quality, can I help you?'

'Anthea, it's Pat.'

'Pat. What can I do for you?'

'There's a chance that Romy Favel may contact Ritchie, and if she does – '

'That's the person you had dinner with last night?' Anthea's voice had become a little cold. I wondered if Ritchie had been unwise enough to sing Romy's praises to his own secretary. 'No. She hasn't 'phoned.'

'If she does, would you give her a message?'

'Mm hmm.'

'Tell her that if anyone asks her any questions the Neapolitan gentleman whose name begins with V does not exist.'

'Are you being serious, Pat?'

'Yes. Have you got it?'

'The Neapolitan gentleman whose name begins with V does not exist,' Anthea repeated the phrase in the prim tones she used for discouraging undesirable customers.

'That's right. It's really quite important.'

'You astonish me,' Anthea said and broke the connection.

Time was rapidly running out and I was beginning to become worried about making Sagrano's deadline. I'd had no chance to try and figure out what lay behind the visit of the two detectives, nor why the tubby one had produced his trick card just when Bannerman had me by the short hairs. I knew that I ought really to have left a message with Anthea telling Ritchie that the Saab had been recovered, but I was afraid that he might insist on my bringing it round so that his Middle Eastern customer could see it. Recovering the car had been my first really good stroke of luck and I intended to take full advantage of it.

When I had replaced the receiver I went into the kitchen and emptied the sugar bowl onto the table. The diamond rolled out among the lumps, glittering wickedly. It seemed, if anything, to have grown even larger. I inserted it in the small ticket pocket under the waist-belt of my trousers. The belt pressed the angular shape against my skin, reminding me of its presence with every move.

I got out my set of quarter-inch Ordnance Survey Maps and the AA Gazetteer. The village of Monxton turned out to be not far from the motor-racing circuit at Thruxton, which I knew. An hour and a quarter would be sufficient to cover the seventy-five miles but I wanted to leave myself some extra time in case of possible checks.

Down in the street I found myself glancing to right and left before crossing the road to where the Turbo was parked. Since the incident of the bogus painter I had been taking more interest in anyone who had found a reason for lingering in Elton Square. It was a bright, crisp June day with fleecy white clouds drifting across the blue sky. A lot of the men were in shirt sleeves, and most women in light dresses. They all seemed to be behaving in a perfectly natural way.

I drove round the square once just to make sure that no car had pulled out to follow me. Then I headed for the Cromwell Road. Whoever had stolen the car had apparently treated it with respect. There was no damage that I could see. I even had the impression that its performance had improved. The engine was revving very freely as I swept up onto the Hammersmith Flyover. There was enough power to induce slight front-wheel spin in the up-gradient.

At this lunch-time hour the traffic on the roads leading out to the M3 had slackened. Many lorry drivers had already pulled in somewhere for their midday meal. I slid back the sunshine roof and took it gently, not attempting to challenge the Minis and small vans that buzzed around me, weaving and thrusting to gain a few places. Once on the M3 I brought my cruising speed up to 80 mph and keep it there. Since I was once involved in a multiple pile-up I have had a prejudice against being in a bunch of vehicles moving along in close company at 70 m.p.h. A burst of acceleration can take you clear of them, and for my money the fast lane is the safest place. Consequently I had developed a habit of keeping a constant eye on my mirror. I liked to be whine and the Saab swept quickly to 120 mph. Behind me

Some miles after the first interchange with the A322 I became interested in a black Ford Granada which had been keeping station a steady quarter of a mile behind me. I gently depressed the accelerator. The turbocharger came in with its characteristic whine and the Saab swept quickly to 120 m.p.h. Behind me the Ford responded, though a good deal more slowly, and within a minute was back in station again. When I eased back to 70 it did the same. As I approached the interchange with the A322 I saw it creep closer.

I decided to subject the other driver to a little test. At the interchange, I cut across the traffic and peeled to the left off the motorway. I turned right at the roundabout and crossed the bridge over the M3. The traffic lights two hundred yards ahead were green. I used the full power of the Turbo's acceleration to send the car rocketing forward and crossed them at 120 m.p.h., just as they changed. Half a mile ahead I braked sharply and peeled off left for another climbing loop. It brought me onto the A30 opposite the Cricketers Inn. Now I was heading back towards London on a normal main road. I knew that there was a turning to the right a quarter of a mile on. Again the lights favoured me and I took the right-angle turn with squealing tyres. After a series of curves I was back at the traffic lights I had crossed a minute before. Once again my fierce acceleration enabled me to get across them while they were still green. Ahead was the roundabout where I had left the M3. I crossed the bridge, kinking first left and then right to rejoin the motorway. The little excursion had taken exactly two and a half minutes and had been rather like one lap of a small and very tortuous racing circuit. This time I ignored the speed limit. The Turbo gobbled up the other vehicles as it built up its maximum speed and took me over the brow of the hill at 120 mph.

I checked the traffic behind me carefully for the next ten miles but the black Ford Granada did not re-appear. When I came to the big roundabout on the Andover bypass I had ten minutes in hand. The road sign indicated that the village of Monxton was two miles down the minor road on the left. At the entry to the village the road narrowed and I almost overshot the entrance to the lane. I had to stop the car and reverse before turning in. There was nothing on the road behind me. I felt confident that since I had shed the Ford Granada nothing had been following me.

The narrow, rough and slightly uphill track soon broadened out into a wide, grass-covered medieval highway of the kind beloved by ramblers. The car jolted over deep ruts left by farm tractors. I found myself surrounded by fields of corn patterned by catspaws of wind. There was no other car in sight. I drove on till I came to a junction of four grassy tracks, then stopped. I checked my watch against the car's quartz clock. It was exactly three o'clock.

I stopped the engine and got out. Overhead between me and the blue sky a heavenly host of larks were singing their hearts out. A glider was circling to make its landing at Thruxton and from the old RAF airfield at Andover a parascender was rising mysteriously at the end of a long hawser. High above the larks a couple of helicopters from the Army Air Corps base at Middle Wallop stooged about the sky.

The only other human beings visible were the driver of the tractor near the farm buildings half a mile away, and two people on foot trudging up the grass track towards me from the opposite direction. As they came nearer I could make out that they were a man and a girl. I guessed they had been lying in the long grass and been disturbed by the unexpected arrival of a car in this lonely spot. Both were wearing most unsuitable shoes for a walk in the country. The girl's jeans were tucked into high leather boots with sharp heels which kept sinking into the grass. The man was padding along on blue and white canvas sports shoes. At a distance of fifty yards I could see their faces. The girl would not have been bad looking if she'd bothered to deal with her spots and wiped the petulant scowl from her face. The man was a nasty-looking bit of work. Even on this hot day he was wearing a leather motor-cycling jacket and his chin was dark with sprouting bristles.

When they were twenty paces away the girl stopped. She reached into the canvas bag slung from her arm and took out a pistol. I recognized the familiar .38 Smith and Wesson. She cocked the action then held the weapon beside her thigh, the barrel pointing towards the ground. The confident way she handled the pistol and her balanced legs-apart stance showed that she'd had plenty of practice in its use.

I'd been leaning against the car. Now I straightened out, nerves tensed. There were the people I had come to meet. They must have left their own vehicle beyond the railway embankment a quarter of a mile away.

The man came closer, taking care not to mask her line of fire. 'Mister Maloney?'

I did not bother to correct him. I nodded and felt for the diamond in my fob pocket. Above Andover airfield the parascender had detached his tow-line and was floating rapidly towards the earth. I held the diamond up between index finger and thumb. The sunlight struck it and bounced off, shattered into all the colours of the spectrum.

'Just put it on the seat of the car,' the man commanded.

I opened the door of the Saab and placed the diamond on the driver's seat.

'The keys. Where are they?'

'Still in the slot.'

'Right. Now you walk.'

'What?'

'You walk. We take the car.'

'That wasn't part of the deal.'

'It's part of the deal now. You start to walk. Git!'

I turned to check what the girl was doing. She had half raised the pistol to a firing position. Her whole expression had changed. She looked like a randy woman anticipating sexual action. I did not like the emotional feed-back I was receiving from these two. The man was standing well back from me watching my face warily with his beady little eyes. There was no doubt that they were professionals. They would not crowd in close enough for me to attack, nor jab guns into my body like television crooks.

I knew I had no choice. I turned and started to walk back in the direction of the village. After a few seconds I heard the car being started up and the doors slamming. The sound of the engine and the gears grating told me that it was being turned. Then in low gear it began to come after me. The broad grass track stretched for a good three hundred yards ahead. There was no real cover on either side. The hedges had been cut to ground level by the farmer. I felt like a victim of pirates being made to walk an endless plank.

I turned round to take a quick look. The Turbo was about fifteen paces behind me. The girl was standing on the passenger's seat, the upper part of her body sticking out through the sliding panel, her gun hand resting on the front of the roof. I knew with absolute certainty that she was lusting to kill me.

The world suddenly seemed a very attractive place. Danger had tuned my senses more finely to its riches. I could smell the wild flowers growing by the track, hear the rustle of the wheat ears in the wind, feel the warmth of the sun on my body. Never had the singing of a lark sounded more joyous.

Then the sound of the engine told me that the Saab was stopping. It could only be because she wanted a steady support for her forearm. When the car halted she would fire and the bullets would smash into my back. The instinct to live took over. I ducked sideways, raced towards the low bank bordering the track. I cleared it head first, landed somersaulting and went into a forward roll which carried me in amongst the ripening wheat. I rolled sideways, crawled fast for another few yards and then lay doggo.

The Saab had stopped. I heard the doors opening as they scrambled out.

'Why didn't you plug him, you stupid bitch?'

'Don't worry. I'll soon flush him out. Watch for the grass moving.'

I froze and listened for the noise of footsteps crashing into the wheat. Her voice, when she spoke again, sounded very close.

'You in there. Stand' up or I'll shoot the shit out of you.'

I cringed low, my nails digging into the ground. Then the first bullet came. It passed a couple of feet to my left. The next just missed me on the right. The third went above my head, the fourth just short of my feet. She was firing to a pattern.

At battle school I had been put through an experience like this, stuck in a narrow trench with my head sticking out while four Bren guns on fixed lines sent a stream of bullets past my head. The experience had been shattering, even though it had only been a simulated situation. This was for real and the fear I felt was degrading. It could only be a question of time before she hit me.

Odd things happen to your mind when you're under maximum stress. I had crushed a butterfly in my scramble for cover and its beautiful wings were hopelessly damaged. It would never fly again, but die a slow and agonized death. As I crushed it with my hand to release it from suffering. I had time to think that this was probably the last conscious act I would perform on earth.

The whirlwind seemed to come from nowhere. All at once the wheat stems bent under the wind and a roaring noise filled the air. Feeling myself being stripped of my cover, I scrabbled at the earth, obsessed by a primordial instinct to burrow further into it. Then the roar of an engine and the whirling clatter of vanes restored my capacity to reason. I rolled onto my back and stared up. One of the cruising helicopters had swung low over the cornfield. It was close enough for me to see the faces peering down at me.

On the track the man and the girl had piled into the Saab, slamming the doors. As the engine was started and rammed into gear the girl stood on the seat again and loosed off a string of shots through the sunshine roof at the helicopter. The noise of the whirring blades was so great that the detonations sounded like dull thumps. The engine of the car was inaudible as it accelerated towards the main road, leaping and bumping over the ruts.

The helicopter rapidly gained height, canting crazily as the pilot manoeuvred it to follow the Saab. Then it rose rapidly to a couple of hundred feet and clattered off towards its base at Middle Wallop.

I picked myself to my feet. The ascending lark had been scared out of the sky by the helicopter, but all over the field I could see butterflies identical to the one I had mercy-killed. I took a deep breath of the good air. Then I went back to the track and began to run towards the railway embankment. Beyond it I could see vehicles moving east and west along the A303. Already the helicopter must be radioing its base. Within minutes the police would be converging, and I was not in the mood to answer questions.

'Just a small service,' Varzi had said, before putting forward his proposition. The deal I had made with him had abruptly turned very sour. Now that they had the diamond in their possession they did not need me alive any more. In fact, it figured that from their point of view I was better dead.

And the same argument could apply to Romy.

It was after five when I at last got back to the flat, having thumbed a lift into Andover and caught a train to Waterloo. I would have taken a taxi across London if I'd thought it would save time, but I knew that during the rush-hour the Underground would be quicker. From West Kensington Station I ran most of the way to Elton Square. As usual the lift was at the top of the building. I ran up the nine flights of stairs. All three locks on the door of the flat were fastened. I had a premonition that no one had opened it since I had left four and a half hours earlier, but I was calling Romy's name as I entered. No answer. I went into the bedroom. Her clothes were still strewn about as she had left them. In the kitchen the empty sugar bowl stood on the table with the lumps scattered around it. She obviously had not been back.

I still had the number of the publishers in my head. I went to the telephone on my desk and rapidly dialled the seven digits. The same receptionist replied.

No. Miss Favel had not been there. Unless, the receptionist added, she had come and gone during the lunch break.

Next I rang the showroom.

'Automobiles of Quality, can I help you?'

'Anthea.' I paused and made an effort to keep the anxiety out of my voice. 'Has Romy been in touch with you or Ritchie? It's Pat here.'

'You sound very breathless, Pat. Is everything all right?'

'I hope so. Has she 'phoned you?'

'Not while I've been here, but I had to go to the dentist this. afternoon. Would you like to speak to Ritchie?'

'If he's in, yes.'

'Hang on. I'll see if he's free.'

I waited and guessed that the delay was because she was telling Ritchie about my earlier message and present enquiry.

'Pat!' His robust voice sounded in my ear and I moved the instrument a few inches away from it. 'What are you and Romy up to? All this cloak and dagger stuff.'

'I haven't seen her since this morning and, as she doesn't seem to know her way round London all that well, I told her to get in touch with you if she had any problems.'

'Good advice, old soul, but she hasn't been in touch with me. More's the pity.'

'Oh, well,' I said rather lamely, 'I just thought I'd check.'

'You sound a bit fraught, Pat. What's happened?'

'Nothing,' I lied. I had not told Ritchie that the Turbo had been recovered and I could not bring myself to do so now, only to have to cap it with the news that it had gone again. 'If she does contact you ask her to ring me without delay, will you?'

'Will do. But I wish you'd tell me what this is all about.'

'I will, Ritchie. But not now. I want to try a few other places where she might be.'

'Hope you find her, old pal. Will you be coming to work tomorrow? I've had an interesting proposition from a Scottish Baronet. A Derby drop-head that's been in his family from new.'

'Yes, I'll be in tomorrow – barring accidents,' I told him, and broke the connection.

Despite what I had said there were no other numbers I could try. I prowled aimlessly round the flat attempting to persuade myself that I had no real reason to worry about her till after all the shops and offices had closed. The attempt was not successful. To use up some time and give myself something to do I went into the kitchen to make some tea. I'd had nothing to eat since breakfast, apart from a sausage roll and a Kit-Kat which I'd wolfed at Andover before my train pulled in.

The kettle was coming to the boil and two slices of bread had popped up in the toaster when I heard the sound of someone trying various keys in the front door. Romy was the only person besides Juliet to whom I had given a set so I knew it must be her.

She got the door open just before I reached it and as she came in I seized her and gave her a hug which made her gasp. Behind her the door banged shut.

She seemed astonished by the warmth of my welcome. 'What's all this about, Patrick? You haven't been worrying about me, have you?'

'As a matter of fact, I have. I'm bloody relieved to see you. I've been telephoning those publishers and the showroom trying to contact you.'

'You needn't have worried about me.' She went into the sitting-room, depositing three parcels marked Harrods, Harvey Nicholls and Russell & Bromley on the sofa. 'I've managed very well. And I think I've got a job.'

'I wanted to warn you. I had a visit from the police – '

'I know. They were arriving just as I left, you remember? I met them down below as I came out of the lift. Fancy putting two detectives on a case of car stealing. That's what I call service.'

'The car theft was only an excuse to come in here and interrogate me. They were on to something but I could not make out how much they knew. That's why I wanted to get in touch with you, so that you could tell them the same as – '

She spun round as a loud whistle sounded from the kitchen.

'It's all right,' I said. 'It's the kettle. I'm just making some tea.'

She followed me into the kitchen and while I made more toast and brewed the tea I told her about my conversation with Bannerman and his anonymous colleague. She was strangely on edge and I wondered whether she had 'managed' quite as well as she claimed. She had to make an effort to concentrate on my account of the police questioning. When I told her about the recovery of the Saab she shook her head and two worry lines appeared between her eyebrows.

'Why would someone steal a car and leave it at London Airport? And if it hadn't been damaged at all, how did they get into it without keys?'

'I didn't have time to go into all that. I was running late already and I did not want to miss my rendezvous with Varzi's friends.'

'Yes. I've been thinking about that and hoping you were all right. You're not the only one who worries, you know.'

She touched my arm, but I had both hands occupied. I carried the tray with the cups and slices of Marmite toast into the sitting-room.

'You had good cause to worry. Sit down and I'll tell you what happened.'

My account of the afternoon's events was broken by bouts of quick chewing and hurried swallowing. Before I had finished Romy had put her second slice of toast down and forgotten all about it.

'You think she really meant to kill you?'

'I still don't know for sure whether she would have shot me in the back while I was walking down that track, but I was just not prepared to risk it. Once I was in amongst the corn it was really lethal. She's paranoid, that girl. She'd get more kicks out of shooting a man than being screwed by him.'

Romy had paled. She picked up her cup and took a long drink.

'So the Saab's gone again.'

'Yes. Of course I realize now why there was all that insistence on my going to the rendezvous in that particular car. That complicated rigmarole about the registration number being additional identification was just a cover. I never really quite believed it.'

'What was the point, then?'

'They want a bullet-proof car. It's obvious when you think of it. Bullet-proof cars are not easy to come by and anyone buying one is certain to attract attention to themselves. Varzi intended all along to have that Saab as part of the deal and he very cleverly conned me into delivering it for him.'

'The only thing is, Patrick – I can't see how he'd have known it was bullet-proof. It looks like an ordinary model. That's the whole point.'

'You can spot the extra thickness of the window glass when you get close. Remember the helpful Italian you met outside the customs in Naples.'

'It still doesn't explain why he'd want to have you killed.'

'Because I'm the only person who knows about the diamond and his plan to come to England. Or rather, I *was* the only person.'

'And I'm the other.'

I nodded. 'That was why I got into such a stew about you.'

'Do you think there's another cup of tea in the pot? I could do with it. No, don't bother. I'll get it.'

I lit a cigarette while she went into the kitchen to refill her cup.

'What are you going to do?' she asked me, as she sat down again. 'Will you tell the police?' '

I offered her a cigarette. She nodded. I took one out of the pack and threw it to her. She rescued it from her lap and then made a successful catch of the lighter.

'I'm not sure. I was stalling when they questioned me because I did not want to say anything about Varzi. Partly because I didn't think his threats were empty and partly because I had given him my word. Admittedly things are very different now that his people have taken the Saab and tried to kill me. But it would be embarrassing to go to the police now and confess that I'd smuggled a valuable diamond into the country for someone who is obviously a big-time criminal.'

She flicked the lighter and put the flame to her cigarette. She gazed at me thoughtfully for a moment and I saw that she was going through one of those changes of mood that I found so baffling.

'That was a wonderful welcome you gave me when I came in just now. You really were glad to see me, weren't you?'

'Of course I was.' Her face had the same expression as when we had been sitting together on the sofa the previous evening. This time I was not going to let myself be taken in so easily. But her next remark surprised me. 'You do not know much about women, do you, Patrick?'

'No,' I answered rather curtly. 'But I'm learning fast.'

'That evening in Naples I literally threw myself into your arms. A woman should never do that. I was very cross with myself afterwards. Surely you realized that next time I had to make it harder for you. When I said no last night, why did you not just take me?'

Her eyes were veiled and I found it difficult to read them. At that moment the Arab blood seemed to be flowing very strongly in her.

'Use force, you mean?'

'Yes, if necessary.' She bit on her lower lip as if my expression had made her suddenly apprehensive. 'But not too much force would have been needed.'

We sat at opposite ends of a deep, foamy bath, sponging the sweat off our bodies. The love-struggle had been energetic and there were marks on Romy's sun-tanned skin. She tossed her head scornfully when I expressed concern that I had been too rough with her.

'I gave as good as I took. Look at your shoulder.'

I glanced down and saw the clear imprint of teeth on my flesh. We were still laughing when we realized that the telephone had been ringing for some minutes.

I left wet patches behind me on the carpet as I headed for my desk, wrapping a large towel round my middle.

'Malone speaking. Who is it?'

'Write down this number,' said a man's voice. 'Then go to a 'phone booth immediately and ring it.'

'Balls to that,' I replied. 'If you've got anything to say to me you can say it on this line or not at all.'

'Malone, what game are you playing?'

It was a new voice, and though there was a touch of foreign accent in it, the speaker sounded more educated than the gruff Sagrano.

'What exactly are you talking about?'

'You've double-crossed us.'

'*I* double-crossed *you*?' I retorted, my anger at being shot at suddenly boiling over. 'The boot's on the other foot. It was never in the deal that you should have the car. And what about that paranoid girl of yours? Was it part of her orders to shoot me down?'

'You've double-crossed us,' the man repeated doggedly. 'That we do not forgive.'

'Listen! I went to the meeting-place exactly as I was told and handed the thing over. If they haven't passed it on to Sagrano then they are the ones who are doing the double-cross.'

'Sagrano warned you not to tell the police. Why did you inform them – '

'I told the police *nothing* about it – '

'Why did they come so quickly, chase the car?'

'Because that crazy girl of yours fired at an Army helicopter. Of course they radioed back to their base. The police would know about it in minutes. This is England, not Italy, you know.'

I could hear the man breathing as he digested this statement. I glanced up at Romy. She was standing at the other side of the desk, her eyes wide and apprehensive, trying to make sense of the half of the conversation she could catch.

'Maybe you tell the truth about the police but it is still a fact that you steal the merchandise. Maybe you try to sell to somebody else?'

'That is not true!' I almost shouted. 'You ask the two you sent. They are the ones who are double-crossing you – or Varzi if you like – '

'No names on the 'phone,' he cut in quickly. 'Be careful what you say.'

118

'Then you be careful, too. As far as I am concerned I have kept my part of the deal. What is more I want that car returned.'

'You try to pretend you do not understand, Malone, But you understand very well what I mean. Where was the car last night?'

'In a private garage, like I told Sagrano. You wouldn't expect me to leave a bullet-proof car in the streets of London, now would you? Or perhaps,' I added sarcastically, 'you did not know it was bullet-proof.'

He grunted. 'That had better be true. If you have been to the police you have signed your death warrant. And the same goes for your little Arab half-breed.'

'Keep that line for your next appearance.' I snapped, angered at his slighting reference to Romy. 'Can't you get it that I have not told the police about my deal with Varzi, that you're being double-crossed by your own people?'

'We will give you one more chance,' he said, as if I had not spoken. 'Tomorrow you receive new instructions – '

'It's no good sending me instructions,' I insisted, exasperated by my inability to get my message across, and the man's infuriating way of repeating phrases he must have learned from outdated thrillers. 'I am trying to tell you – '

'Tomorrow you receive new instructions. You make sure you have the goods ready to deliver. Otherwise Sagrano will send more orchids. This time not such a sweet flavour.'

He disconnected and I was left listening to the dialling tone. I put the receiver down and stood up. Romy watched me with a tense expression while I went over to the drinks table and poured myself a hefty Scotch.

'Now I know why those two wanted to kill me. They've pinched the diamond for themselves and they're making out I never handed it over.'

CHAPTER 9

I made Romy stay in the flat when, later that evening, I went round the corner to the Chinese take-away shop. We had decided it would be best to eat at home. When I came back, she had the door open the moment I rang the bell.

'Patrick, I just heard something on the news – '

'Let me get this stuff into the kitchen. I think the sauce carton is leaking.'

I put a hand under the plastic bag to stop the leak from dropping onto the carpet and rushed through to the kitchen.

'There's been a car chase in Slough with shots fired and everything,' Romy told me excitedly, as she followed me. 'I was wondering if it could have been the Saab – '

I put the bag down on the draining-board and began to unpack the warm cartons.

'What did they say?'

'It was just a short news flash. Something about the police chasing a car along the M4. The crooks tried to elude them by turning off into Slough. They abandoned the car and there was a shoot-out before they escaped through the back streets.'

'They say what kind of car it was?'

'No. Just something about a 120 m.p.h. chase.'

I turned the hot tap on and put my hand under it to rinse the sauce off. 'I wonder if I would find out by ringing the Slough police.'

'What will you tell them?'

'That's a point. But if it is the Turbo they're going to trace it back to me in any case.'

'Is it not going to look suspicious if that car really is the Saab and you have not reported it as stolen again?'

'But Varzi, or Sagrano, or whoever is conducting the English end of the operation has remarkably good sources of information. They may even have a contact inside the police.'

Romy turned the oven on and set the temperature to 150. She

put the cartons side by side on the metal bars of the shelves, closed the oven door and straightened up.

'All the same, I think you should go to the police. You were lucky to come back from that meeting alive. I am sure you are in very great danger, Patrick.'

She had gone very pale. Her eyes told me how deeply concerned she was. I was surprised that she cared so much. I glanced at my watch. It was ten past eight.

'All right. I'll ring Scotland Yard and see if I can contact Bannerman.'

I looked up the number in the directory and dialled 230 1212.

'I'd like to speak to Inspector Bannerman, please.'

'Inspector Bannerman?' the switchboard operator asked. 'Which department is he in?'

'I don't know, I'm afraid.'

'One moment, please.'

After a short delay a second voice came on the line. 'Welby speaking.'

'Is that Inspector Bannerman's office?'

'Who is this calling, please?'

'My name's Malone. I know it's rather late but I thought perhaps if he's not there you could give me his 'phone number – '

'The Inspector is out on a case, sir,' Welby cut in, his tone somewhat reproving at the idea that a Scotland Yard detective would have gone home by such a civilized hour as 8.15. 'If you leave your number I'll ask him to telephone you.'

'All right. It's 603 3987.'

'I'll tell him as soon as he gets in, sir.'

'Is he likely to be in tonight?'

'I can't really say, sir. It could be tonight, it could be tomorrow morning.'

Bannerman had not telephoned when Radio 3 closed for the night. By that time Romy and I had discussed every aspect of the situation and still found no good way out of it. The Chinese dinner had been washed down by some of the *vin ordinaire* we had brought back and digestion had been aided by more brandy from the bottle we had broached the previous evening. When I went to switch off the radio, Romy uncoiled her legs and got up from the sofa. The prospect of bed suddenly became very alluring.

She finally fell asleep in my arms some time after two and she did not wake when I gently extracted my numbed right arm from under her head. Myself, I did not get to sleep till the first light of dawn was creeping round the edge of the curtains. I kept hearing noises in the flat which could have been caused by someone moving stealthily around. Twice I got out of bed to check up, verifying that the chain was still on the door and that the window catches were intact.

It was half-past eight when she woke me. She'd been up for half an hour and had already prepared breakfast. We were still sitting at the table drinking a third cup of strong coffee when the 'phone rang.

I made a grimace at her and went to answer it. '603 3987.'

'Mr Malone?' The voice was a strange one. It was not Bannerman or Welby, but I somehow knew that this was not a message from Varzi's people.

'Yes. Malone speaking.'

'This is the Thames Valley Police, sir. Slough station. You reported a car stolen.'

'Er – yes?' It took me a moment to collect my wits. I had not reported the second theft of the Saab, so this man must be referring to the 'phone call I had made to the police the previous evening. The details must have gone into the police pipeline and when the Saab was returned, there must have been some slip-up in procedure so that the registration number had remained on the list of stolen cars.

'Can you confirm the number, sir?'

'It's a Saab Turbo with a Tunis registration – 30.4392.'

'We have the car here, sir. The Superintendent would like you to come and claim it without delay. How soon can you be here?'

'How urgent is it?'

'How soon can you get here?'

'Oh, give me forty minutes,' I told him casually.

This was too much to be coincidence. I was sure now that the car involved in the police chase was my Saab. I returned to the kitchen, picked up my cup and finished the coffee. Romy watched, questioning me with her eyes.

That was the Slough police. They've got the Turbo and want

me to go down and collect it right away. I'll use the Alfa. I'd like you to come too and then you can drive it back.'

As it turned out, forty-five minutes had passed before the Alfa nosed into the forecourt of the red brick building which housed the Slough H.Q. of the Thames Valley Police. I had lost five minutes in a traffic jam at Datchet.

The constable on duty at the counter in the entrance hallway had only been warned to expect me. He obviously regarded Romy as an unexpected bonus. We were shown without delay to the office of the Superintendent himself.

The Superintendent in charge of the Slough station was wearing uniform. He came from behind his desk as the duty constable closed the door on us. A man with ginger hair and a shiny leather jacket was standing with his back to the window. The venetian blinds had been lowered to deflect the low morning sunlight.

'That was quick, sir,' the Superintendent remarked with a smile. 'Our section which watches the motorway reported an Alfa Spyder moving at remarkable speed, but we told our patrol cars to leave you in peace.'

'Thanks.' I was nodding to the man who had turned away from the window. I was not really very surprised to find Bannerman here. His eyes were red and heavy and I guessed that he had not slept the previous night. 'I had the feeling that you wanted me here in a hurry. I brought Miss Favel. I hope you don't mind.'

'I'm glad you did, sir. And I apologize if my man was rather abrupt. The telephone is not as private as people think.'

'Did you get the impression that my line has been tapped?'

'It could have been, sir,' Bannerman answered in an off-hand way. 'Now, if you and Miss Favel would like to be seated we can talk. We have to thank Superintendent Nash here for letting us use his comfortable offices.'

Nash sat in the chair behind his desk while the rest of us settled ourselves in easy chairs arranged round a low table facing the Superintendent.

'Can you answer one question that's been bothering me?' I asked him. 'Was the car involved in that car chase reported on the radio my Saab Turbo?'

'Indeed it was, sir, and my people had quite a problem in

catching it. I'm afraid they had to use a firearm and the body work has suffered some damage.'

'I didn't know your road patrols carried firearms.'

'They don't, sir,' the Superintendent said equably. 'This was not a patrol car. You had not reported the car stolen a second time, sir?'

'I tried to ring Inspector Bannerman at Scotland Yard last night. I spoke to someone called Welby. Did he not give you my message?'

'I got your message this morning,' Bannerman answered. 'By that time the car recovered by the Superintendent's men had been identified as yours.'

'A valuable car, sir,' the Superintendent said. 'I'm surprised you didn't report the second theft earlier.'

'Yes, and a very unlucky one. It had brought me a load of trouble. That was why I wanted to talk to the Inspector before I reported the second theft.'

'Did you leave anything of value in the car, sir?'

I glanced from the Superintendent's face to Bannerman's. The expression of neither of them told me anything.

'Why? Did you find anything in the car when you recovered it?'

'Yes, sir. The thieves abandoned it in a great hurry but they left this in the glove pocket.'

The Superintendent opened the top drawer of his desk and brought out an object wrapped in tissue paper. He unwrapped it carefully so that his finger tips would not touch the contents, then placed it in a clean ash-tray, which he raised so that I could see it. The diamond twinkled mischievously against the amber of the tray.

'They left that behind?'

'You have seen it before?'

'Yes,' I said quietly, glancing again at Bannerman.

'Does it belong to you. sir?'

'No. I was asked to bring it to England by someone I met in Naples.' I turned to face Bannerman. 'I'm afraid I didn't tell you the whole truth yesterday morning, Inspector Bannerman. I hope you'll forgive me when you understand the position I was in. That's why I tried to contact you last night.'

Bannerman may have believed me or he may not. He simply nodded and left it to the other man to continue his questioning.

The Superintendent tilted the tray, causing the diamond to reflect and diffuse a scatter of coloured reflections.

'It's a substantial stone, sir. Have you any idea of its true value?'

'I'm no expert on diamonds, but it's the biggest one I've ever handled. I assume it's worth a very great deal of money.'

'Yet you brought it into the country without declaring it to Her Majesty's Customs and Excise?' Bannerman interposed.

'Yes, I'm afraid I did.' I swung round to face the Inspector. 'When you came to my flat yesterday you asked me whether I'd made contact with anyone in Naples and I said no. In fact, some-one made contact with me. I had reasons for keeping quiet about that yesterday morning, but last night I decided that I'd better tell you the whole story.'

'That was a wise decision.' Bannerman glanced at the Super-intendent and received a nod. 'I'd like you to tell me in your own words. Later I may ask you to make a statement.'

'The statement I made to you yesterday was substantially correct, so I don't need to go over all that again, do I?'

'Not at the moment, sir.'

'What I did not tell you was this. During the night I was in prison I was taken from the cell by a warder who conducted me to some sort of interview room. In it was waiting a man who gave his name as Varzi.'

As I told about my conversation with Varzi and the deal I had struck, Bannerman listened with half-closed eyes, still not taking any notes. The Superintendent gently tipped the diamond this way and that, apparently captivated by the way it reflected the light.

'So the deal was that in exchange for the influence he would use to secure your release, you would deliver the diamond to his relatives in England?'

'Yes.'

'You didn't agree to do anything more than that?'

'No. A small favour, I think he called it.'

Bannerman grunted, then prompted: 'Go on with the story,

sir. You had reached the point where you were taken back to a special cell.'

I was committed now. The man on the 'phone had told me that if I talked to the police I would be signing my death warrant. Even if I had taken that melodramatic warning seriously I now had little alternative.

I picked up the thread of the story, describing how I had been released from prison, but had been unable to arrange for the release of the Rolls. When I came to the events at the Bella Napoli both the Superintendent and Bannerman looked at Romy, but neither of them interrupted my statement. I glossed over our drive back to England, the brush with the customs, and the peculiar incident of the orchids, but I went into more detail about the 'phone call from Sagrano and my encounter with the two who had been sent to meet me.

'When they rang up and accused me of not handing the diamond over I realized I was not out of the wood. I thought I'd carried out my part of the deal and the whole thing was over and done with but when they started threatening Romy as well as me – . There was no way I could get out of that jam so I decided to come clean with you.'

There was silence in the room. The Superintendent put the ashtray down on the middle of his blotter. Bannerman opened his eyes.

'And that is the full story, sir?'

God, I thought. What more does he want? 'In its essentials, yes.'

'It was not in the agreement you made with this man Varzi that you would hand over the car?'

'No, it certainly wasn't.'

Bannerman tapped the pocket where he kept his notebook. 'You omitted to mention in your statement that the car was armour-plated.'

'That did not seem to be a point of any importance. The old lady who'd owned it before had a persecution mania. She thought that her life was threatened. Anyway, I told the customs people at Ramsgate all about it.'

The Inspector nodded, as if he was prepared to concede that point.

'So the diamond was the only thing you agreed to deliver?'

'Yes. I've told you. I know I was contravening Customs and Excise Regulations but there was no personal profit in it for me. I'm willing to accept the consequences of smuggling the thing into Britain. Do they make the punishment fit the crime? I mean, will my sentence be commensurate with the value of the diamond?'

Bannerman's usually serious face creased into a wry smile.

'If so, you'll get off very lightly, sir.'

'I'm not with you.'

The Inspector stood up and went to pick the diamond off the ashtray.

'What do you suppose it's worth, Superintendent?'

The Superintendent also seemed to be sharing in this mysterious joke.

'Oh, I don't know.' He put his head on one side to look at the diamond. 'It's a craftsman job. Say, about a hundred quid.'

'A hundred thousand you mean,' I corrected.

'No, sir. This isn't a real diamond. It's a synthetic one.'

I could find nothing to say. Romy and I exchanged a bitter glance. I reached for a cigarette and lit up. The two policemen were watching me but I don't really believe I outwardly showed any reaction. I drew on the cigarette a few times, adjusting to this extraordinary announcement, trying to work out the implications. It was difficult to accept the fact that a man of Varzi's stature would have allowed himself to be deceived by a synthetic diamond as easily as I had been. Nor could I any longer believe that he had devised such an elaborate plan merely to acquire possession of a bullet-proof car.

'So, what are you going to do about it? I mean, what is my position now?'

'We don't intend to prefer charges against you at present, sir.' Bannerman's smile had disappeared and he had again adopted his stern policeman's expression. 'Though the case could be made that you attempted to obstruct the police in the performance of their duties. We would all have been saved a lot of trouble if you had told me the full truth when I first interviewed you.'

I nodded, trying to appear repentant. 'I know. I'm very sorry about that. But I was in a hell of a situation. They'd threatened to harm not only me but Miss Favel as well if I informed on them. In fact, the same threat was repeated last night. As I tried to explain, they think that I've still got that diamond.'

'In cases such as this,' the Inspector said, with an admonitory pursing of the lips, 'people find out sooner or later that the only sensible course is to come to the police. May I take it, sir, that you are now willing to cooperate with us?'

Romy had remained completely outside all this discussion, leaving the talking to me but listening attentively to every word that was said. I shot her a quick look before answering the Inspector's question, but she did not meet my eye.

'Yes, of course. What do you want me to do?'

Bannerman stood up and crossed to the Superintendent's desk. The latter held out his hand with the diamond resting on his palm.

'I want you to take this stone away with you. If you are contacted again agree to any arrangements the other party propose for handing it over, then let us know the time and place.'

It sounded a reasonable and moderate request, but a vivid memory of the shooting at the Bella Napoli had flashed across my mind. I took the fake diamond which Bannerman dropped into my hand and stowed it away in my fob pocket.

'Can you assure me that there will be proper protection for Miss Favel and me? I don't dismiss the threats that have been made as bluff. You've got to remember that they've already tried to kill me once.'

'You will have adequate protection, Mr Malone, so long as you follow certain rules. I would like you to stay in your flat as much as possible, and notify us when you are going out. That applies to both you and Miss Favel. In fact, if you stay close together it is easier for us to cover you. Above all, do not indulge in any "shaking-off" tactics when you are travelling in your car – like that performance on the M3 yesterday.'

'So the black Granada was a police car?'

Bannerman did not answer the question but I thought that for a moment he was on the defensive. I could imagine that he had given his driver a lambasting for losing me.

'If and when these people contact you, let me know immediately by telephoning this number. It is always manned and if I am not there a message will reach me without delay.'

He handed me a card on which he had ringed one of the two telephone numbers. I put it in my wallet inside the cellophane panel which protected my bank card.

'And the Saab? I understood you wanted me to take it away?'

'If you would, sir,' the Superintendent said, somewhat to my surprise. 'We've checked it for fingerprints and as we don't require it any further I would like to record that it has been returned to its owner.'

That suited me. Madame de Sonis's fears about mysterious assailants may have been unfounded, but until I had successfully handed Varzi's property over to him it would be comforting to travel in a bullet-proof car.

'I'm afraid it has suffered some superficial damage, but it is driveable,' the Superintendent added. 'I'll have it brought round to the front of the building.'

When I saw the Saab parked in the forecourt of the police station beside the Spyder it was obvious that someone had given it a rough ride. Mud was splattered along the bottom of the bodywork, there was a dent in the panel enclosing the near-side front wheel and the front bumper was hanging askew at an angle of several degrees. Perhaps it was driveable in town conditions, but it was not fit to travel at motorway speeds. However, the ignition key was still in its slot. The criminals had baled out in too much of a hurry to engage reverse and withdraw it.

From the constable who made me sign for the Turbo (I'd already signed for the synthetic diamond) I ascertained that there was a Saab agent in Slough.

'I'm not going to try and drive it back to London like this,' I told Romy. 'Will you follow me in the Spyder and I'll take it to the Saab agents straight away?'

The service manager at the Saab agency took one look at the bumper and shook his head. He squatted down and rocked the loose end of the bumper up and down. It was a massive fitting, about six inches deep, covered with a black rubber-like material.

'Never seen one in this condition before.'

'Yes, it's had a hefty bash. I wasn't in the car at the time.'

He nodded at the dent in the wing panel. 'I can see that. But this bumper is supposed to be crash-resistant. It absorbs the first five miles an hour of any impact, and then if it's distorted it resumes its original shape.'

He lowered his head, tilting it sideways till his ear was almost touching the ground.

'Someone's had this off recently. It's only held by two Allen screws – '

'What's that about resuming its original shape?'

The service manager resumed his squatting position.

'You never seen inside a Saab bumper? It's filled with compressible cellular plastic blocks in sections. They bend on impact instead of breaking but the material remembers its original shape and goes back to it.'

He prodded the bumper with a finger. The black covering yielded to his touch.

'Have you had this bumper off, sir?' he asked me accusingly.

'No. I haven't had it off. Why?'

'The plastic blocks have been removed. No wonder the thing's been knocked off its mounting – '

'Just a moment,' I cut in. 'Do you mean that the bumper is mostly hollow?'

He straightened up, a true enthusiast and an obvious devotee of the cars he dealt with.

'You want to see what a bumper looks like? There's one in the workshop we took off a crashed Saab.'

I signalled Romy to wait while I followed the service manager into the workshop. The mechanics working on the lines of engines and cars looked up with interest as he led me to a bench at the side of the shop. He picked up a Saab bumper from half of which the black covering had been stripped. The interior structure was visible. It consisted of a number of sections of whitish plastic, about four inches deep, like extra deep ice-cube trays. He showed me how they could be slid in and out of position once the covering of the bumper had been removed.

'That's what absorbs your impact, see? It's a special Saab feature. You've not seen one of these before?'

'No. That's a new one on me.'

The agents did not have a replacement bumper in stock, but the service manager promised me that if I could give him a couple of hours he would send a van to the Saab works at Marlow and collect a new one. To slap it on would be a matter of minutes. I told him we would go and lunch locally and I'd ring him in an hour's time to confirm that the job had been done.

'We'll find somewhere to eat nearby,' I told Romy when I rejoined her. 'The Turbo should be ready in an hour or so. Let's head down towards the river.'

I let her drive the Spyder down the road which led towards Eton and the Thames. She was still familiarizing herself with the car and we did not talk as we passed the playing fields of the school on our left. Classes were just ending as we passed between the brick buildings of the College and a host of boys in black tail-coats thronged the pavements and spilled over into the road. At the far end of Eton High Street we found that the old bridge was closed, blocked off by bollards and transformed into a pedestrian footway. Romy parked the Spyder on a piece of waste ground reserved by the restaurant on the opposite side of the road. A Vauxhall Magnum, which had been behind us all the way from Slough, cruised past, wending its way towards the town car-park. It was still early for lunch and we were in time to secure a good table by the window, looking out across the river to the castle.

I ordered cocktails and told the waiter that we needed a little time to study the menu.

'Did my driving scare you?' Romy asked me, as the menus were put before us. 'You've been very silent.'

'No. You drove very well. I've been trying to make sense of what happened this morning.'

'That diamond turning out to be a fake? I wonder what Signor Varzi's going to say when he finds out that his precious diamond is synthetic. Somebody must have conned him in a very big way.'

I smiled at her idiomatic and trenchant way of expressing herself. A couple of days in the United Kingdom had restored her familiarity with English, and she had almost lost that attractive accent.

'He didn't strike me as the kind of man who'd let himself be conned. I was the one who was conned.'

'You mean the diamond was just a blind so that he could get hold of the Saab Turbo?'

'No. He would not have gone to those lengths just to secure possession of the car.'

I looked over my shoulder. A party of four had come in. They were talking German and were obviously tourists who had been visiting Windsor Castle.

The waiter came to take our order. Romy ordered Vichyssoise and a rainbow trout. I chose avocado pear with prawns and a steak Diane. To the waiter's disappointment we decided against a bottle of wine. Romy opted for a glass of Chablis and I asked for beer.

The sunshine slanted through the window onto our table. On the river below motor cruisers were chugging by, wives and daughters stretched sunbathing on the decks, father standing skipper-like at the wheel. The vast shape of the castle was outlined against the sky. The Royal Standard floating in the breeze from the Round Tower showed that the Queen was in residence.

The Germans were conversing uninhibitedly in their strong voices, providing good noise cover so that I could talk to Romy without being overheard. I leaned forward across the table.

'I'm sure I was right when I said that the diamond and the elaborate arrangements to use the car as a means of identification were a blind to divert my attention from the real object of the exercise. They wanted the car but not because it was the bullet-proof version.'

The waiter came to make some readjustments to the cutlery laid in front of each of us, then sped away to answer a summons from the German party.

'I thought there was something odd about the way Varzi's man referred to his merchandise when he 'phoned me last night. I jumped to the conclusion that he was talking about the diamond, but I suspect it was something else which he did not want to mention openly on the 'phone.'

Romy's eyes moved and focused on two more new arrivals. I could see them reflected in the glass of a picture on the wall. Both were wearing very fine leather coats and open-neck shirts. They had the dapper assurance of male models and were spruce enough to have stepped out of a clothing catalogue. The waiter put them at the table in the window embrasure beside ours.

I leaned closer to Romy and lowered my voice. 'Varzi's story about the diamond and his plan to escape from Italy sounded a harmless, almost romantic scheme and I fell for it. But I'm sure now that we were carrying something else for him – something much more valuable.'

'More valuable than a diamond?'

'The diamond would have been chicken-feed – even if it was genuine. There's a commodity which fetches far higher prices and I should have cottoned on to it when Varzi's man used the word merchandise. When I was in that gaol in Naples my cell-mates were mostly drug smugglers – '

Romy warned me with a frown. I leaned back as a waiter brought out first course.

'Vichyssoise?'

'That's for me.' Romy picked up her paper napkin and spread it on her knee.

'Avocado with prawns for you, sir?'

I nodded. More customers were coming in and nearly all the tables were now full. The tape deck had been switched on and low music with a lot of bass was coming from invisible loud-speakers.

'You think we were being used to smuggle drugs? I know there's a lot of cannabis resin being produced in Algeria.'

'Cannabis resin, maybe. But I think heroin is more likely. I read about a case the other day when the Customs and Excise seized fifty pounds of heroin and the street value was put at four million pounds. And I know for a fact that there are at least half a dozen Britishers serving sentences in Continental gaols because drugs were planted on their cars without their knowledge. Remember that the Saab was standing in that car-park under the Hotel Verona for a good twenty-four hours.'

Romy was holding her soup-spoon in her hand, the Vichyssoise still untouched. She was obviously very shaken by what I'd said.

'But, Patrick, the car was thoroughly searched at Ramsgate. If there had been any heroin in it they'd have found it, surely.'

'They didn't look in the bumpers. I've just discovered that the bumpers of a Saab are held on by two Allen screws. You know how massive they are – and most of the space inside them is air enclosed by deformable plastic. There is room for about a thousand cubic inches of powder in each bumper.'

'What would that be in weight?'

'Oh, I'm not sure. Think of two-pound bags of sugar. About fifty pounds altogether, say twenty kilos.'

Romy's lips moved silently as she made the calculation. 'So we could have been carrying four million pounds' worth in the bumpers?'

I nodded. 'Yes. Those Saab bumpers make an ideal storage space. The slide-in plastic sections are almost made for the purpose. All anyone had to do was take the bumpers off, insert the heroin and replace them again. Then do the same in reverse to recover the stuff.'

I picked up my spoon and embarked on the avocado and prawns. Romy had put down her spoon and pushed away her bowl of soup. She was studying every newcomer with wary suspicion. It was evident that her nerves were on edge.

'I can't believe that anyone would take the risk involved in putting stuff of that much value in someone else's car. So many things could happen.'

'They may have been forced to take a risk. Heroin is only valuable if it can be put on the market and sold for outrageous prices. Varzi had everything to gain and not much to lose. You can bet that he would only risk a proportion of his total stock on this run. Besides, he had my name and address and the registration number of the Saab. It was unlikely that we'd ever know we had been carrying heroin, and even if I hadn't gone to the rendezvous he would sooner or later have been able to collect.'

The waiter came to remove Romy's soup bowl and the dish on which my avocado had been served. The sound of conversation in the restaurant was hushed as a harsh roar vibrated the windows. Looking out I saw the unmistakeable shape of Concorde soaring over the battlements of Windsor Castle.

Romy put her forearms on the table again. 'What was the word you said Sagrano used when he was talking to you last night?'

'Merchandise. It made me wonder at the time. Not the kind of word you'd use to describe a diamond. But obviously he did not want to refer to heroin over the 'phone. Perhaps he was not certain that I had realized what I was carrying.'

'So, where is the heroin now? Do you think there is a rival gang and they stole the Saab?'

'I'm beginning to think it was the police who stole it.'

Normally I find taped music in restaurants maddening, but now I was thankful for it. It would have been difficult for anyone to overhear what we were saying. Romy's eyes were continually exploring the room, scanning the faces of all newcomers suspiciously. I thought there was an even chance that somewhere among them was a plainclothes man from Bannerman's department.

'If it was the police,' I went on, 'or perhaps even the Customs and Excise, it would explain a lot of things. You remember the way we were kept waiting at the Italian frontier and then allowed to go through, and the abrupt decision of the customs men at Ramsgate to abandon the search and let us go on? I think that the police must have an informant in Naples and through Interpol we've been under observation since the moment we left there. They suspected we were carrying heroin and they wanted to find out who the contact in England was.'

'If that's so, it wouldn't make sense for them to steal the Saab. Still less to let you have it back.'

'They may have got cold feet, knowing that so much heroin was standing out there on the streets of London. For all they knew Varzi's friends were going to collect the car from outside the flat. And you remember the bogus workman who was painting the railings when we arrived? Then, once they had the heroin in their hands they could afford to return the car and watch to see what happened next. At that point they knew damn well that I was not telling them the truth. They wanted to find out where I'd go, who I'd make contact with. For all they knew I had been corrupted and in a sense I was – though, Christ, I'd never have agreed to carry heroin! And, you see, they still have not come clean with us. And do you know why? Because they want to use us as decoys to flush out the drug traffickers. That's why they asked me to agree to meet Sagrano if he contacts me again.'

I leaned back to let the waiter put my steak Diane in front of me. Looking out of the window across the Thames I saw a dark-blue van come round the corner from the direction of Windsor railway station. It turned onto the quayside opposite the restaurant, found a space between the vehicles parked there and reversed into it. No one emerged, but a moment later a wisp of cigarette smoke drifted up from the open window on the driver's side.

'Mustard, sir?'

'Yes, please.'

'French or English?'

'A little English, please.'

The usual ample dishes of vegetables, slightly overcooked, were brought. Romy asked for a green salad with a French dressing. I accepted sauté potatoes and spinach.

'Do you think,' she asked when we were left alone again, 'that they know we have been talking to the police?'

'I don't see how they could,' I answered. Then an unpleasant thought struck me. 'Unless my 'phone is tapped.'

'You think it could be?'

'That could explain why someone gained entry to my flat and left again without touching anything.'

'The police do tap 'phones, don't they?'

'They have to get Home Office authorization and then they can do it at the Exchange. They don't need to enter people's residences.'

Romy contemplated her rainbow trout dubiously. It looked and smelled delicious but she did not appear to be very enthusiastic about starting it.

'It's an uncomfortable feeling, isn't it? The police not sure about us and waiting to see what happens next. Sagrano thinking we've stolen his heroin and stashed it somewhere. What are you going to say when he contacts you? Are you going to do what the police want?'

I had no answer to that just then. Either way it seemed that I could not win. I was beginning to think I needed a strong ally and was coming round to the idea that when we returned to London I would take Ritchie into my confidence and put him fully in the picture.

The tape of canned music had come to an end and in the comparative silence snippets of conversation from nearby tables became audible. The German family had already finished their meal and were sorting out the problems of English currency and how much they should give for a tip. The two male models had their heads close together and were sharing a secret joke. From over by the wall came a roar of hearty laughter from a group of be-suited young executives.

'Look, Patrick. What's that flashing from across the river?'

I was just in time to see a glint of light from inside the blue van. It could have been sunlight reflected from some small mirror or glass object, but I had a feeling that it had been a double flash, as if from twin lenses. Then the window was wound up and I could no longer see the driver. The van was a Ford Escort without any trade markings. An aerial fitted at the side of the windscreen showed that it was equipped with radio.

I had chosen a table in the window so as to enjoy the view, but I now saw that this had been a mistake.

I finished my steak off and put down my knife and fork. Romy had lost her appetite and had only managed to eat half her trout. Now she was toying with the salad.

'I'm just going to 'phone the garage,' I said, pushing my chair back and putting down my napkin. 'Shan't be a moment.'

From a coin-operated telephone outside the Toilets I dialled the number of the Saab agents in Slough and was put through to the service manager.

'The car's ready, Mr Malone. I hope you'll approve but we've fitted two new bumpers. The one at the rear was in a sorry state as well.'

'Thank you very much. I didn't think to look at the rear one. Now, I want to ask you a favour. Is there any chance you could garage my Alfa Spyder for a few days?'

It took a little persuasion but after a few minutes he had agreed to send a man down with the Saab and take the Alfa back to Slough. They would find a place to park the Spyder for a few days until I was able to come and collect it. I gave him instructions on how to find the car-park and told him his man would find us in the restaurant.

'Send the bill with him and I'll write him a cheque. Yes, I've got a banker's card. And thanks for your help.'

The waiter had removed our plates when I got back to the table. I had noticed that a number of people were waiting in the cocktail bar for tables to become free, so I understood why he had become so busily attentive. They wanted us out so that they could seat another couple.

'Dessert, sir? Would you like to see the trolley?'

'Do you want a dessert, Romy?'

She shook her head. 'No. I don't seem to have much of an appetite. I'd like some coffee, though. A big cup, not a small one.'

'Just coffee, please.'

'Very good, sir.' The waiter, pleased at these signs of early departure, bustled towards the service door.

I glanced casually in the direction of the blue van and let my eyes roam over it without seeming to stare. Just for an instant I again caught the double reflection of light. It could have been caused by the sun striking the driver's spectacles – or alternatively the lenses of a pair of binoculars.

'Is everything all right, Patrick?'

'I hope so. Perhaps I'm being unduly sensitive but I've arranged that when we leave here we'll go together in the Turbo. They're going to collect the Spyder and keep it in the garage in Slough.'

Romy was disappointed. 'Oh. I was looking forward to driving the Spyder on the motorway.'

'You'll get the chance one day.'

She scanned my face, guessing that something had happened to make me nervous, but I shook my head slightly. She took the hint and did not ask any questions.

We had finished our coffee and I was just writing out a cheque for the bill when a young man came into the restaurant. His shirt and trousers were clean but I could see from his hands that he had recently been working on a car. I nodded to Romy. We stood up and went to meet him.

'Mr Malone, sir?'

'That's right. Where have you put the Saab?'

'In the park alongside your Alfa.'

'Good. Let's go into the bar and sort this out.'

We sat at a table in the cocktail bar which had been vacated by the couple who were going to take over our table in the window. I wrote out a second cheque for the repair to the Saab. The mechanic, briefed by the service manager, carefully checked it and compared the number I had written on the back with the number of my bank card. He handed me the keys of the Saab and I handed him the keys of the Alfa.

'You go ahead,' I told him. 'And don't forget she's got five forward speeds. And I have a note of the speedometer reading.'

His expression of anticipation modified a little and I guessed that I had saved the Spyder a burn-up along the M4.

We gave him five minutes start before leaving the restaurant ourselves. On the bridge which had once carried vehicular traffic from Bucks to Berks the seats provided by the council were occupied by picnicking tourists. From a landing-stage on the opposite bank, upstream from the bridge, a boatman was shouting the merits of a river trip to Dorney Lock. Outside the door an irate mother was spanking the reddening thigh of a screaming infant.

I took Romy's arm, and wondered why I had such a strong sense that out here in the sunlight we were exposed to danger.

'We're not going to hang about,' I warned her. 'Get into the Saab as quickly as you can and slam the door.'

She sensed my nervousness and gripped my arm more tightly. Though no traffic was passing, I looked carefully to left and right before stepping off the pavement.

Walking deliberately slowly we crossed the road towards the car-park opposite. On the bridge a woman threw a handful of bread-crumbs for the swooping seagulls which had come inland to escape a storm.

Two cars were parked, regardless of the yellow lines, with their rears towards the bollards blocking vehicular access to Windsor Bridge. One was the green Vauxhall Magnum which had followed us down from Slough. Two men were sitting in the front seats. They wore bored and supremely disinterested expressions. The other car was a blue Opel Ascona, also with two male occupants. The driver was wearing a hat and at that moment held his cupped hands in front of his face to shield the flame of a match. Alongside the pavement to my right a yellow Allegro had drawn up and was waiting with its engine ticking over.

Beside the Turbo was a blank space, recently vacated by the Spyder. I went round to the passenger's side to unlock the door for Romy. As I verified that a new bumper had been fitted I heard

139

her slam her door. Wasting no time I unlocked my own door and got in.

'Fasten your seat belt,' I told her and clicked my own into the secured position.

I fitted the ignition key into its slot, switched on and, with my foot on the clutch, stayed in reverse. I backed out before turning the car to point towards the car-park exit.

'If we hit anything, press back hard into your seat and brace yourself.'

Romy stared at me but she did not say anything.

Knowing that the bridge was blocked gave me a feeling of claustrophobia. We were, so to speak, penned in down at this end of the town. I had two routes to choose from. The obvious way was straight up the narrow High Street. An alternative was the lane which turned off the High Street just before the bridge. It looped round the back of some new council flats and rejoined the High Street a quarter of a mile further down.

I decided to take the less obvious route. On emerging from the car-park I turned left into the lane. In my mirror I saw the blue Opel Ascona move out to follow me.

I had gone fifty yards when a car and caravan, which had been masked by the old pub, pulled out across my path, completely blocking the road. I braked hard, engaged reverse and backed into the entrance to the service area of the council flats. As I selected first gear and moved out, left hand hard down on the steering wheel, the blue Opel was twenty yards away. When he saw me coming the driver swung to his right, swerving over onto the wrong side of the road in an obvious effort to block me. Still in first gear I accelerated hard and felt the full power of the compressor come in. I veered towards the right and just before the front of the Saab hit the rear of the Opel I had a quick but vivid view of the driver's frightened face. The Saab gave a faint shudder as it brushed the other car aside with a glancing blow.

Beside me Romy gasped.

The green Vauxhall and the yellow Allegro, which had been facing each other, had both decided at the same moment to join the party. Turning into the lane simultaneously they had collided head on and were now halted in a V formation, blocking the road. The Vauxhall was at a better angle for my purposes, so I aimed at the rear end, just behind the wheels at the point where the aeriel protruded from the wing panel. There was a shuddering crash accompanied by the tinkle of breaking glass. The green car rocked for a moment before deciding not to capsize. The Saab had stood up to the impact well, the bumpers taking most of the shock. My safety belt had held me firm.

I threw a quick glance at Romy. She was braced rigid, her arms stiffened, her hands gripping the sides of the seat.

The Vauxhall had been forced through an angle of forty-five degrees but there was still not room for the Turbo to get through. I backed off twenty yards and charged it again, still aiming at the extreme rear to get maximum leverage. Just before impact I heard the crack of a pistol being fired from the window of the Allegro and the thud of a bullet embedding itself in the thick glass beside my passenger's head. Then we hit the Vauxhall. This time it swivelled through another forty-five degrees, rocking dangerously. The Turbo brushed past it, one wheel on the pavement.

I kept my hand on the horn button. A party of tourists scattered as I swung into the High Street with tyres squealing. People were not used to cars moving at speed in this area, so I dared not use my full acceleration. As it was I had to brake hard. A dear old lady on a bicycle had unwisely tried to look round. She swerved into the middle of the road and had to get her feet down to save herself from falling. She smiled at me seraphically as she dragged her bike out of my path.

Before I got going properly again three more bullets thudded into the back of the car. One of them was deflected by the sloping rear window and went whining away between the houses.

I switched on my headlamps and with my hand on the horn button bullied my way down the length of the High Street. Opposite the chapel of Eton College I turned left. I did not want to go back into Slough and there was a minor road leading through Dorney to the Old Bath Road.

'Are you all right?' I asked Romy as we emerged into open country again.

'I think so. Apart from a few bruised ribs and a crick in the neck. What was happening back there?'

'I'm not sure. When I saw those cars converging on us I knew we had trouble.'

'What were you trying to do?'

'It was an ambush. They were trying to snatch us – or one of us. I'm sorry if I frightened you, Romy, but it was better than – '

I put out a hand and touched her. Just to confirm that I really did have her beside me still. Then I put my foot down. I wanted to be out of the area before some too observant busybody notified the police of the registration number of the car that had gone berserk in Eton High Street. After a few miles a bridge took us over the M4 motorway. I rejected the idea of using it to travel to the Severn Bridge and the mountains of Wales beyond it. The motorway was too conspicuous and too well policed. We crossed the Old Bath Road before any call could possibly have gone out for us on the police network. From now on I intended to stick to minor roads, using my sense of direction to work my way northwards.

'Where are we going? London's the other way, isn't it?'

'We're not going back to London.'

'I'm cold, Patrick. Do you think we could have some more heat?'

It was the effect of shock. She must have thought that I'd gone mad back there. I readjusted the heating controls and turned the radio on. A little soft music would help to soothe her nerves.

We had been travelling for half an hour and had wriggled our way into the hills north of Henley-on-Thames when I stopped and reversed fifty yards. We were on a quiet country lane and I had seen at the back of a tumbledown barn something I had been keeping my eyes open for. I took a couple of screwdrivers from the tool-kit in the boot and climbed over a wired-up gate. The Morris 1000 which had been abandoned in the field was badly rusted but its number-plates were in fair condition. It took me five minutes to detach them and another ten to put them on the Saab in place of the Tunisian registration number. I spotted a hole in the rear of the body and a V shaped mark on the back window where the shot had ricocheted off the toughened glass. They were not too noticeable. But the bullet was still embedded in the glass beside Romy's head, though the glass had not crazed. I pulled the Hoverlloyd sticker which we had acquired on the cross-Channel ferry off the rear window and stuck it over the blemish.

When I drove on I felt happier. The Turbo was still a noticeable car but now at least it had a registration number that did not cause people to look twice. Maybe it dated back to the 1960's but cherished numbers were all the vogue now. It was half-past three on a brilliant summer's afternoon. We had seven hours of daylight and the whole of England before us.

Romy had recovered sufficiently to ply me with questions.

'You think all that happened because they found out we'd been with the police?'

'It's a fair assumption. They must have realized that the Saab was at the Slough police station and they were probably watching the place. So it would have been no problem following us to that restaurant. They had someone watching us from the other side of the river all the time we were having lunch. I expect the whole thing was co-ordinated by walkie-talkies.'

'It just shows how much protection we can get from the police.'

I slowed down as we approached the village of Fingest. 'The police may not be best pleased with us. I have a horrible feeling that one of the cars I crunched was a CID car. How much money have you got on you?'

'Not much. About twelve pounds, I think. Why?'

'We're going to have to buy some things – like toothbrushes and toothpaste and a razor for me.'

She turned to study my face. 'You've decided not to go back to the flat. Won't that put you in the wrong – with the police, I mean?'

'We're going to disappear for a while. I'm in an absolutely hopeless situation. If I thought that the police would believe my story and trust me I'd feel different. But so many things have happened to undermine my credit with them. In any case, they could never allocate enough men to give us one hundred per cent protection. That operation in Eton proved it. Then there's Varzi. He's not going to let four million pounds' worth of heroin slip from his fingers so easily. He may be wondering whether the police have got hold of it but I still remain his principal hope of getting it back. So he'll continue to threaten and bring pressure on me.'

'He wanted to kidnap and torture you?'

'I don't think so. If I was in his shoes that's not the way I'd go about it.'

'How would you go about it?'

'Look out for signs for Thame,' I told her, dodging the question. 'It's a nice little market-town and we should be able to get what we want there.'

In Thame we parked the Saab in a quiet street and went shopping. Our first purchase was a couple of suitcases into which we could put the things we bought. My banker's card was used half a dozen times and when we'd finished we had all we would need for a week or two. As I closed the hatchback on our brand-new luggage I felt as carefree as a cormorant.

Romy smiled at me over the top of the car. I should never have let her persuade me to bring her back with me. She made me too vulnerable. I cared too much about her now. I could not bear the thought of them using her to bring pressure on me. So far as I was concerned the police and the drug traffickers could fight it out among themselves. I wanted out – for both of us.

Darkness was falling as we rolled quietly into the little town of Sedbergh, in what used to be known as the West Riding of Yorkshire. Two hundred and fifty miles of minor roads had ticked up on the trip mileage recorder. The Cumbrian Fells were etched clearly against the evening sky and already London seemed a long distance away. We were lucky that a cancellation had left a double bedroom free in the White Bull. The proprietor brightened when I told him that we might very well be staying for several weeks, and assured me that the Saab would be perfectly safe tucked away at the back of the hotel. I had no intention of doing any motoring for some time to come. We would use our own two feet for transportation across the fells.

There was time for us to have sandwiches in the bar before closing time and afterwards we went out to walk the length of the almost deserted village street.

'You've been here before, haven't you, Patrick? What made you come to this place? Sentimental memories? You were very quiet during the last few miles.'

'I was at boarding school here. At least, until I was expelled.'

'You were expelled from school? What for?'

'Nothing much.'

'Go on. Tell me.'

I hesitated. The thing rankled still. 'One of the masters had a very attractive daughter. I used to climb out of my House at night to go and visit her. One night her father walked into her bedroom and found us in bed together.'

'But that's nothing to be ashamed of! What age were you?'

'Fifteen – rising sixteen.'

'Did you ever see her again?'

'No. I never came back. Not till now.'

'Why now?'

'I don't know. It just came into my head when I was wondering where we could hide out.'

'You were in love with her.'

'I guess I was. It was the first time.'

'The first of many?'

'No. Not many. Perhaps three – or four.'

'Were you in love with your wife?'

'Oh, yes. I loved her as much at first as I disliked her later.'

'And since then?'

'No one since then. Not till now.'

We both woke early. Through the window I could see blue sky and the hump of a green mountain. I wanted to be on top of those hills with Romy. We got up and dressed. She put on a snazzy pair of trousers she had bought in Thame. I made her take a cardigan too. Like schoolchildren we tip-toed downstairs. The hotel was still locked up and silent. A smiling cook let us out through the back door beyond the kitchen.

I led her up a well-remembered track at the back of the town and soon we were clear of the houses and on the fells. It took us half an hour to reach the first summit and when we got there we flung ourselves down panting on the heather. A fresh, clean morning breeze was blowing from the west with a tang of the sea in it. On the slopes below the sheep called to each other and stared at us distrustfully. The grey town nestled a thousand feet below and above us there was nothing but empty sky.

145

'That one's got a bad touch of smoker's cough,' Romy said, laughing.

'Where?'

'That sheep. Look, we're not the only ones.'

She pointed to the higher hill above us. A string of figures in blue shorts and white sweaters were moving up it.

'Probably a football team from the school on a training run. We used to do that, get up before breakfast and come up onto the fells. It kept us fit during the cricket season.'

The breeze was blowing her hair across her cheeks. Her face was flushed and her breast was still rising and falling from the exertion of the climb. I reached down, took her hands and pulled her to her feet.

'I'll show you a different way down.'

'Can't we stay up here a bit longer? I feel we've got the world to ourselves. I don't want to go back where people are.'

'What about breakfast? Don't you fancy breakfast?'

'Yes! I could eat a real English breakfast. Two eggs at least and half a dozen rashers of bacon.'

'Come on, then. I'll show you the technique we used for going down steep slopes. You run till you're going as fast as you can then you sit down and slide on your bottom.'

'Ouch! That sounds painful.'

I led the way, careering down the hill until I was sure I was about to fall on my face. The hill was furrowed with the slide-grooves carved in the hillside by the boys. It all came back as if it had been yesterday. At full tilt I sat down on one heel and stuck the other leg out ahead of me, skidding and bouncing twenty yards till I came to a halt. Then I turned and signalled Romy to follow.

She started to run, going faster and faster.

'Sit down!' I yelled at her.

'I daren't.'

When I thought she was certain to crash headlong, she sat down with a bump, both legs stretched out ahead of her, slid down the grass for ten yards then began to roll over and over. She wound up at my feet. I helped her up and she flung her arms round my neck, helpless with laughter.

146

'That was great,' she said, as soon as she could speak. 'Come on, let's do it again. I'll be better this time.'

In this fashion we proceeded down the hill. Miraculously when we reached the gate leading into the lane our trousers were still intact.

'It'll brush off,' I assured her, as she looked over her shoulder to see how much of the hillside she had collected on her seat.

'I hope so. This is my only pair of slacks.'

We climbed the gate and holding hands started down the lane towards the town about half a mile away. I pointed to a range of hills to the south.

'You see that white cloud over Baugh Fell? That's a sure sign it's going to be a beautiful day. After breakfast we'll go up that way. I know an inn where we can have a ploughman's lunch. Their ale used to be very good.'

She jerked her elbow against me and nodded towards a car that was parked in the lane fifty yards further on. It was facing away from us. Through the back window I could just see the heads of the couple in the front seats. They were very close together and the man's arm was round the woman's shoulders. It seemed an odd time of day to be canoodling in a car. But who were we to criticise?

We were silent as we approached them, feeling a kind of conspiratorial empathy with another couple of lovers. Subconsciously I assessed the car, noting its good and bad points. It was a habit I'd developed since I'd been in the car trade, to measure up every car as if I'd been offered it in a part-exchange deal. This was a fairly new Ford Cortina 2.8 litre, with a T registration. It was fawn in colour with a black vinyl roof, heated rear window and a towing attachment. A set of cross-ply tyres had been fitted recently, Michelin's, by the look of them. As we came abreast of it, taking care not to stare at the couple inside, I noticed that there was a patch on the near-side front wing panel where the cellulose did not quite match. An expert panel-beating job had been done at some time, but the paint sprayer had not been quite so good at his job.

We had only just passed them when I heard one of the doors being opened. I did not look round. Then the other door was opened. That struck me as odd. I was about to turn to see what they were up to when another couple stepped out from the cover of a wall ten paces ahead of us. The woman was pale and tight-lipped, with black hair cut close like a boy's. She wore jeans tucked into high black boots and a tight black sweater. The man was clad in what looked like an Al Capone suit and bore a remarkable resemblance to Humphrey Bogart playing one of his less pleasant roles. They both had hand-guns, and I thought I recognized the new U.S. Ruger automatic.

Romy's hand clenched on mine. We halted. I turned round, knowing already that I was going to see again the couple I had met amid the wheat-fields near Monxton. This time the man was carrying the gun. The female was holding a couple of skeins of nylon parachute cord.

The lane was bordered by high stone walls. We were in a trap. Now when it was too late I realized that I should have abandoned the Saab after the first ambush attempt. Somewhere along the line a bugging device must have been planted on it, but I did not have time to work out where or when. I loosed Romy's hand.

'Lie down on your faces,' Bogart commanded, jerking his gun. Romy and I looked at each other. Our eyes said much. A sad farewell to the brief moment on the sunlit hill.

'Come on, now,' the man said. 'We don't want anyone hurt, do we?'

They wanted us alive. The choice was between a quick death and slow torture – with a possibility of survival.

'Don't lie down,' I muttered to Romy. 'Force them to come closer.'

I had reckoned without Bogart's vicious hatred. He must have guessed what I was thinking. He put a bullet between our two heads. It ricocheted, whining off the walls. The report had sounded very loud in the morning air.

'Your boy-friend gets it next time,' he said.

Romy dropped on her hands and lay on her face. I could not blame her, but I cursed inwardly.

The short-haired girl beside him sprinted forward to sit on Romy's back. I moved faster than she did and hit her hard on the hip with a rugby tackle before she could reach Romy. After that things became a little confused. As we rolled to the ground together I kicked clear of her and came up crouching. Just in time, because Bogart was coming at me, his gun held in a clubbing position. I parried the downward sweep of his hand with my forearm and smashed my fist into his diaphragm. He doubled up, choking. The second, younger man was already coming for me with bare hands. Their guns were really useless to them if they wanted us alive. They were only good for threatening. But the odds were still four to two.

I went down on my knees, always a good position for unarmed combat. The move surprised my attacker, who had been trying to come in under my guard. Impelled by his own momentum and aided by me, he went flying over my shoulder.

As I stood up a miniature tigress landed on my back and a boney forearm was clamped across my windpipe with astonishing strength. I stooped, trying to throw her off me. The man I had sent flying was scrambling crabwise towards me, aiming clawing hands at my genitals. I kicked out at him, but he caught my foot. All three of us rolled to the ground. I managed to twist as I fell, so that my full weight landed on the girl. I jabbed backwards with my elbow and felt it make contact with her teeth. She grunted and the bone bar across my windpipe slackened. I was going with everything now – knees, elbows, head – and getting the better of it when a sharp call pierced the red fog swirling round my brain.

'Malone! Do you want her cut?'

The message got through, shaking me enough to break my concentration. In that split second I lost the fight. The girl's forearm tightened across my throat, completely blocking the air passage. The man got two hands on my arm, bending my wrist so painfully that I was forced to my feet even though I had the weight of the girl on me.

Bogart and his female had got to Romy, who was still face down on the ground. The girl was sitting astride her. He had grabbed a handful of her hair and yanked her head back. Her eyes were wide and shocked, staring at the blade of the flick-knife which he was holding an inch from her cheek.

I let my muscles relax. Immediately my two attackers grabbed an arm each, holding me so that I could not move. The knife remained aimed at Romy's cheek.

149

'Tie his hands,' Bogart commanded. 'No tricks, now, Malone, or I'll slice this pretty cheek.'

Romy was cringing away from the blade. I knew that the best policy was to go on fighting till the end, never let them tie you, but I had not the strength of mind to do it. I let them tie my wrists.

The man folded his flick-knife and put it away. 'Throw us that other cord.'

From behind me a coil of parachute cord went sailing through the air. Bogart's partner caught it, grabbed Romy's unresisting arms and bound her wrists in the small of her back. Then she took off her own thick leather belt and used it to pinion her ankles.

Then the two of them lifted her and carried her to the car. They thrust her face onto the floor at the back and closed the door on her.

Then Bogart walked slowly back to where I was still standing helpless, held by the other two. On his face was an expression of sadistic anticipation.

'So you like rough games, do you? Hold him still for me, now.'

He smacked the sides of my face hard with each hand in turn. I dropped my head to avoid the blows.

'Grab his hair and hold him still, for Christ's sake.'

My hair was seized and my head yanked back. He slapped me a few more times. He was really enjoying himself.

'That's just for starters,' he said, and bunched his fist.

He smashed his fist into my mouth and I wondered if he'd hurt himself as much as me. His knuckles were bleeding before he hit me first on the left cheek and then on the right. A pistol whipping would have done more damage to me and less to his fists, but he was getting a big kick out of this personal physical contact. Moving to softer parts he crashed a blow into my abdomen and I would have doubled forward if I had not been held.

'Don't be chicken,' the girl with the bleeding mouth told him. 'Let him have it in the bollocks.'

'Give me time. This is only just starting.'

They were all enjoying this, the other three taking a vicarious pleasure in watching the performance. As a result I was the first to see fifteen hefty boys come careering down the hillside and start vaulting over the gate.

'Hold it!' I mouthed at him through bloody lips. 'I've got friends.'

He followed the direction of my eyes. 'Christ, what's this?'

The lads had seen us and had slowed their pace. They had realized that something odd was going on and were not quite sure what to do about it. The leader was a young giant of about six foot two with shoulders to match.

'Let's go,' Bogart said, making an instant decision and gesturing his companions to the car. As they moved to obey he put his face closer to mine. 'You'll be hearing from us. We'll contact you at your flat. And remember, one word to the police and she goes into a coffin.'

He gave me a shove and expertly tripped me up. With no hands to save me I crashed onto the stony lane. As I struggled up I heard the car doors bang and the engine start. It swerved past, just missing me, and accelerated down the lane, stones clattering against the wheel arches.

CHAPTER 10

'Are you all right?'

I looked round into the youthful face of the rugby captain. The rest of the team had trotted up and were surrounding me, their faces alarmed and concerned. They were all in brown or blue jerseys. Some of them had taken their sweaters off and wore them tied round their waists by the sleeves.

'Yes. I'm just fine.'

A sharp stone on the track had gouged my forehead above the right eye, adding to the damage done by Bogart. The blood was blinding me in that one eye. Breathing was difficult, as my nose had been squashed and I was chewing on tatters of flesh from the inside of my lips.

'Can you untie my hands, please?'

A second boy quickly stepped forward and got to work on the cord knotted round my wrists. Even in that short time it had bitten into my flesh and my hands were starting to tingle.

I stared down the lane. The car was hidden by the walls but I could still hear the diminishing scream of its over-revved engine. I thought of Romy lying on the floor with the boots of those female thugs digging into her back. My bile rose. I bent double, clutching the stones of the wall and vomited onto the grassy bank bordering the lane.

'Parkinson, you stay with me.' The captain issued his orders with authority. 'The rest of you get back to the house. Melville, tell Matron that we'll be bringing in a casualty.'

Twenty minutes later I was sitting in the Matron's room of a boarding house flanking the village street. The rugby captain and his friend Parkinson had been sent off to change for breakfast. I'd discovered that the big boy's name was Dorward. I intended to remember that. One day I might be able to do something about repaying him. He'd saved the parts of me which I most valued from Bogart and handled the whole situation with remarkable presence of mind.

The Matron was a fresh-faced lady in her late thirties. She tut-tutted as she dabbed at the cuts and bruises on my face, and applied dressings where the skin was broken.

'What *have* you been doing to yourself? Fighting, if you ask me.'

'I'm afraid so, Matron.' I felt very much as if I was a small boy back at school again. 'But please don't report this. Someone's life may depend on it.'

She thought I was joking and laughed. The cuts certainly needed dressing but I resented every minute of delay.

'There,' she said presently. 'I've done my best, but you'll have to see a doctor. You'll probably need stitches in that cut and your nose looks as if it's broken. And those teeth will have to be seen to. You're not local, are you?'

'No.' I stood up and searched for a mirror. There was a big one above the fireplace. 'Jesus Christ!'

I looked like an advertisement for car safety-belts – the man who hadn't fastened his and went through the windscreen.

'Now,' she warned me. 'We don't like that sort of language here.'

If my lips had not been bloody I would have kissed her. 'Matron, what's your name?'

'Constance Wetherby.' She blushed.

'I can't stay to thank you properly but I'll write you as soon as I have a chance. You've been wonderful.'

'Aren't you going to see Mr Spooner?'

'Who's he?'

'The Housemaster. I'm sure he'll want to speak to you.'

My personal memories of interviews with Housemasters were not altogether pleasant. I excused myself from that one. Miss Wetherby reluctantly showed me how to get out into the street.

It was still too early for the shops to be open but the entrance to the hotel had been opened. My watch told me that it was twenty minutes past eight. I slipped in unseen by anyone except a maid who was hoovering the hall and did not look up from her work.

When I entered the bedroom and saw Romy's things lying about I was very nearly sick again. Despair and grief hit me with an almost physical impact. I flung myself down on the rumpled bed where we had made love, grabbed the pillows to muffle my alternate sobs and curses.

It was pitiful. Then I seemed to see myself from outside, lying there on the bed, broken and useless. My own voice commanded me to get up, quit bawling, start doing something positive.

I got the two suitcases down from the top of the wardrobe, opened them and put them on the bed. I piled all Romy's things into one and all mine into another. We had not bought enough to fill them so there was plenty of room. Then I wrote a cheque payable to the White Bull. I left the amount blank and endorsed it "not more than fifty pounds". I put the number of my banker's card on the back and weighted it with the Cinzano ashtray on the table.

Some of the other guests were coming down to breakfast. They gaped at my plastered face as I humped my suitcase down the stairs. The hoovering maid chose that moment to straighten up from coiling the lead round the vacuum cleaner. Her mouth dropped open when she saw me. Then her eyes went suspiciously to the suitcases.

'Would you tell the manager I've had to leave urgently,' I lisped at her, my speech blurred by swelling lips. 'I've left a cheque in my room to cover the bill.'

She did not care for that. As I went out the back way she had turned towards a swing door reserved for 'Staff Only'. I wanted to get away from the place without having to enter into explanations about the absence of Romy or the condition of my face. The Turbo started instantly for me. As I bumped out into the street I saw faces peering at me from the kitchen window, but fortunately the maid had not been able to find the manager.

Set among the hills as it is Sedbergh suffers from a heavy rainfall. I had never seen it look more glorious than on this sparkling summer morning. I looked back once at the hill where we had lain together in the heather, then turned my attention to the road ahead.

Five miles of narrow, curving roads, climbing and dipping over the hills, brought me to junction number 37 on the M6 motorway. It was just coming up to nine o'clock. Anthea would be unlocking 'Automobiles of Quality' any minute now, but it was unlikely that Ritchie would arrive before nine-thirty.

I swung down off the interchange road, checked the traffic coming southward, then moved over into the fast lane. The roar of the wind rose with the whine of the compressor and the car swept to the maximum speed permitted by the revolution limiter. My speedometer needle went right round the dial to 120 m.p.h. I switched my headlights on to warn the cars I was overtaking that here was a man in a hurry. I knew I was inviting police interest but there was no way I could have restrained myself to a plodding 70 m.p.h. The best I could do was keep an eagle eye on my mirrors, check the bridges crossing the motorway for radar vans and monitor the traffic joining the carriageway behind me from interchanges.

In forty minutes I had travelled eighty miles, and was level with Liverpool and Manchester. I turned off into a service area, found the public telephones. They were all occupied. I served myself with a plastic cup of coffee from an autovendor and drank it while I waited for a green-overalled transport driver to finish his call.

The sight of my face may have induced him to hurry it up. I saw him grinning and twisting his face into amicable expressions as if the person he was talking to could see him. I jingled the coins I had ready in my hand. At last he hung up and came out, muttering: 'Sorry, mate.'

I nodded but did not try to crack my aching face into a smile.

'Automobiles of Quality, can I help you?'

'It's Pat.'

I heard her gasp. 'Pat! Pat, hold on. Ritchie's here beside me.'

I heard her say to Ritchie: 'It's Pat. He's in a call-box. Ask him for the number.'

The instrument was transferred and I heard Ritchie clear his throat.

'Ritchie here. That you, Pat?'

'Yes.'

'What number are you on, so that I can call you back if the pips go?'

I read out the number on the disc and heard him repeat it so that Anthea could write it down.

'Right, got that. Where on earth are you?'

'On the M6 somewhere between Manchester and Liverpool. I'm on my way back to London.'

'Not before time. We've had the police here twice. First yesterday afternoon and then again this morning. They've only just gone. What are you up to, old soul?'

I'd had my tenpence worth. The pips told me that my time was up. Instead of putting in another coin I hung up and waited for Ritchie to ring me back. Outside the booth an impatient commercial traveller put a hand to the door, thinking I had finished. He scowled as I pointed to the telephone. Luckily at that moment it rang.

'You alone in the office now, Ritchie? I mean, except for Anthea.'

'Yes. There's nobody here except us. But remember you are on the 'phone.'

Ritchie, with his background, was obviously alive to the possibilities of 'phone-tapping. I was going to have to take a chance on that. If any 'phone was tapped it was more likely to be my own.

'I'll remember that, but there's nothing else for it. I have to talk to you.'

I told him the story, as briefly as I could, right up to the moment when Romy had been taken away in the Ford Cortina.

'The bastards!' he grated. 'That poor kid! How about yourself? Are you all right?'

'Not so bad. A broken nose, a few teeth missing and some cuts. We were interrupted before he got going on my more tender parts.'

'Mm. Your speech is very blurred. Have you been in contact with the police?'

'Good God, no! That's why I'm ringing you. I can't go to the police, Ritchie. Those people are quite capable of killing Romy as if she were a fly on a sausage. They know every move I make. They must have planted some tracking device on the Saab but I can't see – '

'Listen to me.' Ritchie was speaking very earnestly. 'This is far too big for you to handle on your own – '

'I thought you might help me – '

'I will help you. And the best help I can offer is to give you the right advice. Even the two of us have no hope of dealing with what you're up against. I know how you feel but you're more emotionally involved than I am. That's what they're counting on. That show of brutality was to soften you up. You'll never see Romy again if you try to go it alone.'

'Jesus, I wish I knew – '

'Listen. Kidnappers take hostages so that they can do a deal. There's usually something they're demanding. Right?'

'Yes,' I agreed reluctantly.

'Can you deliver what they're going to demand in exchange for Romy?'

'No. I see what you mean.'

'Pat, will you give me permission to contact this Inspector Bannerman and put him in the picture? You can rely on me to insist on absolute secrecy and discretion. Will you trust me to do that?'

I heaved a big sigh. Ritchie's voice was so calm and confident and I knew that I had been hysterical. The commercial traveller had been joined now by a middle-aged woman who was equally impatient. She must have wondered why I stared so deeply into her eyes, even though I was not really seeing them.

'Yes, all right,' I said. 'You can get him by ringing 230 1212. 'I just hope it's the right thing.'

'That goes for me too. Now, Pat, you get back to London as fast as you can. Don't come to the garage or go to your flat till you've contacted me again. Stop at a call-box as soon as you're in London. I'll stay here till you ring. I'll try and get the word sent out to the patrols on the motorway not to stop you for speeding.'

'That would help. Oh, I forgot. The registration number's changed.'

'You surprise me! What is it now?'

'CWU 303.'

'Right – I've got that. So we'll talk again in a couple of hours.'

England seemed small in a car like the Turbo. If there were radar traps on the motorway they did not stop me. Just two hours after talking to Ritchie I was on the outskirts of London. The fuel warning light on my instrument panel was telling me that my tank was nearly empty. I pulled in to fill up at a self-service petrol station. The cash-desk was in a miniature shop where anoraks, folding chairs, picnic sets and car accessories were being offered at bargain prices.

I asked the Indian at the till if there was anywhere I could telephone. He nodded his head towards a coin-box telephone mounted on the wall at the back of the shop. As I was already in the London area all I needed was twopence. I put a coin in the slot and kept another in my hand in case I needed it.

Ritchie himself answered before the number had rung for more than a couple of seconds.

'Hello?'

'It's Pat.'

'You're in London?'

'Yes. I've just come off the M1.'

'Good going. Now listen. I've made an appointment with the dentist for you.'

'Oh, for God's sake, what does a tooth more or less matter when – '

'He wants to see you without delay,' Ritchie cut in, using his most commanding tone. 'In case you've forgotten the address, it's 73 Brewer Street. That's just off the Fulham Road.'

I did not argue. My dentist was in the Holland Park area.

'Okay. I'll go straight there.'

I replaced the receiver and went back to the car. The time was ten minutes to midday.

Brewer Street was lined with terrace houses dating from the beginning of the century. They had been designed for the most modest buyers in the lower middle-class, and had probably sold originally for about a hundred pounds. Now they were sought after by the new rich class of executives, television personalities and professional men. They had all been redecorated and looked as smart as bandboxes. The cars parked in front of them reflected the affluence of the residents.

I had to go a couple of hundred yards past number 73 before I found a parking space. As I walked back, it was just beginning to rain. To my slight surprise there really was a dentist's plate beside the door of the house. PUSH, the glass-panelled inner door told me. I pushed and found myself in a flush-carpeted reception cum waiting-room.

I went to the desk where a dark and pretty girl in a blue overall looked up smiling from an appointment sheet.

'My goodness!' she exclaimed, when she saw my face. 'What have you been doing to yourself?'

'I met an old acquaintance and we had a difference of opinion. I understand Mr Bryer made an appointment for me to see someone.'

'What name is it, please?'

'Malone.'

The smile disappeared and a worried frown put creases between her neat eyebrows.

'Oh, yes, Mr Malone. Mr Flynn is expecting you. Would you take a seat, please? He won't keep you long.'

I sat down on one of the chairs lining the wall. The other patients stared at me briefly and dropped their eyes when I looked in their direction. I put a finger to the dressing above my right eye and looked at it. Blood had oozed through the pad. One of my broken teeth was aching painfully, and I had to hold my lips open to prevent the broken flesh from sticking. My breathing was noisy because my nostrils were filled with blood. From a chair opposite a giant and very cuddly panda, provided to distract frightened toddlers, gazed at me with a frank, beady stare. I leaned my head back against the wall and closed my eyes. From twin loudspeakers mounted in the corners soothing music crept into the room.

Nearly five hours had passed since I had seen Romy bundled into the car and driven away. Where was she now? What were they doing to her? Would they torture her to try and make her talk? When would the first message come?

My mind spiralled into a series of horrific scenarios and I could hear my own breathing become faster and faster.

'Mr Malone.'

The pretty receptionist's voice brought me back to my present surroundings. I opened my eyes.

'Mr Flynn will see you now.' She pointed to the corridor leading out of the reception area. 'It's room number 4.'

Room number 4 was the second on the right. I opened the door and walked in. The room was equipped with a reclining chair and all the paraphernalia of modern dentistry. It was occupied by four men. They were Ritchie, Bannerman, the balding man who had accompanied him on his visit to my flat and a white-coated stranger who I assumed was Mr Flynn.

'What a surprise,' I said drily.

'Come in, Pat.' Ritchie came forward to meet me, his face concerned. I could tell by the attitude of the two officers that it was he who had insisted on this very cloak and dagger arrangement and they'd had to agree to it whether they liked it or not. 'You look really rough. Sorry I had to be so abrupt on the telephone but I didn't want to say too much. I've never been able to trust the bloody thing.'

'That's all right. I got the message.'

I was not altogether happy to be having this rendezvous with the police, even though Ritchie's logic had been sound. In spite of myself I had already been softened up in exactly the way the kidnappers intended me to be.

The balding, older man was standing under a wall poster depicting a blown-up section of a human skull.

'Mr Malone, we've met before, but I did not introduce myself. My name's Ray and I'm a Senior Investigating Officer of Her Majesty's Customs and Excise.'

'Dod a bolishbob?' My swollen lips boobed the words and I had to try again. 'Not a policeman?'

'No. Inspector Bannerman and I are working on this case together.'

'Why don't you sit down, Mr Malone?' Bannerman said. 'You'd better take the patients' chair.'

'I'm sorry we're not better provided with chairs,' Flynn said apologetically. In fact, apart from the reclining chair, there were only two stools for the dentist and his assistant.

'That's all right,' Ray said. 'I've been sitting at the wheel of a car all morning.'

I sat down in the big chair a little nervously. My own dentist has a habit of canting me backwards without delay, leaving me staring at a ghastly Antarctic landscape which he's had fixed to the ceiling. I placed my forearms on the arms and then folded them on my lap. I'd had an unpleasant vision of straps securing my wrists, neck and ankles, and of a less amiable dentist than Mr Flynn approaching with a drill.

Ritchie sat on the assistant's stool. Mr Flynn was behind me on his own little perch. The Scotland Yard detective and the man from the Customs and Excise remained standing in front of me, looking down on me.

'Now, Mr Malone,' Bannerman said with a patience and forbearance which were remarkable under the circumstances. 'Will you fill me in on what has happened since you gave us the slip yesterday? Did you know that you had knocked out the car which I detailed to keep an eye on you?'

'I was afraid I might have, but at the time I thought it was one of the bandits'. All I knew was that I was in an ambush situation and my reflex was to get out of it at any cost.'

'The cost was perhaps a little high. One officer concussed and the radio equipment seriously damaged – '

'I'm sorry about that – ,' I began, but Ray interrupted, in his quiet, almost academic voice.

'Let's not waste time with recriminations and apologies. Can you keep your story brief, Mr Malone? We can go back over it and pick up details if necessary.'

I leaned back in the chair, which was rather on the hard side. My stomach muscles were still aching and stiff. I related briefly how I had navigated my way northwards on minor roads and taken refuge in Sedbergh, believing I had thrown off all pursuit.

'I just wanted to get out of the whole situation,' I explained. 'I did not think that you trusted me or believed that I was telling you the truth, and I was not keen on being used as a bait to trap the perpetrators. On the other side Varzi's people were threatening both me and Romy if I did not hand over his heroin.'

'Did you say heroin, sir?'

'Yes.' I looked Ray in the eye. 'There was heroin concealed in the bumpers of the car, wasn't there?'

'Go on with your story,' Bannerman said.

'When that ambush in Eton was attempted, I realized that they knew I'd been talking to you and had decided to get rough. I didn't think you'd have the resources to give us one hundred per cent protection so I made a snap decision to disappear.'

'Tell us about what happened this morning, sir.'

From a massive metal plate secured to the ceiling a stainless steel column thrust downward towards the chair, carrying the power for the X-ray cameras and drills. Mr Flynn had not switched off the small spot-lamp which sent a beam into the patient's mouth. Beside me the swan-necked pipe over the spittoon emitted an indecent gurgle and then fell silent.

My voice may have faltered a little as I told them how we had been trapped in the lane under the fells in the bright morning sunlight.

'I don't know whether their plan was to grab us both or Romy only. If those boys hadn't turned up I think they'd have taken me too and then dumped me out somewhere. What bewilders me is how were they able to find us so very quickly? I'm absolutely certain we were not followed, and yet they'd got to us after only one night.'

'Your car may have been bugged,' Bannerman said. 'We didn't spot anything like that when we examined it, but then we were looking for something different.'

Ritchie spoke from behind my left shoulder. 'The car they took off in, Pat. Did you get a good look at it?'

'Yes. It was a 2.8 Ford Cortina with a T registration. The prefix may have been XDP and there were two digits. If I had to guess, I'd say the number was 69, but that may be wishful thinking. Fawn with a black vinyl roof. Tow-bar fitted and Michelin cross-ply tyres.' Bannerman had whipped his notebook out and was writing rapidly. I paused to let him catch up. 'The car had been damaged on the left front wing panel. It had been beaten straight and resprayed, not too expertly. The silencer box had been holed and she was burning oil.'

I must have winced, because Mr Flynn came round in front of me. His glasses reflected the light from the window as he examined my face.

'That mouth of yours is in bad shape. Are you having pain?'

'Yes,' I admitted. 'The nerve of one tooth seems to be exposed.'

Flynn turned towards the two officers. 'I think I ought to have a look at this man's mouth. He's in real pain.'

Bannerman looked at Ray. Ray nodded. Flynn operated an unseen pedal and I was tilted into an almost prone position. He drew his stool round beside me and aimed the spotlight at my mouth.

'Open wide, please.'

162

'Can I talk while this is going on?' Ray asked.

'Yes, of course,' Flynn assured him. 'I just want to – oh, dear! Things are in a bit of a mess in here. I'll do what I can but you will have to see a doctor.'

'Ugh, ach, a gug-gug.'

'I'm just going to give you an injection before I tackle this tooth. You've had quite enough pain already.'

'I would be less than frank,' Ray began, 'if I did not tell you that we have been very suspicious of you since the moment you entered this country – in fact, before that. And it did not help matters, sir, when you withheld the truth from us on that first interview.'

Flynn's hand, holding the needle, was in my mouth, so I could not make any reply.

'However, we appreciate that you were in a difficult position and in view of this latest development we have decided that it is only fair to put you fully in the picture.'

A slight prick in the gum made me stiffen. Even an insignificant pain like that produced a reflex. All my nerves were very sensitive.

'We'll just give that a minute to take effect,' Flynn said, and removed his fist from my jaw.

'It appears that you were the victim of an elaborate confidence trick,' Ray went on, moving along the wall a few feet so that he could see my face over Flynn's shoulder. 'One might almost think that the Arab stowaway was planted in your Rolls-Royce and the Guardia di Finanza in Naples tipped off to expect you.'

'I don't think anyone planted Ahmed,' I said lop-sidedly. 'He stowed away of his own accord.'

'Well, in any case you were put in prison and softened up by stories of the dire consequences of being caught smuggling. Then this Mr Varzi came along with his offer to help you and you jumped at it – '

'Wouldn't you have done the same? He acted as if he had a lot of authority.'

'In Naples, Mr Malone, the police only exercise their function in partnership with organizations such as the Mafia, the Camorra and the Red Brigades. Even the Guardia di Finanza has been penetrated. However, these things cut both ways and we also have our own informants within the organization.'

'Do you know who Varzi is?'

'Was,' Bannerman corrected me. 'He was murdered the night after you left Naples and his body bore the marks of extreme torture.'

'Oh, God! The poor bastard! Do you know who killed him?'

'Almost certainly the same lot as shot up the café. It had all the characteristics of a gangland vendetta. Varzi must really have been desperate to create funds for himself outside Italy.'

'But if Varzi's dead,' I objected, 'why hasn't the English end of his operation crumbled?'

'It has. The body of your friend Sagrano was found in the Thames at Greenwich this morning. He'd suffered the same treatment as Varzi – been viciously tortured and then shot in the back of the neck.'

Flynn was hovering over me with his drill. I waved him away. The left side of my face was beginning to feel numb and speech was becoming more difficult than ever, but there were questions I had to know the answers to.

'What I'd like to know is, when did you get onto the fact that there were drugs on the Saab? And what was the point of letting me through the customs at Ramsgate? And was it you who stole the Saab from outside my flat?'

'The anaesthetic will wear off if you don't let me do this tooth,' Flynn warned. 'I'm only going to use the drill for a moment.'

'Oh, all right.' I once again gave my imitation of a baby cuckoo in the nest. The high-speed drill whined viciously. Though I could not feel a thing, I was surprised to see Bannerman's normally stern face wince in sympathy. After a moment Flynn withdrew his drill, hooked it up on the stainless-steel arm and swung it away.

'Mouth open still, please. I'm just going to put a temporary cap on that tooth.'

I remained gaping. All I could do was lie there and listen to Ray, who made the most of this opportunity to talk while I was unable to answer back.

'To answer your questions in order, Mr Malone. We in the

Customs and Excise are better informed than the public realize. They think that our resources are concentrated at the point of entry into this country. In fact, our information – you might say intelligence service – operates much further afield. And through Interpol and the Customs Co-operation Council we have close contact with our colleagues on the Continent. The war against drug trafficking is carried out on an international scale. Last year we seized one hundred and twenty pounds of heroin in the UK alone – '

Bannerman, who had become restless as he listened to Ray's slightly pompous delivery, broke in: 'Mind you, that's only one twentieth of the total UK consumption.'

'Fair enough,' Ray conceded. I guessed that there was a little inter-departmental rivalry here. 'But our measures are proving more and more effective. So much so that what has been referred to as a heroin mountain has piled up in Naples, which is the route now favoured for the trade from Afghanistan. The traffickers have had to resort to such measures as planting the drugs on the vehicles of unsuspecting travellers who look innocent enough to escape the attention of customs officers. But thanks to Interpol we are gradually beating it. That was why it was agreed that you would be allowed to make your home run, Mr Malone. The Italian authorities had received a tip-off about you. We wanted to see who your contacts in this country were, to try and get at the principals behind this operation. That is why you were passed through the Italian and French customs. Unfortunately you reached Ramsgate before we expected you and our message only just got through in time.'

I pushed Flynn's hand away and removed the saliva extractor tube myself.

'So you were observing me from the moment I entered this country. Was it your people who stole the Saab?'

'Please, Mr Malone,' Flynn entreated me.

I replaced the extractor and he bent again to his work.

'My colleague here was worried about so much heroin standing in a London street,' Bannerman remarked rather acidly. 'So we decided to take a closer look at it.'

He saw that I was trying to speak again and anticipated my question.

'We had the chassis number from the Customs and Excise in Ramsgate so we asked SAAB Great Britain to provide us with a key. They were loath to hand one over to anybody except the registered owner but the Commissioner prevailed on them in the end. As I think you have guessed, we found sixty pounds of heroin packed in the bumpers.'

'The painter was one of yours, I suppose.'

'The painter?' Bannerman looked puzzled.

'The character who was doing a rather messy job on the railings outside my flat.'

'Oh, him.' Bannerman stole a sly glance at Ray, who appeared just a little embarrassed. 'We can't claim credit for him. He was one of Mr Ray's flock.'

Ritchie had been listening carefully to all this. Now he chipped in : 'Why didn't you arrest Pat then and there?'

'There were certain things that did not make sense.' Ray took up the thread again. 'I wanted to take a look at Mr Malone, put a few questions to him, see how he reacted. We decided that, although he was not the type to indulge in drug trafficking on a serious scale, he was still hiding something from us.'

'Did you tap his 'phone?'

Bannerman said : 'That's something I'm not prepared to divulge.'

When Flynn turned away for some more amalgam I took the opportunity to put another question.

'Was yours the black Ford Granada that tailed me on the motorway when I was going to the rendezvous at Monxton?'

'Yes, that was ours,' Bannerman admitted. 'We had you under observation from the moment you drove out of Elton Square. When you gave us the slip we put a helicopter onto you. You should be thankful, because otherwise you would not have walked away from that meeting.'

'But you still didn't trust me after our meeting in Slough, did you?' I accused Bannerman. 'You wanted to use me and Romy as decoys to see if you could flush out the criminals.'

'Nearly finished,' Flynn said, smiling. 'If you'd put the extractor in again, please. The mouth is becoming a little moist.'

'It seems to me,' Ritchie said slowly, 'that if you were prepared to take chances with something like five million pounds' worth of heroin, there's more in this than meets the eye. Am I right?'

Ray and Bannerman consulted each other with their eyes. Bannerman shook his head.

'You could be right, sir, but I can't say any more without authorization from my commander at Scotland Yard.'

'There!' Flynn said, removing the extractor tube from my mouth. 'I think that will hold till you can have a permanent cap put on by your own dentist. Would you like to rinse?'

I leaned over, took the glass of purplish water from its holder, rinsed my mouth out and spat into the little glass basin.

'Could you do anything about my eye?' I asked Flynn. 'I may not be able to get to my doctor in the near future.'

'Well,' the dentist said doubtfully, 'it's not really my – . Still, I'll see what I can do.'

'I think we've wasted enough time talking.' Ritchie got up off the radiator in the window embrasure. He had been using it as a seat. 'The point is, what are we going to do about this hostage situation?'

Flynn moistened some cotton-wool in the basin and began to remove the dressing over my eye.

'Well, for a start we have Mr Malone's very good description of the car. That gives us something to work on, though they are certain to change cars at an early stage. I'd also like to have the fullest possible description of the two men and two women concerned.'

'The odd thing is that they did not look like criminal types, though their behaviour was certainly rough. And their way of talking sounded almost educated. The whole thing was strangely contradictory.'

Bannerman nodded, as if what I'd said made sense to him.

'Can you describe them?'

He made notes while I gave the most detailed description I could of the four.

'This should really have stitches,' Flynn shook his head unhappily. 'All I can do is patch it up for you. You should really see a doctor.'

'We'll see what the PNC can make of these.' Bannerman tapped his notebook with the pen. 'There's not much else we can do till they contact you. For the moment the initiative rests with them.'

'What do you think our chances are?'

Bannerman sighed. He still looked just as tired as the day before and seemed even more uncomfortable inside his clothes. 'We'll do our best, sir. That's all I can promise. But I can assure you of one thing. It is our rule that in all such cases the safety of the hostage is our first priority.'

'They're going to want their heroin. Are you prepared to hand that over in exchange for Romy?'

Bannerman glanced at Ray. Ray chose not to answer and dropped his eyes to the floor.

'We'll cross that bridge when we come to it, sir. Let's see what demands they make first.'

'Do I lead them to believe that I still have the stuff, or do I tell them that the police have got it – or rather, the Customs and Excise?'

'You tell them that you'll do your best to meet their demands. Keep them talking as long as possible. Try to keep the dialogue open. But don't worry too much about that, sir. We'll have a man with you night and day round the clock and we will monitor all calls on your telephone number – '

'You bloody won't!' Flynn chose that moment to operate his foot lever and I was pushed upright by the back of the chair. 'These people have ways of knowing *everything* that I do. If they get an inkling that the police are in this with me, or that I am not in a position to hand over the heroin, Romy will not stand a chance. You've got to think of something better than that.'

I knew that my voice had risen and that I was trembling. Bannerman pursed his lips.

'Without your full co-operation, our hands will be tied – '

'I've had a taste of your full co-operation,' I told him bitterly. 'Look at what happened yesterday at Eton!'

'Take it easy, Pat.' Ritchie came over and put a hand on my shoulder. 'I've got a suggestion to make, Inspector. Let me act as liaison between Pat and you. I can keep both parties fully informed on what is happening. As I'm a friend of Pat's it won't seem unnatural if I'm with him a lot during this time of crisis. You and I, Inspector, can fix up some way of communicating so that it will not be apparent that you're in on this. What do you say to that?'

Bannerman and Ray again exchanged one of their glances of silent consolation. Though the police and customs had been co-operating on the case so far the hostage situation obviously came under the jurisdiction of the Metropolitan Police.

It was Bannerman who answered. 'Yes, I'm quite prepared to agree to that arrangement.' He gave me a measuring look. 'Later on, Mr Malone may decide to work more closely with us.'

'What are the prospects, do you think?' I asked, repeating my former question.

'Well, the Met has a good record in hostage and kidnap cases. Time is generally on our side. We could help you more if we were in closer contact, but you have made your decision. I just hope you realize what you are in for?'

'Would you enlarge on that?'

'If things follow the usual pattern, they'll let you sweat for twenty-four hours so that your nerves are affected. Much depends on how strong your feelings for the hostage are.'

The Inspector was watching my reactions with his shrewd eyes.

'Go on.'

'Then they'll exert more pressure. You may hear unpleasant sounds over the telephone, or receive photographs through the post. Perhaps articles as well.'

'Articles?'

Bannerman was uncomfortable. He answered reluctantly. 'There have been cases where a fingernail or an ear or something like that has been sent to the relatives of a hostage.'

I shivered.

'It's possible that some deadline will be given for handing over the ransom money – or rather, in this case, the heroin. The deadline is usually extendable. That is the time when the kidnappers are at their most vulnerable so they often take elaborate precautions. We'll just have to play it by ear. At that point it is vital that you keep in touch with us.'

Bannerman's expression softened for a moment. I really believed that he felt very sorry for me, but that did not give me any cause to feel more cheerful.

169

'Well, I think that's it,' Ray said. 'Thank you for fixing this meeting, Mr Bryer. And thank you too, Mr Flynn.'

'Yes. Thank you both,' Bannerman chimed in, picking up his mackintosh from the floor. 'Mr Ray and I will leave first and you can follow after a few minutes. You'll be in touch with me, Mr Bryer? You have my number, haven't you?'

'Yes. I'll ring you from my office later today – or before, if anything happens.'

Ray had gone out and Bannerman was already at the door when he stopped and turned back.

'Oh, Mr Malone. One thing more. I would advise you from now on to keep a diary of events.'

'What's the point of that?'

'They are going to try and wear you down, sir. To play on your nerves. You may be deprived of sleep. You will be subject to great distress. Things may become confused in your mind.'

CHAPTER 11

Bannerman's advice about keeping a diary turned out to be sound. If I had not followed it I would now find it very difficult to recall the sequence of events during the nightmare days which followed. Tension, anger, fear and exhaustion made my mind unreliable and as things built up to a crescendo I believe that the discipline of keeping a record did a lot to prevent me from losing my grip.

After leaving the dentist's surgery in Brewer Street, I followed Ritchie round to the showroom in the Turbo and left it there. Bob Jensen, one of his fitters, was an expert on electronics and Ritchie wanted to have the car checked over for bugging devices. He lent me a Bentley Continental which had just come in so that I could get back to the flat. I was on edge in case the kidnappers were already trying to telephone me, so I only stopped at a snack-bar for long enough to buy half a dozen sandwiches.

The flat felt terribly empty. Everything was as we had left it the previous day when we rushed off to Slough – things unwashed on the kitchen sink, the bed not made, her clothes lying all over the bedroom. I wolfed the sandwiches and washed them down with a beer from the cold larder. Then I dealt with the dirty dishes and did what I could to straighten the bedroom out. It was impossible to think about anything except what might be happening to her. The fact that two of her captors had been women made matters worse. I knew that certain groups of terrorists are trained not to think of their hostages as being human, so that they are insulated from any possible feeling of pity or compassion. They deliberately degrade them so that if a time comes when they have to kill them they can do so without compunction.

The first time the 'phone rang I rushed to my desk and scooped the instrument up. It was my solicitor. He'd had another letter from Juliet's legal representatives. They claimed to have uncovered new evidence and were trying to upset the settlement we had agreed on. I told him rather curtly to write back and tell them to get themselves stuffed. All I wanted was to clear the line. I was afraid that the kidnappers might try to ring me and would find my number engaged.

They did not ring that afternoon, but half a dozen other people did. I choked them all off as quickly as I could. A few budding friendships came to an abrupt end before the afternoon was out. The time dragged unbearably. I could not settle down to anything with concentration.

A little before six the door-bell rang. I opened it to find Ritchie outside with his arms full of plastic bags from the supermarket. I took some of the load off him and slammed the front door with a flick of my foot.

'Ouch!'

'What's up?'

'My stomach muscles. I forgot they were so tender.'

We took the parcels into the kitchen and dumped them on the table. Ritchie subjected me to a keen inspection with his one good eye. I found myself warming to him in a way I'd never done before. He had already given me the feeling that he was in this with me up to the hilt. It was good to feel I had such a strong ally.

'No communication yet?'

'No. Nothing.'

'I didn't think there would be.'

'What about a drink? Will you have your usual gin and French?'

'No, thanks. I could use a beer, though.'

I got two cans from the cold larder and filled a couple of glasses. We went back into the sitting-room.

'I got Bob to look at the Turbo. You were bugged all right, and in a very sophisticated way. He found a loop aerial concealed under the edging of the vinyl roof and traced it back to a small transmitter cum receiver about the size of a box of Swan Vestas matches. It was fixed behind the head lining next to the interior light and wired to its battery connection.'

'That's not the same as a bleeper?'

'Good God, no! We've come a long way since those days. There's been a lot of spin-off from space exploration in this field. If you can get back messages from a space station orbiting Mars, it's not too difficult to do the same with a motor car swanning around England.'

'If you have the technological back-up. This must mean they've got considerable resources.'

'And presumably a control centre somewhere. That may work in our favour.'

'I never had much chance, did I? What was the point of fitting an extra aerial when the car's got one already?'

'As far as I can understand Bob's very technical explanation, you were bugged with a device known as a transponder. Working on VHF skywaves the car aerial would not have been any good. The receiver part of it was permanently switched on, but consumed only a few milliwatts – less than an electric clock. That was enough to detect the interrogation signal, which was – '

'The interrogation signal?' I asked, a little dazed by the technical jargon.

'The clandestine transmitter sent out a coded, one-second burst of a hundred characters. Your bug recognized the code and answered by sending back a one-second VHF tone.'

'Clever little bug.'

'This would be picked up by the pre-tuned and highly-sensitive receiver at the control centre. Only a small computer would then be needed to work out the signal angle and time interval, which would determine its direction and distance. The same principle's used in the electronic interrogation of aircraft approaching our shores.'

'But we hardly used the radio. I know it was switched off long before we got to Sedbergh.'

'The car radio did not have to be on. The on/off switch was by-passed by this equipment. That's why an extra aerial had to be fitted so that when the automatic aerial was retracted the device would still work. So long as your battery wasn't dead the incoming signal would trigger the electronic switch and – hey presto – your little transmitter sends its signal. The car could be locked up and standing in a garage – so long as it wasn't an underground garage.'

'What's the range of these signals?'

'Oh, enough to cover the whole of Britain. And the beauty of it is that mountains make no difference to sky waves – which they would to ground waves. The signal is bounced off the ionosphere and back to earth again.'

Ritchie was waxing as enthusiastic about this exotic piece of equipment as if he had thought up the idea himself.

'It must have pin-point accuracy, enough to find the car in the backyard of the hotel.'

'Ah, the final location would have been done by cars. The control centre would give the approximate area. Then they'd get, say, three cars with receiving equipment into the area, trigger the transmitter and pin-point you by triangulation. Simple. It's a nasty reminder of how efficient modern methods of surveillance can be.'

I poured what was left of my can of beer into the glass.

'I suppose it was fitted by the racketeers and not the police?'

'If it had been fitted by the police they would have found you, wouldn't they? Obviously the people who found you were the ones who were using the equipment.'

'What make was it?'

'Japanese, of course.'

'The only place it could have been fitted was Naples. Why would Varzi make such elaborate arrangements for a rendezvous if he had me bugged all the time? It doesn't make sense. If he had resources on this scale at his disposal he'd never have needed to resort to such a shaky deal as the one he made with me.'

'There's a simple explanation for that, old soul. You've been promoted.'

'Promoted? How?'

'You've been taken over by a much bigger organization. A lot must have happened that day you left Naples. Varzi may really have been desperate to get some loot out of Italy and into Britain, but he was just too late. A rival organization liquidated him and his gang and took over his operations. That included you and your run to England. Any muddling there has been can be accounted for by the normal difficulties of a takeover.'

'You think the bugging device was fitted to the car by the people who killed Varzi and Sagrano and took over the operation?'

'It's only a theory, but it makes sense of what's happened, doesn't it?'

'Not entirely. If they had this means of tracking the car, why did they make such complicated arrangements for the rendezvous at Monxton?'

'I understood from you that was fixed by Varzi's contact in this country. The other lot simply took over the existing arrangement. It had certain advantages for them as well.'

'What is worrying me is that they – I keep saying "they" because it comes to the same thing whether it's Varzi or a rival gang – they must have fantastic resources to be able to operate a control centre such as you assume. Do you think the police realize what they are up against?'

'I think they do, though they are playing their cards close to their chests. I know they've fed all the information you've given them into the National Police Computer and the Swansea Computer. What we're waiting for now is a message from the kidnappers. We'll be able to tell a lot from the way Bannerman and Ray react to whatever they demand.'

Ritchie departed at about seven, taking the Bentley Continental and leaving the Saab. He had an evening engagement which he said he could not break. He gave me a telephone number where I could reach him if anything happened before he got back to his own house in Pimlico. That was vitally important, because he had promised to come and be with me as soon as the kidnappers made contact. After his description of the bugging device which had been concealed on my car, I was more than ever convinced that it would be fatal to have direct communication with Bannerman. If the kidnappers had such sophisticated equipment they might find ways of tapping my telephone. And in a closely built-up area such as this they might even be able to beam laser microphones into my rooms.

I cooked myself a meal, but drank very moderately to keep my head clear. Then I tried to concentrate on television for a couple of hours. The telephone remained silent. At least twice I picked it up and listened to the dialling tone to make sure it was still functioning.

At one o'clock I went to bed – in the old dressing-room, not the double bedroom. I had put the light out and was trying to relax enough for sleep when the 'phone rang. I was at it within twenty seconds.

'Hello?'

No reply. Just the faintest sense of a presence on the other end of the line.

'Malone here. Who's calling?'

A pause, then the other person gently put their instrument down on the cradle.

I went back to bed and resumed my attempts to sleep. I think I had dozed off when the 'phone bell rang again. I answered, gave my name and the 'phone number. As before, after a short pause, the connection was broken. When the same thing happened for the third time I came to the conclusion that it was a trick to erode my nerves and prevent me from sleeping. I steeled myself to leave the receiver off its cradle before going back to bed and deliberately emptying my mind of thought.

I woke when the first ray of sunlight shone through a chink at the side of the curtains. My first action was to go through to the sitting room and replace the receiver. After a few minutes I checked to make sure that the normal dialling tone was coming through.

The time from five-thirty till nine dragged terribly. The telephone remained silent. My chill loneliness was relieved a little by the sound of the morning traffic building up on the Cromwell Road and nearby streets and the companionable noises from neighbouring flats.

At nine Ritchie rang. I told him that I'd had no positive contact, only the three mute calls in the small hours.

It was now more than twenty-four hours since I had seen Romy driven away in the Ford Granada.

At exactly ten o'clock the 'phone rang.

'Malone here.'

'Malone. We're going to give you a code-word. You'll know a message is genuine if it is preceded by that word.' The voice was a man's, but I could not identify it as belonging to any of the kidnappers I had encountered. There was no trace of coarseness or illiteracy in it. 'The word is Torquemada. Have you got that?'

My legs were shaking but it was more from anger than apprehension.

'Torquemada,' I repeated the word, and before I had time to say any more the connection was broken.

176

I immediately 'phoned Ritchie at the showroom to tell him.

'Torquemada. That rings a bell.'

'It should. He was head of the Spanish Inquisition – '

'That doesn't mean a damn thing!' Ritchie came back angrily. 'A cheap attempt to soften you up. Don't let them get to your nerves, Pat. Ring me if you feel like it. I'll be here all day. Anthea will bring some lunch in for me.'

We had agreed that in our conversations on the 'phone we would make no reference to the police. I knew that he had arranged a method of passing on information to Bannerman.

Just before midday I answered the 'phone again. Several people had called me during the intervening two hours and I had tried not to cut them off too impatiently.

This time the voice was a female one.

'Malone? Torquemada calling. We have a question for you. Be careful how you answer. Why did you not return to your flat directly yesterday? Why did you go to Brewer Street?'

'I went to see my dentist,' I replied tersely. 'Your friend broke two of my teeth and one of them was giving me hell. You can check on that if you want. The dentist's name is Flynn.'

'Have you been in contact with the police?'

'No.'

'That had better be true. Now, hold on. There's something we'd like you to hear.'

It was obviously going to be a tape recording and I guessed what was coming. That did not make it any easier to hear.

'No, please! Please don't! I can't bear it any more.' Romy's voice, no doubt about that, calling out with a desperate appeal and urgency. Then a scream of agony which made me shut my eyes tight and grip the telephone so hard that it creaked. The ghastly fugue of gasps, cries and screams, amplified by a slight dungeon-like echo continued for an interminable half minute. I could not bear to listen and I could not disconnect. Then the tape was switched off.

'There's more, of course,' the voice said. 'That's just a sample.'

Then came the dialling tone. I managed to put the 'phone down gently. Then I sat in my desk chair and pounded the table with my clenched fists.

'Christ! Jesus! God!'

It took me a few minutes to get a hold of myself. Then I pulled the telephone towards me and dialled a number.

'Automobiles of Quality, can I help you?'

'It's – ' I choked on the words, then bit my lip so hard that I tasted blood.

'Pat. You want to speak to Ritchie?' Anthea had guessed from my voice that I was in trouble. 'Hold on.'

While waiting I took some deep breaths and slowed my pulse rate down.

'Hello, Pat.'

'Ritchie. Can you – could you come over?'

'Have they been in – '

'Yes.'

'All right. I'll be with you in ten minutes.'

I found myself compulsively checking my watch as I waited. Time was passing so slowly. I went to the drinks cupboard, poured a couple of fingers of Scotch and drank it neat.

Nine minutes after he had rung off Ritchie was at my door.

'Jesus!' he exclaimed when he saw me. 'You look like Lazarus. What's happened?'

I told him. His colour heightened and his false eye flashed as if it was alive. He was very angry.

'Those things can be faked – '

'This wasn't a fake,' I almost shouted, and realized that I was losing control of my emotions. 'Bloody hell, I know her voice – '

'Well, amplified anyway.' Ritchie quizzed my profile. 'I'm not saying it wasn't Romy, but a lot can be done by editing and cutting tapes. You can get electronic effects that sound extraordinarily human.'

'Ritchie.' I stood facing him, waiting for him to turn and meet my eye. 'Are you trying to tell me that they're not capable of hurting her – '

'No, of course not,' he said quietly. 'But what you heard was an edited recording of something that has already happened. The danger is that it will repeat continually in your mind and if you let it do that you'll go round the bend. Now, get a hold of yourself, Pat.'

We glared at each other. I forced myself to relax, tried to drive the sounds from my memory.

178

'I spoke to Bannerman about half an hour ago.' Ritchie dropped his voice deliberately to a lower key. 'The police have made some progress. The getaway car – the one you described – has been traced to its owner in Liverpool. It was stolen some time during the night of Wednesday-Thursday and of course the number-plates were changed. Last night a car answering your description was found abandoned in Chester. There were blonde hairs on the back carpet and analysis of the mud showed that it came from the lane where the kidnapping took place. The kidnappers must have changed cars in Chester. On the assumption that they are using stolen cars, the police are collecting details of every car stolen in the Chester area on Thursday.'

'That means not only Scotland Yard but the Chester police must know about it,' I protested. 'How are they going to keep it out of the papers? If that happens I'm sunk.'

'Pat, you had to bring the police in. You can't fight a thing like this without help. They've got computers and masses of modern gadgetry at their disposal and I promise you they are being as discreet as possible – '

'I expect you're right, Ritchie. I just hope so.'

'Bannerman asked me to put this to you. He says it would make it much easier for the police to crack this if they could put a man in here with you. It would be done very discreetly – '

'Not bloody likely. I've gone as far as I'm prepared to in that respect. They can perfectly well get their information through you.'

'Well, I've said my piece. I told him that's what your reply would be.'

Realizing I needed human companionship, Ritchie stayed and watched me drum up a couple of toasted sandwiches on my infra-red machine. We ate them standing up in the kitchen. When he left to go back to the showroom he advised me to try and get some sleep.

'I'm going to send my doctor to see you,' he warned me. 'Those dressings need changing and you're still wheezing through your nose.'

The doctor came at five o'clock. He stuck a thermometer in my mouth and felt my pulse. He told me I was running a fever and ought to be in bed. I replied that I'd tried bed and it hadn't done me any good. He made me lie down while he prodded my stomach. I winced and he nodded with satisfaction. Then he turned his attention to my nose, decided it was broken and ought to be reset under a general anaesthetic. That would mean being admitted to hospital. I said that it was impossible at the present time. At that he seemed to wash his hands of me, but I persuaded him to put a fresh dressing on the cut above my eye before he packed his things in his little black bag. At the door he paused, pricked by medical conscience.

'You're under great nervous strain, I can see that. I'll prescribe you a sedative if you like.'

'Would it make me less alert mentally?'

'Well, it would take the edge off things for you.'

'No, thanks. I want to keep the edge.'

The edge was there all right. Every time the 'phone rang I went to it dreading to hear the sound of Romy under torture. But Torquemada had temporarily sent me to Coventry.

Ritchie came soon after six. He'd brought a small suitcase. He told me that he intended to move in for the weekend, so that he could take his share of answering the 'phone and I could get some sleep.

'Oughtn't you to be going out to Naples?' During the hours of waiting I'd started worrying again about the Phantom II, which had gone completely out of my mind since the abortive ambush at Eton. 'You've got a pile of money tied up in that car. I feel very bad about what has happened.'

'Don't worry your head about the Rolls,' he reassured me. 'I've been on the blower to your friend Dempster. I think someone at the Home Office must have been on to him too, because he promised that the Consulate would keep tabs on the car till one of us can get out there. You just be guided by me, old Pat. My doctor phoned me after he'd seen you. He says you are under acute strain and in no condition to be left on your own.'

I did not hesitate long before agreeing. Even the kidnappers would have to admit that the person they were putting under pressure could not meet their demands without some help from a friend.

I was grateful for his company. The silence and waiting were beginning to have their effect on me.

'I've had another talk with Bannerman. I gather there's a massive combined operation going on, orchestrated by a senior officer at Scotland Yard. The Drug Squad and the anti-Terrorist Squad are in on it as well as the Customs and Excise people. But they're being very cagey about it. I have the feeling that your drug-smuggling exercise is only part of a much bigger game. Bannerman is obviously working under somebody very high up but he's being used as the officer to liaise with us.'

'Is he on our side? I mean, what's his priority? To get Romy back safe or to catch the kidnappers?'

'He keeps telling me that the safety of the hostage is paramount in operations like this.'

'Do you believe that?'

'When I stop believing it I'll let you know.'

We dined off fish and chips from a shop in the North End Road and tried to keep our minds occupied by playing poker. I'd dealt a hand and he'd exchanged two cards when he suddenly looked up.

'How strong do you really feel about Romy, Pat?'

'More strongly than I realized,' I admitted. 'Since Juliet and I broke up I've tried not to get emotionally involved with anyone, but during that time in Sedbergh Romy and I became very close. I've really only been able to measure it by the gap she's left.'

Ritchie grunted. We played the hand. My four sevens beat his three Queens and I won twenty-five pounds.

'She's a lovely person, Pat, and I don't like to say this, but are you sure she hasn't been playing you along? You'd never met her before. She persuaded you to let her come along and bring the Saab. Have you considered that the heroin may have been on the Saab and the bugging device fitted before it left Tunisia?'

'If it was she didn't know about it. I'd stake my life on that.'

That night I got to sleep in the end. Ritchie woke me with a cup of tea. He'd already started preparing breakfast. It was Saturday.

I shaved and took a cold bath. Dressed, I went into the kitchen to the smell of coffee and bacon and eggs.

'I brought your mail in.' He nodded at a half-dozen letters on the table. 'I think you should open that one on top.'

The envelope was of normal size but a bulge indicated that it contained a small object wrapped in paper. The post-mark was Bristol and it was date-stamped the previous afternoon. My name and address had been composed of letters cut from a newspaper. I slit it carefully with a knife. There was no writing-paper. Just the small parcel. I shook it out onto my hand and unwrapped the paper. The paper was marked and stiffened by partly-dried blood.

The object which had been wrapped up was a drawn tooth with small fragments of flesh and blood still adhering to the roots.

When Ritchie had gone I took my plate of bacon and eggs out of the oven and forced myself to eat. He had taken the tooth and the envelope with him and was going to make an arrangement to hand them over to Bannerman in case the police forensic experts could make any useful deductions from them.

At half-past ten I answered the 'phone.

'Torquemada. Are you ready to talk business?'

This was the third Torquemada call. It was the man who had first given me the code-word.

'Yes.'

'Is your 'phone tapped?'

'Not that I know of. Why should it be?'

'If it is you have only yourself to blame. Now, I want straight answers. Where is the merchandise?' Even now they were hesitating to use the word heroin.

I'd had plenty of time to work out what answer I was going to give to this question. I had to convince them that I was holding some cards, even though my hand was pathetically weak.

'You must be joking. I'm not going to tell you that.'

'Why did you go to the Slough police station on Wednesday morning?'

'To get the car back. You know all about that.'

'They must have questioned you.'

'Of course they did.'

'How much did you tell them?'

'Fuck all.'

A pause. 'Are you still in a position to hand the heroin over to us?'

'You mean you want to make a deal?'

'We have your girl-friend. Plus a nice tape of the love scene in the Hotel Verona. You're quite a lover-boy, aren't you?'

'I asked you if you wanted to make a deal.'

'All right. We'll release her when you've delivered the merchandise in accordance with instructions. You can do that?'

'What guarantee have I that you'll release her if I do?'

'Be practical. Of course there's no guarantee. But that's the deal. Take it or leave it.'

'How do I know she's still alive?'

'You can talk to her if you want. Do you want to?'

I should not have fallen into that trap. The answer had come too pat.

'Yes.'

I waited for ten long seconds, then I heard her voice, very flat and unemotional. 'Patrick'.

'Yes, it's me. Are you all right, Romy?'

'They're – going to kill me – if you don't – .' She was speaking in jerky, broken phrases. 'I can't stand – much more. Oh God! Please, you must – get me away – '

'I'm going to. Just hold on, Romy. I'm making a deal with them now – '

'That's enough,' the kidnapper's voice cut in. 'This conversation must end now. Just answer this. How soon can you deliver?'

'I'll need time. The stuff's been stashed in a number of different places.'

'You're lying. We'll give you twenty-four hours, no more. Be ready to act on our instructions.'

Ritchie was back before the end of the morning. The police had obtained Home Office authorization to tap my line. The Torquemada call had been made from a call-box in South Norwood.

'They've almost certainly got several units going. Firstly their communications centre. That could be mobile, concealed in something like a motor-racing team's transporter or one of those American motor-homes. Then there's a London-based group for keeping contact with you and arranging for the collection of the heroin. And there must be a hide-out, where the hostage and those guarding her are holed up. So the police have three chances of locating them. All police forces and the Post Office surveillance teams are on the look-out for any vehicle that could be a communications centre – .'

'Did they get anything out of the tooth or the envelope?'

We'd gone into the kitchen. Ritchie was unpacking the parcels of fresh supplies he had brought from the supermarket.

'I haven't heard yet. But thanks to the Swansea computer we've had a bit of luck. There was an incident in Llangollen yesterday when a boy on a bicycle was knocked down by a car which failed to stop. Someone got the number and the police checked up with Swansea. The car came from a Chester suburb. The owner did not even know that his car had gone till the police called on him!'

'Llangollen. That's the place where they have the Festival. What do they call it? The Eisteddfod.'

'Yes. Very Welsh. It gives them a line. Sedbergh, Chester, Llangollen. And the envelope was posted in Bristol. They're concentrating their search now in mid-Wales. Something's bound to turn up soon. They're sure to have switched cars soon after that accident.'

'Was Bannerman listening in on that conversation I had with them?'

'No. But he got a transcript of it. I understand that you made a deal to deliver the heroin. Wasn't that a bit premature?'

'If they ever suspect that it's in the possession of the police, or get the idea that I'm not in a position to deliver, then I'm really sunk. Bannerman's got to meet me on this. You've got to persuade him, Ritchie.'

Ritchie opened the fridge and put a six-can pack of beer into the lower compartment. 'It's this man Ray who's the problem. This is his biggest haul of heroin yet. Now that he's got his hands on it he's not too keen to part with it.'

'Bannerman said that the life of the hostage was always paramount. You've got to persuade them, Ritchie. I must have that heroin by midday tomorrow.'

I could feel myself being manoeuvred into an impossible situation, a race which I could not possibly win. On the one hand I wanted to arrange a handover of the heroin to the kidnappers before the police located the hideout and began a siege. On the other hand, I dreaded what could happen if I agreed to a rendezvous and then turned up without the precious merchandise.

'I'll do what I can,' Ritchie promised doubtfully. 'But you realize you're asking for enough heroin to provide fifty thousand addicts with a fix?'

The weekend in London has never held much appeal for me. That Saturday and Sunday reinforced my distaste for the metropolis on non-working days. The monotony of waiting was broken by two events.

Late on Saturday night Ritchie arrived with a couple of suitcases. He put them on the sofa and we opened them up. Each one contained twenty opaque plastic bags about the size of a 3 lb. bag of sugar. They were all sealed except one, which had been refastened with Sellotape. I opened it. It contained a white powder not unlike fine salt. I licked my index finger, dipped it in the powder and put it in my mouth. It had a sharp, acrid taste.

'How do I know this is heroin?'

'Jesus, Pat, what more do you want?' Ritchie exploded. 'Don't you realize what this means? I've been down on my bended knees to Ray and Bannerman. It was only with the greatest reluctance that they let me have this stuff.'

'All right, Ritchie,' I said quickly, calming him. If the white powder was not heroin I didn't want to know, for the very good reason that there was absolutely nothing I could do about it. Perhaps it would have been asking a lot for the Customs and Excise to hand over four million pounds' worth of drugs to a not very satisfactory private citizen. 'As far as I'm concerned this is heroin. You've done a bloody good job.'

The second envelope from the kidnappers must have been pushed through my letter-box at some time during the night. The white rectangle lying on the mat inside the front door caught the corner of my eye as I walked from my bedroom to the sitting-room to draw the curtains. This time it bore no name or address. I took it to my desk, feeling the shape of the contents with my fingers. Cards of some kind, and slightly curled.

I took a paper knife and carefully slit the top of the envelope. I withdrew two photographic prints, obviously taken with a polaroid camera. The subject of both was Romy. The first was taken from behind and showed the top half of her. Her torso had been bared and her wrists were tied above her head to a spike hammered in between the stones of a wall. Her back was criss-crossed with ugly weals. The second photograph was more horrible, but in a different way. She was seated in a chair facing the camera, her wrists strapped to the back legs. Round her neck was a noose with an imitation of a hangman's knot under her left ear. The rope had been drawn tight, probably on a beam above, forcing her head to tilt at an angle. Propped against her chest was a copy of the previous day's *Express*.

I must have uttered some exclamation, for Ritchie came out of the bathroom, one cheek still covered with shaving soap. He came and stood behind me, looking over my shoulder at the photographs.

'Oh, sweet Jesus! The bloody bastards!'

'She's been flogged,' I answered dully. 'And if I don't deliver the heroin they're going to hang her.'

'So it would appear.'

'What else can it mean?' I shouted. 'Christ, Ritchie you're always trying to make out that she's being treated like a guest at the Hilton.'

'Well, at least we know that she was still alive yesterday. Let's have a look at those pictures.'

I handed them to him over my shoulder and stared unseeingly out of the window. This time I was not going to crack. The kidnappers were in danger of over-playing their hand. Some sort of film had settled over my emotions, hardening them so that I did not feel things so acutely now.

The fourth Torquemada call came two hours later. Ritchie had gone off to meet Bannerman, taking the photographs with him.

'Malone? Torquemada here.' It was the same female as had made the second call. 'You've seen the photos?'

'Yes.' I saw no point in indulging in protests, pleas or threats. That would only be playing their game. But once again I experienced that trembling of the legs and a drying of my mouth.

'You want to know why she was whipped?'

I did not answer.

'Because you went to the police.'

'That's not true.'

'Then who's the man who regularly leaves and enters your flat?'

'He's a friend. Actually the person I work for at Automobiles of Quality. He's moved in to help me. You don't think I can handle this on my own, do you?'

'You'd better be telling the truth. If you try to trick us, she'll hang.'

'I hope I'll have the pleasure of meeting you again some day,' I said, unable to keep the venom out of my voice.

She laughed. 'Perhaps the pleasure will be mine. I wouldn't treat you in such a gentlemanly fashion as Ivan did, you fucking bastard.'

I held my peace. After a moment she said: 'You have the goods?'

'Yes.'

'The real stuff? No tricks?'

'Yes.'

'Be ready to leave your flat with it as soon as you receive our instructions. You will use the Saab and come alone. No one must follow you. If you inform anyone else your woman will be executed.'

Disconnection.

I went into the bathroom and cleaned my teeth. I felt fouled even by talking to her.

When Ritchie came back he'd brought hot Cornish pasties from the fish and chip shop, which always opened for a few hours in the middle of Sunday. I did not want to tell him about the 'phone call and the instructions I'd been given, but he'd heard about it from Bannerman.

'You'll be followed, but it will be done very discreetly. Bannerman thinks they'll probably send you on a dummy run, just to test whether you've got something to hand over. They've traced all the Torquemada calls and they're coming from an area of about two square miles round the Crystal Palace.'

'What about the Welsh end? I'm more interested in that. That's sure to be where they've got Romy.'

'They're following up another stolen car. This time it's a Cavalier GLS, which they think was used after the Llangollen accident, but the trail has petered out in Gwynedd. There's a lot of uninhabited country in that part of Wales. They're going to ask the RAF to fly an IRLS over the area tonight.'

'An IRLS? What the hell's that?'

'An infra-red line scan. It's a long strip of air photo taken with an infra-red camera. Any hot spots show up. If you see a bunch of houses glowing where no habitation is supposed to be you sit up and take notice. Human bodies make enough heat.'

'Terrorists usually conceal their hostages in densely populated areas.'

'That's true so far as this country is concerned. But in Italy they often choose remote mountain areas. And Bannerman thinks these are some new breed of terrorist. The patterns are different from anything he's been up against before.'

When Ritchie came back he found me pacing the flat. I had been waiting all day for a 'phone call which never came.

'That's all to the good,' Ritchie observed when I told him. 'The more time they waste the better. It increases the police's chance of getting closer to them.'

'Did they get anything from those photographs?'

The photographs had been constantly materializing before my eyes, just as the screams and cries had gone on echoing in my mind.

'Not so far. As Romy's dentist is in Tunisia, they haven't been able to identify the tooth. But the area of search in Wales has been narrowed down. The IRLS has revealed several possible hideouts. The RAF suggested doing a run over the area with one of their training Phantoms and taking some photos. They're doing that this evening. Thank God for weekend flyers. Don't look so worried, Pat. There's always a lot of Air Force activity over the mountains of Wales. That's where they practise their hedge-hopping techniques.'

The 'phone rang. I rushed to answer it.

'Patrick. It's Juliet.'

That was all I needed.

'Juliet, I can't talk to you now – '

'Listen, duckie. You'd better take what my solicitors said seriously. You've had a letter from them, haven't you? We're quite prepared to take you to court for perjury – '

'You do the listening, you bitch!' I said savagely. 'I know now why you couldn't find your keys to my flat. You gave them to that little squirt of a private detective and he's been in here snooping around among my things.'

'How dare you talk to me like this!' she spluttered. 'I've never – '

'Get this straight, Juliet.' My voice rode over her protest. 'If you do that again you can take me to court but it'll be for assault and battery because I'll come over and give you the biggest thrashing you've ever had in your life and enjoy doing it – '

She hung up. I took a deep breath and did the same.

'An old flame?' Ritchie enquired, with a lift of one eyebrow.

'Juliet. God, I feel better for that!'

'Good juicy stuff, old pal. I hope the dicks monitoring your calls enjoyed it.'

'Lord, I'd forgotten about them.'

The evening passed and the expected call from Torquemada never came. At midnight we went to bed and had an undisturbed night.

The messages had been bad enough. This lack of contact was even worse. Had the police been clumsy and betrayed their tap on my line to the kidnappers? Had they carried out their threat to kill her? Would the next package contain some awful proof that she was dead?

The first call of the day came at a quarter-past nine on that Monday morning. I was the one who answered it.

'It's the library,' a pleasant woman's voice informed me. 'Is that Mr Bryer?'

'No. Do you want to speak to him?'

'Would you tell him that we have the book he ordered?'

189

'Okay.' I could not keep the irritation out of my voice. 'I'll tell him.'

Ritchie's reaction to the message was surprising. He dropped the spoons he was drying back into the sink and whipped off the incongruous frilly apron he was wearing. 'That means they've got something! I'd better go round straight away.'

'Must be quite a book. The unexpurgated *Fanny Hill*, I suppose, or *Confessions of a Teenage Call-Girl*.'

'It's Bannerman, you berk! That's the message we agreed he'd send if there was an important development.'

Left to myself I began to wonder why Bannerman had not wanted to speak in clear over the 'phone. It could only be because he suspected that someone else besides the police were listening to my calls.

Monday was the day when nobody wanted to know me. At eleven o'clock I rang Anthea but she had heard nothing from Ritchie. I did not dare to 'phone the number Bannerman had given me in case the call was overheard. All I could do was wait.

Once I rang the operator and asked her to give me a test ring. I'd got the idea that my 'phone was out of order and that no one would be able to contact me. But there was no fault in my telephone.

At three I rang the showroom. Ritchie had not turned up there and Anthea had received no message from him. She was beginning to get worried about him.

This was the fifth day since Romy had been snatched and it dragged more than any of the others had done. The shock, horror and fatigue which I had experienced in the early stages had been replaced by a mixture of frustration and anger. Inactivity was eating into me now more than fear. Sometimes I was certain that the kidnappers' plan had gone wrong, that the whole thing was already finished and Romy dead. Then I'd tell myself that this long silence was just a new refinement in the war of attrition on my nerves.

I had my answer at eight o'clock.

'Torquemada.' It was the woman. 'This call's going to be short, so listen carefully. We have reason to believe your telephone has been tapped. That is why we were unable to give you instructions on how to deliver –'

'You're wrong about that. I'm quite certain – '

'Don't talk. Just listen. Your woman's been punished again. We haven't time to send you a photo but her back's not a pretty sight.'

'Jesus! What's the point – '

'Listen! This operation has only twelve more hours to run. It's six o'clock now. If the heroin is not in our possession by tomorrow morning we're going to cancel the operation and then she'll hang.'

'Tell me what you want,' I said levelly. It was the first time they had mentioned heroin in clear. 'I'm only trying to do what you want.'

In my hall the buzzer of the intercom sounded. Someone was pressing the button against my name down at the street door.

'We're going to give you one last chance to deliver.'

'Tell me what you want me to do.'

'There's someone in the street ringing your bell.'

'They can wait.'

'No, they can't. Go and answer it.'

I laid down the post office telephone and went to the instrument in the hall.

'Who is it?'

'Malone?' It was the male partner in the telephoning team.

'Yes.'

'At ten o'clock you leave the flat with the goods. Take the Saab and drive by the M4 to Bristol. Do not exceed the legal speed limit. There is a pub called the Crown and Cushion in Campbell Road. Be there at midnight. Naturally it will be closed. But in the car-park at the rear there will be a yellow DAF, registration number ORU 557M. Behind the rear number plate you will find further instructions. Come alone. Be certain you are not followed.'

'Wait! I'll have to leave here before ten if I'm to get there by then.'

There was no answer. He'd gone. I went back to the telephone lying on my desk and picked it up. All I heard was the dialling tone.

I felt a sense of secretive triumph when I realized that although Bannerman or his monitor had heard the telephone conversation, they would not have heard the message which had been passed over the intercom. That meant I now had a chance to slip a possible police tail and make a clean delivery of the two suitcases. The crucial point was, did they contain genuine heroin or not? I felt no qualms about releasing the drug onto the illicit market. It would barely suffice to keep Britain's five thousand heroin users supplied for two weeks. But if Ray and Bannerman were bluffing, if the suitcases contained some harmless substance such as Epsom Salts, with perhaps the one bag of genuine heroin to allay suspicion, how would the kidnappers react then?

Meanwhile, the police search was continuing and if what Ritchie had reported was true, it was on a massive scale. At any moment the hideout might be discovered and then the whole situation would be changed. The kidnappers would know that I had all along been in contact with the police and I was very afraid that, even if they found themselves in a siege situation, they would still carry out their threat to kill Romy.

I was pacing the flat, agonizing over what it was best to do, when I heard a key in the lock of the front door. When Ritchie came in he looked tired, worried and irritable. His usually immaculate jacket and trousers were wet and rumpled. He was carrying an Ordnance Survey Map and a couple of photographs.

'God, I'm hungry! I haven't had anything to eat since breakfast.'

'Where the hell have you been?'

He prowled into the kitchen, intent on food.

'I've a lot to tell you, but I've got to eat first. Fill me in on what's been happening here while I get something inside me. What's this? Luncheon meat?'

While he cut thick slices of bread, buttered and then slapped slices of luncheon meat between them, I told him about my long day of waiting and the message which had finally come from Torquemada.

'They must be getting rattled.' He chewed energetically, took a swig of the beer I'd poured for him and belched. 'They've got wise to the fact that your calls are being monitored and they may have noticed a concentration of CID cars in the Crystal Palace area.'

'We have a deadline now. Six a.m. tomorrow morning.'

'Deadlines are often extended. However, we've got a new problem.' He glanced at his watch. 'I'll need to talk fast. We're going to have to make some decisions.'

He crammed the rest of his crude sandwich into his mouth. I waited for him to masticate it.

'As you know, I left you this morning to go and contact Bannerman. The whole thing had taken a sudden turn. The air photos supplied by the Phantoms following up the IRLS had been very positive. It's amazing what they can do nowadays with aerial photography. I won't go into technical details but they've located the Cavalier, even identified the roof-rack and spot lamps.'

'Where is it?'

'In a disused mine-working about eight miles inland from the Welsh coast. That's where I've been all day. About half an hour after leaving you I found myself in a helicopter with Bannerman and a Chief Superintendent Munden on my way to attend a conference at Meirion.'

'Never heard of it.'

'It's the county capital of Cwmrydd. While the operation was based on London the case was in the territory of the Metropolitan Police. Now that the kidnappers' hideout has been located, the matter comes under the jurisdiction of the Chief Constable of the area.'

'That doesn't mean Bannerman has to drop out of it, surely?'

'No. The two forces will liaise, but it's the sort of situation where personalities count for a lot – '

'What are they going to do? You don't sound as if you had much confidence in the Chief Constable – '

'Steady on, old soul.' Ritchie put up a hand to calm me. I realized that I'd been barking my questions at him. 'Come into the sitting-room and I'll give you a proper briefing.'

He slapped the map and the photographs down on the table and while I waited impatiently got one of his long cigars going.

'Ray and Bannerman did not tell us the full story when we had that meeting at my dentist's. But reading between the lines of what I've heard today, this heroin-smuggling operation is only part of a much bigger operation. The Anti-Terrorist Squad have been working through Interpol with the police forces of European countries. They have identified a new group, calling themselves

IMAG – that stands for International Marxist Action Group. They're mostly intellectuals disenchanted with society and dedicated to changing it by violent methods. A little amateurish still, by comparison with the Bader-Meinhof and the Red Brigades – '

'This hideout, Ritchie,' I cut in, fingering the map. 'Have you located it?'

'I'm coming to that, Pat. This is all relevant, what I'm telling you. IMAG is planning a really sensational kidnapping operation in the UK. They're aiming at the very top.'

I stared at him. 'They wouldn't dare try and snatch *her* – even if they could.'

'Wouldn't they? Why else are they trying to raise four million pounds? Heroin smuggling is just about the most profitable racket in the world. That's why they moved in on Varzi and took over the operation he had planned using you. When you went to the RV to meet Varzi's contact you were really going to meet members of the English section of IMAG. Naturally they were annoyed when they found that you had cheated them – or so they thought. They must have suspected that you had disposed of the heroin for your own gain. I'm only passing on Bannerman's theory, mind you.'

I looked at my watch. What Ritchie was telling me was very instructive, but time was slipping away fast.

'Do you know what the plan is?'

'As soon as it was dark they intended to move up and surround the hide-out. When daylight comes they will use loud-hailers to tell the kidnappers that their escape-routes are blocked and that their only hope is to give themselves up.'

'That'll blow the gaff. They'll know that I've been in contact with the police all this time.'

'Yes,' Ritchie agreed soberly. 'Unless they suspect it already. That's why I'm here. I thought you ought to know.'

I looked out of the window at the darkening night sky. An aircraft on the run in to Heathrow airport had switched on its landing lights and was casting long beams across the misty air. I was concentrating so hard on it that when the telephone started to ring my mind did not register the fact. It was Ritchie who threw down his pen and went to answer it.

I heard him lift the receiver and give the number. Only when

I realized that he had been listening for a full two minutes, interrupting with an occasional grunt, did I turn round. He stared back at me unseeingly then averted his face so that I could no longer read his expression.

'So where do we go from here?' he asked his caller after another half minute. Then, 'I see. So, you'll keep in touch? Right. Thanks.'

He put the receiver down very carefully and deliberately. 'That was Bannerman. They moved in on the hide-out just after dusk – '

'Jesus!' I exclaimed, staring out at the sky. 'It's barely dark yet. If they were seen – '

Ritchie put up a hand to stop my outburst. 'Wait till you hear, Pat. It was done very skilfully and they're sure they were not observed. But there is something funny about that hide-out. Bannerman says there are only two people in the house. And neither of them is a woman.'

I leant back against the sharp edge of the table, trying to keep my anger at bay.

'Now wait a minute! If they are really being all that cautious how can they be so sure there are only two people in the house and that – '

'Obviously they are using the most modern and sophisticated equipment. You know they have miniaturized television probes and can put a laser microphone into a house from fifty yards away. But the occupants aren't even keeping a proper watch. Bannerman's sure it's a false trail.'

'But they might have her in a cellar. That photograph they sent looked like a cellar.'

Ritchie shook his head. 'They don't think so. The Chief Constable wants to move in on them at once but Bannerman insisted on him waiting. He felt we had a right to know the form. But they will go in just before first light.'

I slumped down into a chair. After the brief raising of hopes this abrupt let-down was hard to bear. I looked yet again at my watch. It was just coming up to nine-thirty. Eight and a half hours to the dead-line, and we were still as far as ever from knowing where she was being held.

I got up and walked into the kitchen. I subconsciously began cutting myself some bread and a slice of the luncheon meat. I was not really hungry but I felt I had to be doing something. All of a sudden the map and the air photos had become completely pointless. The police had deployed every conceivable resource and it had got them nowhere.

Ritchie joined me but we did not speak. Over my shoulder I heard him open the fridge and get out two cans of beer. There came a double hiss as he opened them over the sink. He poured a glass and put it down on the table beside me. I nodded my thanks. It was not a time for words.

There was only one course open to me now. Before dawn the kidnappers would know that I had been in collusion with the police. Despite Ritchie's affirmation that deadlines are often extended I had now become convinced that by the end of the coming night I would have run out of time. Before then I had somehow to get a direct contact with IMAG. The only way I could do so was by delivering two suitcases which I was virtually certain contained nothing more harmful than fifty pounds of Epsom Salts.

'Of course, I'm coming with you.'

'What? What did you say?'

I must have done a double-take, for Ritchie laughed as my head jerked round. He had been quietly watching me as I munched my sandwich.

'I'll come with you when you go to the rendezvous. I agree with you. We've been sitting on our fannies for five days and it's got us nowhere. Now it's time for us to take the fight into the enemy's camp.'

In other circumstances his military jargon would have made me smile. I'd always known that the effect of Ritchie's intervention would be to escalate events. It was his character to seek the most active and violent solution to a problem. But whereas before I had been alarmed at the possible consequences of letting him take the initiative I now found tremendous relief in the prospect of doing something positive. Between them the police and the kidnappers had manoeuvred me into a hopeless position. It was no longer possible for me to remain passive. I was far too conscious of what they had already done to Romy, and I could not sit down under the threat of what they had promised to do to her at dawn the following morning.

'They made it a condition that I go alone,' I pointed out, without very great conviction.

'We're making our own conditions now,' Ritchie said. His whole manner had changed at the prospect of action. His shoulders had gone back, and his good eye was sparkling with anticipation. Even his moustache seemed to be bristling with aggression. 'They think they've got you thoroughly softened up. It could be they're going to receive a slight surprise.'

CHAPTER 12

It was ten o'clock precisely when I carried the two suitcases down to the street, stowed them inside the hatchback of the Turbo and locked it. If IMAG had anyone watching they would be able to note that I was meticulously carrying out instructions. I had to take into account the possibility that the police might still have me under observation, so before joining the traffic moving out of town I took steps to make sure that I could not be tailed. They involved violating a number of traffic regulations, murdering the speed limit and arousing the wrath of a good many peaceable motorists. But as I swung over the Chiswick Flyover I was confident that nothing could have tailed me.

I drifted at 70 mph as far as the first service area a couple of miles beyond the beginning of the M4. There was no problem in spotting Ritchie's Bentley Continental in the car park. I stopped the Saab beside it and opened the passenger door. Ritchie got out of the big car and carefully locked it. He placed the canvas shoulder satchel he'd collected from his house on the seat of the Turbo but did not climb in. Instead he pulled a pair of plyers from his pocket.

'Can you open the bonnet a minute?'

'What on earth for?'

'I just want to make a modification to this engine,' he said, avoiding my eye.

I shrugged and, to humour him, released the bonnet catch. He opened it up and I saw him lean over the left side and sever a pair of wires. He then removed the top of the distributor and changed the rotor arm. Next he went round to the other side and leant over the turbocharger. After a moment he straightened up and closed the bonnet again. As he slipped into the seat beside me I was already letting in the clutch to reverse out again.

'What was all that about?'

'Just giving you a bit more power,' he told me with great satisfaction. 'You never know when it might come in handy. But you'd better watch the dial carefully and be careful how you use the throttle. It's liable to shoot up into the red.'

'What the hell have you done?' I asked suspiciously. As I accelerated away the needle of the compressor dial had swung round alarmingly into the danger section.

'With a rotor arm and a pair of pliers you can transform this thing into a bomb in about two minutes flat. All you have to do is nip the pipe from the waste gate on the turbocharger, which shuts off the by-pass diaphragm, and replace the centrifugal cut-out on the distributor with a normal rotor-arm. With the over-pressure sensor bridged you have more than two hundred brake-horse-power under your boot.'

'I'm not quite with you.' I was watching the dial carefully as I swung out into the motorway traffic and built up speed. The car had changed alarmingly, like a racehorse that has got the bit between its teeth and felt the urge to bolt. It was showing an eager readiness to rev right off the dials. The power at my disposal was enormous.

'Well, the centrifugal rotor arm which is standard restricts you to 6,000 rpm,' Ritchie explained. 'Now you've got an extra 1,000 rpm. That will boost your power considerably and increase your available speed to 140 mph, maybe more. But you'll have to watch it. If you use full power the turbocharger will burst with centrifugal force.'

'Are you sure you know what you're doing?' I changed into top gear as the speedometer needle swung towards 100 mph. 'Is this an approved modification?'

'God, no! The makers would have a fit – '

'We're risking damage to the power unit.' I was keeping an eye on the turbocharger dial which had jerked towards the red danger zone. 'It won't help us much if the compressor bursts.'

'You'll have to take care and keep out of the red. The maximum safe turbocharger speed is 220,000 rpm, but for normal use it's governed down to 110,000.'

'I didn't know you were so clued up on turbochargers.'

'I got the idea from Bob the other day,' Ritchie said casually. Then, deliberately changing the subject, he groped in the canvas satchel. 'I picked up some equipment from my house. There's a

Smith and Wesson .38 for you. You're familiar with them, aren't you?'

'Yes,' I said guardedly, 'but don't you want it for yourself?'

'I've got a new toy.' Glancing down I saw that he had withdrawn a neat automatic with an unusually thick butt. 'It's the latest from Beretta. A 9 mm semi-automatic with a double action. The magazine holds thirteen rounds. You can have it, if you like, and I'll take the old Smith and Wesson.'

'Thank you, Ritchie. But six rounds will be enough for me.'

On the outskirts of Bristol we stopped. Ritchie moved into the back and went to ground behind the front seats. We'd covered the journey from London in an hour and three quarters. That gave me half an hour to find the Crown and Cushion. I had to ask directions from a late-night service station before I located Campbell Road. The public house was half way along on the left. By this time there were few pedestrians about and the place already had a closed and shuttered look.

I drove into the car-park at the back as the hands of the dashboard clock centred on midnight. Only one car was left there. It was a yellow DAF. I parked the Turbo near it and got out. A smell of urine and stale beer assailed my nostrils as I walked towards the other car. Ritchie was crouched in the Saab, with instructions from me to keep a low profile and not start a shooting match unless it was absolutely necessary. I felt sure that my pick-up would be observed and I strongly sensed the presence of a pair of eyes behind one of those closed windows above my head.

The number plate of the DAF was on a hinge and the petrol filler cap was behind it. When I pulled it down I saw a long brown envelope. I put it straight into my breast pocket and let the number plate snap back into place. As I walked to the Turbo the urinals in the outside Gents lavatory began to gush gustily.

Back in the Saab I took a torch from the glove pocket and directed its beam at the envelope. It contained a section cut from a 1:50,000 OS map and a sheet bearing three lines of typewritten instructions. For Ritchie's benefit I read them aloud.

'Proceed via the M3, A4042, A479, A470 to Machynlleth. You will then be on this map. Enter Dovey Forest at the point marked X at exactly two o'clock. The forestry road is not marked on this map. Using side-lights proceed along it for five miles at between 20 and 25 mph.'

It was one fifty as we drove through the mid-Wales township of Machynlleth. The brash sodium street lights shone eerily on empty pavements and anonymous cars. As my headlamps illuminated the clock-tower at the T junction a dark figure moved out of sight behind the columns at its base. I was glad I had made Ritchie curl up on the back seat.

I turned right and a mile out of town crossed a narrow hump-backed bridge. Reflected moonlight flashed from the surface of the river. My own headlights glared at me from a row of cottages facing the bridge. I turned right, but kept my speed down. From my memory of the section of map I knew that the point marked X was only a couple of miles further on.

'Where are we now?' Ritchie's voice sounded muffled from the back of the car.

'We've just crossed the river. We should be at the entry to the forest in a couple of minutes.'

'Anything following us?'

'A car came out of Machynlleth behind us but it turned left at the bridge. There's nothing else in sight.'

It was evident that the kidnappers intended to commit us to the lonely forest track so that they could be absolutely sure that no other car was following us before they made their presence known. If they were not happy about it they could simply let us drive through the forest and emerge on the other side of the hills.

I could easily have missed the point marked X if I had not been looking for it. The entry to the forest was not gated. A wire fence stretched away from a pair of railway sleepers embedded upright about ten feet apart. Beside them were two notices. One stated that this was a private road not open to the public. The other bore the usual warning against the risk of fire. The Turbo lurched as I swung into the narrow opening and the wheels rattled sharply on the cattle grid. It was just two o'clock.

I was certain that at this point we would be under observation, but I could not see any car parked in the shadows. I wondered whether the police at the hide-out had betrayed their presence to the two occupants of the deserted house. If that had happened Romy was as good as dead and Ritchie and I were putting our heads into a noose. The rattle of the cattle grid had been unpleasantly suggestive of a portcullis closing behind us. Ahead lay thousands of acres of deserted woodland. No one remained in these forests at night. I was on an unmapped road and there was no way of telling where it led.

'We've just entered the forest,' I told Ritchie, instinctively keeping my voice low. 'That noise was us going over a cattle grid.'

'Any pursuit yet?'

'None that I can see.'

The forest closed us in darkly on either side. On only sidelights I was finding it hard to navigate and it was difficult to drive at the speed that had been stipulated. As my eyes grew accustomed to the darkness I could see the open strip of sky between the trees ahead. Stars were out and the moon was low down to the East.

Soon we were climbing. Loose stones slapped against the wheel arches and occasionally the underside of the chassis grated against the humped surface. The turbocharger whined quietly to itself as the needle of the rev counter rose and fell. Dark tunnels led away between the regimentally planted trees. It was hard to imagine that any form of animal life thrived in this shadowy world.

We passed an open space where tree trunks sawn the length of pit-props were piled up beside a new wooden hut. The ground was covered with off-white saw-dust. A mile later a deserted farm-house loomed up, its stone walls crumbling, a tree poking out through its roof. This had once been sheep farming country, before the habitation line moved down and the shepherds forsook the solitude of the hills for the bustle and throb of the shop floor.

We had covered about four miles in a little under twelve minutes when I glanced in the mirror for the fiftieth time. On the track behind had appeared two lights, like the eyes of a predator stalking me.

'There's a car behind us.'

'How far back?'

'About two hundred yards. He's maintaining his distance. I shall just keep going.'

'Right.'

The car behind did not attempt to close up for another mile. Then it increased speed and moved near enough for me to hear the clatter of stones against its wheel arches.

'He's closed up to about a hundred yards. I don't think it's going to be long now.'

I had set out from the flat without any coherent idea of what I intended to do. All I knew was that I simply had to have some kind of confrontation with the kidnappers. The instructions which I had picked up in Bristol made it clear that they intended our meeting to take place in circumstances where any kind of surveillance would be virtually impossible. But they were bound to be on the alert for any kind of trick or trap. I had let myself be persuaded by Ritchie that our only course was to act offensively from the start and ask questions later. I was reluctant at first to accept his arguments in case our action rebounded on Romy but I had to accept his clinching argument.

'We are running out of time, old Pat. And you don't think they'll just take what's in those suitcases on trust, do you? How do you think they'll react when they find you've conned them again?'

Behind me I heard the crisp metallic sound of an automatic being cocked. The Smith and Wesson reposed in the pocket of the door behind me. I did not think I would be given much opportunity to use it, but I had in my hands a weapon in which I had far more confidence.

The road had levelled and with eyes that had now become accustomed to the darkness I could see that ahead of me stretched a straight section of about six hundred yards. At the far end of it a set of side-lights had appeared, rocking slightly to the undulation of the ground.

'There's another car coming towards us. We're in a sandwich.'

'That's as we expected. How far away?'

'About four hundred yards and closing.'

The forestry workers had been clearing this area. Stacks of pit props on either side confined a vehicle even more closely to the track. The kidnappers had obviously reconnoitred the area and chosen their meeting place with care.

'Which one shall I take first?'

'The one behind,' Ritchie said. I could hear him changing position. 'Give me a second to get myself strapped in.'

The Saab was fitted with seat-belts for the rear passengers as well as the front. I waited till I heard the click of the clasp being fastened.

'All set?'

'Right. Give her the gun.'

I engaged second gear and accelerated hard. As the speedometer needle touched 40 mph I spun the steering wheel in a clockwise direction. Keeping my right foot on the accelerator I slammed my left foot hard on the brake pedal. The rear wheels immediately locked but the power of the engine overcame the front brakes so that the front wheels kept turning. The rear of the car obediently spun through a half circle. When it had completed one hundred and eighty degrees I took my foot off the brake to arrest the spin.

Now we were facing back the way we had come. I changed down to second gear and switched on my headlights. My front wheels were already grabbing at the rough surface.

The driver of the car following me did not have much time to attempt evasive action. He must still have been recovering from the surprise of seeing the Turbo spin round in its own length when he saw it bearing down on him with headlights blazing.

I was not worrying about the compressor gauge now. I was aiming at the front of the other car, building speed fast and ready to react to any attempt on his part to avoid me. But with the pit props piled on either side of the road there was nothing he could do except slam on his brakes.

The impact as the two cars met was not as violent as I expected. Perhaps it was because the Turbo's massive bumpers absorbed the first 5 mph of the shock. I was already bracing my head back against the head rest. At the last moment I took my hands off the steering wheel. I felt myself grabbed by the seat-belt, heard the thump of metal on metal and the crash of breaking glass. The impact of the heavily armoured car on the other vehicle must have been devastating.

I had no time to assess the result. I engaged reverse gear and accelerated. In the heat of the moment I had forgotten that the turbocharger would boost me in reverse just as effectively as in forward speeds. In a couple of seconds I was careering backwards at 30 mph. As before I yanked the steering wheel hard right-hand-down, but this time I declutched as I stamped on the foot brake. All four wheels locked and the car pivoted on its right rear corner. As it spun I rammed the gear lever into first and when it had completed the half circle and was facing in the right direction I gave it another boost of acceleration to set it off along the track again.

At that moment the first bullet struck the front of the Saab and I was dazzled by a blinding glare. The other driver had switched on his headlamps and was coming at me fast. His passenger had an arm out of a side window and was pumping bullets from an automatic weapon. They were ricocheting off the angled front windscreen, scarring it with little stiletto-shaped marks.

The knowledge that I was being fired at by a marksman aiming to kill made me see red. All the resentment and tension that had been pent up for the last five days boiled over. The memory of the drawn tooth, the flagellated back and the noose flashed through my mind. I seemed to hear again the sneering, bullying tones of the kidnappers' voices. I forgot all Ritchie's warnings about bursting the turbocharger and just gave it full blast. The Saab seemed to gather its strength and literally hurl itself forward.

Behind me I heard Ritchie shout, 'Jesus, Pat – for Christ's sake!' But I was berserk now, aiming at those onrushing head-lamps. All I could see was a huge dazzle of light into which I was firing the Turbo like a torpedo.

At the very last moment the other driver's nerve broke and he tried to swerve away from me. I made the necessary correction to meet him. We crashed into each other almost head on. This time the impact was far greater. For a moment I was stunned. The pain in my chest was so great that I was sure that I had cracked most of my ribs. When I opened my eyes there was only darkness. The Saab had smashed the front of the other car, slamming it against a pile of pit-props.

Behind me Ritchie was calling upon every deity known to the World Council of Churches.

I was shaken from my stupor by a sudden WHOOF and the flare of spreading flames. The other car had ignited. I hurriedly engaged reverse gear. The Turbo jerked itself clear with a shriek of rending metal.

The fire spread very rapidly. The petrol tank had been ruptured and fuel had spilled out onto the ground. By the time we had released ourselves from our safety belts and scrambled from the Saab the other car was enveloped in a yellow shroud of leaping flames. We could see the two occupants wrenching at the door handles but they had been jammed by the collision and would not open. Their mouths were open in screams of terror. Even in my most vindictive moments I would never have wished such a terrible vengeance on the two who had tried to kill me in the wheat field at Monxton. Ritchie grabbed me as I tried to move towards the roaring inferno.

'There's nothing we can do, Pat,' he shouted, hauling me back.

I looked round at his face. It was illuminated by the horrific orange light, and the expression he wore sent a quick shiver down my spine. I realized that he was sealed off from all human emotion. 'I'm going to put them out of their misery.'

The two in the car cringed back in disbelief as they saw him raise the Beretta and point it towards them. He fired six shots through the glass. Their bodies jerked and slumped down. Even as I watched, the windows were blackening with the heat and smoke.

'Come on.' Ritchie shook me roughly, 'We've got to check up on the others. Bring the Smith and Wesson.'

There was silence from the other car, which was a couple of hundred yards back down the track. Using the piles of pit props for concealment we approached to within twenty yards.

'You wait here and be ready to cover me,' Ritchie hissed.

He ran to the other side of the track so as not to mask my fire. His Beretta was held at waist level as he approached the silent car. He was a dozen yards from it when I saw a flash from the passenger's seat and heard the crack of the shot. Ritchie's reply was an instant reflex – two shots fired in quick succession from the hip. My own shot, aimed at the spot where I had seen the flash, must have found its mark at the same moment.

Ritchie rushed the car, his automatic in the firing position, but no more shots were fired from the interior.

'It's all right,' he called to me, after a moment. 'One of them is still alive, but he's in no shape to fight.'

It was Bogart. He was slumped in the driving seat, blood dribbling from his nose and mouth. His chest had been crushed against the steering wheel, and his face had been slammed down onto the top of its rim. One leg, perhaps two, were broken, tele-scoped by the collision.

'God, my legs,' he was groaning. 'For Christ's sake, help me.'

'We'll help you, all right,' Ritchie promised him in a friendly, conversational tone which for some reason froze my blood. 'You help us and we'll help you. That's fair, isn't it?'

The girl in the passenger seat beside him was dead. She was the one who had encouraged him to let me have it in the bollocks when they'd jumped us in the lane at Sedbergh. Her eyes and mouth were wide open and there was just enough room for me to see the gap where a front tooth was missing. One of our bullets had found its way to her cold, cold heart.

Back up the track the heat of the burning car had set fire to a pile of logs at the side of the track. The flames were already reaching up towards the branches of the nearest fir trees. Soon we would have a full-scale forest fire on our hands. I had per-formed two 'bootlegger's turns', which are all in the day's work to anyone trained in protective driving, and the results were horrendous.

'Let's get away from here,' Ritchie said. 'We'll talk to him back at that farm we passed. Can you give me a hand with him?'

Only then did I realize there was blood on his left shoulder. 'You've been hit. I'd better get a dressing on that wound.'

'Later.' He brushed the suggestion aside. 'I'm not losing much blood. Let's move our friend down the road first.'

Bogart was hollering and cursing as we dragged him from the wrecked car and put him in the back of the Turbo. I had to use our own car as a bulldozer to shift the other vehicle out of the way. The Saab shouldered it between two piles of timber and I saw it roll over into a dip beyond. We moved off down the track and as we turned a corner the orange glow of the holocaust was left behind. I hit a few switches to test my lighting equip-ments. The two spot-lamps and one headlamp had gone in the

207

collisions but I still had my off side beam and that was quite sufficient to drive on.

At the deserted farmhouse I stopped, the one headlamp directed at what had once been the front door. Between us we lifted Bogart out of the car.

'Lay him on the grass in the light,' Ritchie directed.

The man's face screwed up with pain as we moved him but he gave a sigh of relief as we put him down on the patch of grass in front of the house.

'Now, then,' Ritchie began, in the same casual tone. 'Are you going to tell us where she is?'

'Where who is?'

'You heard me. The girl. Where is she being held? We know it's not the hideout in Aberhosen. That has already been raided by the police.'

Bogart's face became wary. The man was in severe pain but he had plenty of guts.

He said: 'I don't know where she is.'

'I see,' Ritchie's voice was soft. 'So it's going to be like that, is it?'

'Get stuffed,' said Bogart.

Ritchie gave him a long, measuring look. Then he turned to me. 'Pat, you've got a jump-start outfit in the tool-kit, haven't you?'

'Yes. What do you need that for?'

'You'd be surprised how persuasive a jolt can be – even from a twelve volt battery.'

I watched him open the hatchback of the Saab and grope inside it. From the forest behind us the reflected glow of the fire was increasing. I tried not to think of the faces I had seen behind the blackening glass of the burning car, the bleeding fingers scrabbling at the doors, the gaping, screaming mouths. Ritchie had found the twin wires, each with its crocodile clip at either end. He moved to the door of the Turbo, reached in to release the bonnet catch. Then he bent over the engine compartment, attached one wire to the positive terminal of the battery and the other to the negative. His movements were purposeful but awkward. A thick stream of blood was oozing down his arm, turning the sleeve of his shirt scarlet.

208

He tested his equipment out by touching the crocodile clips attached to the free ends of the wires on the body of the car. A series of brilliant sparks cascaded from them with a vicious crackling and hissing noise. Bogart was trying to drag himself away towards the empty farmhouse on his forearms and elbows. He was gibbering with fear.

'Cut his trousers off,' Ritchie told me. Then he grinned. 'But do please take care not to hurt his legs.'

I went down on one knee beside Bogart. The whole thing had begun to sicken me.

I said: 'Why don't you tell us where she is? You will in the end, I can promise you.'

'I don't know, I tell you,' he gasped. His eyes rolled towards Ritchie. 'She went with Cheloui.'

He had slurred the name and I was certain that I had misheard him.

'What? What did you say?'

'Cheloui took her. For God's sake keep that bugger away from me!'

'What do you mean, she went with Cheloui?'

'After the kidnapping performance. We met up with him and he took her in his own car. I don't know where they went.'

I shook my head, but not in disbelief. What Bogart was telling me was incredible but I did not think that he was in the mood to feed me any lies.

'Was she – was she still tied up?'

'No. Why should she have been?'

I sat back on my heels. The forest seemed to rock against the orange-tinted sky.

'You must know where they went,' I insisted, grabbing his arm again and shaking him.

The man's eyes kept veering towards Ritchie, who was extracting showers of angry sparks from his crocodile clips. The suggestive effect was horrible and I could feel Bogart's body shivering under my grip. I never knew whether the former mercenary really meant to put a current through his victim or whether his firework demonstration was merely staged for its moral effect.

'No, I don't.' Bogart told me urgently. 'Cheloui worked on the "need to know" principle. If we didn't have to know about some part of the operational plan he did not tell us. Romy asked him where he was taking her and he made a reply I could not understand.'

'What did he say?'

'It was in Arabic. All I could make out was some crack about putting ham in it. Jesus, my legs!'

'Putting ham in it?'

'That's what it sounded like. I can't tell you any more, I swear it.'

His voice rose hysterically. He had seen Ritchie turn towards him, the free ends of the wires in his hands. He was being careful to hold the crocodile clips well away from each other. With blood pouring down his arm he was not a reassuring sight. Bogart cringed away, clawing at the grass with his hands in an animal attempt to escape.

'It's all right, Ritchie,' I said. 'You can put your toy away. He's told me all I need to know.'

CHAPTER 13

The old gate in the long white wall which surrounded the grounds of the Villa Celeste was open. The gate in the security fence was closed but it was not locked and the electric current was switched off. I got out of the hired car to open it and did not bother to close it behind me as I drove on up the avenue. The water sprinklers were still irrigating the Bermuda grass and beyond the white villa I could see the waters of the Mediterranean shimmering in the afternoon sunlight. I halted the car in front of the doors behind which the Phantom II had stood for half a century, switched the engine off and stepped quietly out.

There was no sound except the calling of cicadas and the faint gurgle of water from a leak in one of the hose-pipes. It was the hot part of the afternoon when all sane folk are having a siesta – or a swim.

In the small hours of that morning I had deposited Ritchie at the Casualty department of Cardiff hospital so that they could dig the bullet out of his shoulder and sew him up. He had promised to give me three hours' start before contacting Bannerman and telling him what had happened. We had set and roughly splinted Bogart's legs, and left him in the abandoned farmhouse to await arrest. I had used all of the Turbo's new-found power and speed to barrel down the M4, collect my passport from the flat in Kensington and race out to Heathrow in time to catch a dawn flight to Paris. At Le Bourget I had boarded an Air France plane to Tunis which landed me at El Aouina just after lunchtime.

I had not told even Ritchie where I was going. He would have tried to dissuade me. I knew that I was in the grip of something not very different from a death-wish. Doubtless, if I had not been in the aftermath of a week of acute tension, which had culminated in a half-hour of explosive and horrific action, I might have studied the situation more calmly. Maybe there was a remnant of pride in me which would not accept the fact that I had let myself be led so blindly up a most beguiling garden path. A hundred questions thronged my mind but there was a particular one to which I had to have the answer. And in my present state of mind it did not matter over much to me if I perished getting it.

As I walked round the verandah I heard the sound of voices from the direction of the swimming pool. I could easily have believed that the events of the past two weeks had never occurred, that I had moved back in time to my first visit to the Villa Celeste. I stopped in the shadow of the bougainvillaea, looking down at the pool. I had been moving very quickly for the past twelve hours and I needed a moment to steady myself before this final confrontation.

All three of them were there. Aziz Cheloui was wearing a snazzy pair of bathing trunks but the women were as I had seen them first – in the state that nature intended. The waters of the pool were stirring and slapping at the edge. Their bodies were still glistening. Cheloui had poured a long drink into three glasses. He handed one to his wife. She had lain back on a sun-bathing couch, her heavy breasts flattened by their own weight. Romy was towelling herself, her beautiful golden body moving pliantly against the rough material. I could see the breath-taking sweep of her back. It was innocent of any weals.

I knew that someone had come silently round the verandah behind me. I did not turn. I began to walk down the steps to the pool.

Romy saw me first. She froze. Her hand flew to her lips and she stifled an exclamation. The other two saw her movement and looked up. Madame Cheloui instinctively clasped her arms over her naked breasts. Cheloui stiffened into alertness and then relaxed. His eyes had gone past me to the person who was following me down the steps.

They watched and waited in silence till I had reached the flagstones surrounding the pool. I stopped there and turned round. Ahmed had halted ten steps above me. He was holding a shotgun at waist level. It was aimed at my stomach. I knew that if he fired at that range the shot would make mincemeat of me.

'So Ahmed got back all right,' I said. 'I'm glad about that.'

Nobody offered any reply. Romy was the first to find her voice, but her words were so low as to be almost inaudible.

'How did you know to come here?'

'Bogart told me you had gone with Cheloui. The only word he picked up from your conversation was Hammamet. But it was enough. When I heard that the penny dropped.'

She shook her head in bewilderment. I switched my gaze to Cheloui.

'Your operation has folded. Two of your people are in police hands, another is in a prison hospital and three more are dead. They did you proud.'

'They were expendable.' One corner of Cheloui's lower lip sagged. 'We have learnt invaluable lessons from that operation. Next time we will not make the same mistakes.'

I took a chance and moved a couple of paces nearer to the group. Cheloui's attitude immediately sharpened. He quickly raised a hand in warning, his sharp eyes searching the verandah behind me.

'Keep your distance!' he rapped out. 'Ahmed only needs one nod from me.'

He barked a few words of Arabic to the old chauffeur and received a brief reply. His gaze came back to me, cruel and mocking.

'I think you are the one who has made the biggest mistake of all.'

'Oh, I realize that my chances of walking away from here are slim, but there was something I had to find out. It is very important to me.'

Cheloui misunderstood me, even though I had been looking at Romy as I made the last remark.

'Ask all the questions you want,' he invited me sneeringly. 'You are one person I do not mind entrusting with the truth.'

Romy had turned away and was moving towards a chair in the vine-shaded arbour on to which she had tossed her bathing-wrap. I wanted to be able to see her face when I asked my question. More to gain time than because I thought the knowledge would be of any use to me I decided to take Cheloui up on his offer.

'There is something that has been bothering me. I appreciate that IMAG is motivated by the highest ideals. How did you come to get mixed up with a common dope trafficker like Varzi?'

'So you know about IMAG!' Cheloui inspected me with fresh interest. I must have been a strange sight, with a patch still over my right eye, a plastic tooth and a nose badly out of alignment. I was still wearing the same trousers as on my first visit and they were beginning to look very second-hand. 'Then you must know also that we are a new movement. We have no links with existing terrorist organisations – the I.R.A., the Bader-Meinhoff, the Brigate Rosse. We cannot dispose of the kind of funds they have. It was necessary for us to use Varzi because only in that way could we gain possession of the heroin and the capital reserve we need.'

Romy was tying the belt of the wrap round her waist. Out of the corner of my eye I saw Madame Cheloui reach for a towel lying under her couch.

'So you persuaded him that the journey of the Rolls and Saab to England provided a heaven sent opportunity to run a larger consignment of heroin to England. Ahmed was encouraged to stow away in the Rolls so that my arrest in Naples would be certain. Then, when you knew the heroin was on the Saab, you disposed of Varzi and his people and took over the whole operation. Did you know that Romy and I were damn nearly killed in your massacre at the Bella Napoli?'

'Romy told me about it.' Cheloui had the grace to look ashamed of himself. 'Of course, we had no idea you were there at the time. If you had been killed it would have invalidated the whole plan.'

I noticed that his English was a good deal more polished than on my previous visit to the Villa. It was hard to believe that his recent sojourn in the sceptred isle had given it such an Oxonian flavour.

'The trouble with your plan,' I told him, 'was that you over-complicated everything. The best plan is always a simple one.'

'I hope you do not think that it was I who planned an operation so full of flaws.' Cheloui bent to a low table, took a cigarette from a red Benson & Hedges tin and rapidly lit it. He inhaled deeply. 'Varzi always tended to over-dramatise, over-complicate. But I had to make the best use of the situation as I found it. I admit that things became a little confused before I was able to fly to England to take over.'

214

The thirty-four hours I had gone without sleep were beginning to tell on me. The sun was beaming down on my bare head and waves of heat were beating up from the flagstones. Cheloui had thrust his feet into a pair of slippers to prevent the hot stone from scorching them. Just for a moment my vision blurred and I saw mirages between myself and the Mediterranean.

'But you'd had the foresight to put a bug on the Saab,' I said, forcing myself to concentrate. This was the one thing that had not made sense, my only real grounds for believing that Romy might not have totally deceived me. 'I cannot see why that was necessary when you had arranged for your personal spy to accompany me.'

Cheloui smiled and his eyes followed mine. Conscious of her appearance even at a moment like this, Romy was running a comb through her marvellous long hair.

'Romy was an additional insurance policy, but I took good care that she knew nothing about the operation. Her main usefulness was to persuade you to take the Saab. I suggested to her that if she could also win your affections it would be very helpful to my purposes. And so it turned out.'

'She obeyed your instructions very expertly.' I was forcing Romy to meet my eyes. 'It was a brilliant performance. Especially during the time we were in Sedbergh.'

'I was not acting then.' Her voice was low, her lips trembling. She kept glancing fearfully at the menacing figure of Ahmed behind me. 'At first I was not being sincere. I admit that. Here at the villa and on the ship I lied to you. But then things began to change. That evening in Naples when you had saved my life and we went back to . . . then the night in London at your flat after they had tried to kill you.' She glared angrily at Cheloui. 'That was when I told Aziz that I would not act any more as his spy. And when we were on the hills together I knew that there could be no going back.'

She could not know how desperately I wanted to believe her, but there was still far too much to be explained. Madame Cheloui was following the conversation with an intent expression, trying to guess from our faces what was being said.

'But when they needed tapes and photographs to soften me up

you were ready and able to co-operate. What about the tooth? I'd hate to think of you losing a tooth.'

The sarcasm was strong in my voice. She winced as if I had slapped her face. Cheloui laughed again and answered for her.

'The tooth was Vanessa's. We had you to thank for that idea. You knocked it out during the fight.'

'You must understand that I had no choice,' Romy besought me urgently. 'It was not so very different from a real kidnapping. I refused to make the tapes and pose for the photographs, but they forced me.'

'But they did not have to whip you.'

'No. They marked me with my lipstick.'

I thought of what I had gone through because of those tapes and photographs. Something must have shown on my face. I saw two worry lines crease her forehead between her eyes.

'Still,' I said bitterly. 'It was good enough to fool me. But as you once observed, I don't know much about women.'

I saw the pain in her eyes before she closed them. I had not come with the intention of hurting her, yet here I was lashing her with my tongue. The two Chelouis were listening with an odd intentness, as if they felt personally involved in the exchange between Romy and me.

'You must try to understand,' she repeated, with the same low-voiced insistence. 'I had no choice. He forced me to do it.'

I had walked into this situation with my eyes wide open, because I had to find the answer to these questions, even if it was the last thing I did. I knew now, as I looked into Romy's face, that the truth was there for me to read. And for the first time since Bogart had blurted out his statement the desire to go on living had returned.

I swivelled my head through forty-five degrees, just enough to confirm that Ahmed was still standing there, covering me with the shot-gun.

I said: 'What I can't understand is how you let him get this extraordinary hold over you. Would it not have been easier to go to the police and tell them the truth about Madame de Sonis?'

Romy raised her chin. She switched her gaze from me to Cheloui. There was defiance as well as fear in her face.

'I am going to tell him,' she said in a voice that was suddenly strong.

Cheloui shrugged and threw down his cigarette. He barked an order at Ahmed, who moved down two steps.

Romy glanced at Madame Cheloui, then faced me squarely.

'That story was invented to gain your sympathy. The real Miss Favel was disposed of days before you ever appeared. I took her place. It was easy for me. Aziz had given me a good education. He had plans to use me for his own purposes.'

'Aziz had given you – . Now, wait! I don't understand – .'

'I was born illegitimate.' She cut in on me. 'Aziz married my mother and adopted me. This is my foster father.'

I stared with incredulity at the older woman. 'Madame Cheloui is your mother?'

At last I had an explanation for the scene of tenderness and affection which I had witnessed when I first looked down on the two women beside the swimming pool. The difference in their ages could not be more than thirteen or fourteen years, but in an Arab country, where child brides are commonplace, that was quite enough. I knew now what was the cause of that indefinable tension which was always in the air when these three were together. It was the hatred which had built up in the heart of mother and daughter against the man who had imposed himself as their lord and master for so many years. And I also knew, as certainly as if I had heard it on oath from his own lips, that Cheloui was impotent and had acquired the baby in order to conceal that fact from the world.

Madame Cheloui, silent as she always was, provided the key to the whole situation. She had correctly interpreted my wide-eyed stare and met it with an unwavering steadiness. It was time to bring her into the conversation, for at that moment an important realization had dawned on me. I summoned up my memories of French.

'Madame does not speak English?' Her response to my addressing her directly was immediate. Her face lit up with animation and I felt an extraordinarily strong rapport with her as she beamed the full concentration of her dark eyes on me. 'You have not understood our conversation?'

'A little,' she replied in her slightly accented French. 'A few words, that is all.'

'It is true that you are the mother of Romy?'

'Yes. It is true. And you must believe – '

'A moment.' I held up my hand. Cheloui had become more wary since I had switched to French, and I could sense that Ahmed's interest had also intensified. The hairs on the back of my head stiffened. I knew that one sign from Cheloui would tighten the old Arab's finger on the trigger. 'I have a question for you, Madame,' I said, still picking my words carefully in French. 'Since Romy was not the person who caused Madame de Sonis's death it has to be someone else. Was it Aziz Cheloui?'

There was dead silence, broken only by the slapping of the waves in the overflow vents of the swimming pool. For the first time Cheloui's composure was shaken. He fired an angry command in Arabic to his wife. But this time she did not cringe. She flung a defiant reply back at him and his brow darkened.

It was Romy, speaking her much more accomplished French, who answered my question.

'Yes. It was Aziz who poisoned Madame. He wanted to use the villa for his own revolutionary purposes and he could not wait for her to die.'

In the hush that followed I could feel that an essential change had come over the whole situation, but I could not define what it was. I only knew that in an instant Cheloui had become totally isolated.

Then the sunlit afternoon was split by a deafening detonation. I was rocked by the blast of the shot as it sliced past me. Cheloui's suntanned body was picked up by a whirlwind of lead and punched clean off the flagstones into the swimming pool. As the scarlet-stained splash subsided he was already sinking in a welter of blood and mangled flesh.

Madame Cheloui was the first to recover her senses. She rose swiftly and ran to her daughter, putting an arm round her and forcibly twisting her head away from the obscene thing in the swimming pool. Old Ahmed had already fled, throwing the gun down and scrambling up the steps. As he disappeared round the side of the villa a woman began screaming on a high-pitched note from behind the bougainvillaea. It was Fatima, who had been watching the whole scene from the concealment of the shrub.

I was still standing on the same hot flagstone, readjusting my mind to the fact that it was not I but Cheloui who had been marked for death that day.

The Tunisian woman spoke a short sentence in Arab to her daughter. She pushed her towards me.

'Take her,' she commanded me in her slightly guttural French. 'Take her away quickly. What has happened here was written in the stars long ago. It has nothing to do with you.'

Romy, white with shock, held back, hesitating to entrust herself to me. She searched my face, trying to read there what my response would be.

'Take her,' the mother insisted for the third time. 'It is true that she loves you. A real love of the heart. I am her mother and I know. Now, go quickly or it will be too late.'

I reached a hand towards Romy. She turned for a last look at her mother, whose face was composed but already resigned to a great sorrow. Then, with a shuddering glance at the horror in the pool, she came to me.

Twenty miles north of Naples I turned off the Autostrada at an exit which led towards the blue mountains of the Appenines. The long, majestic bonnet of the Phantom II stretched ahead of me. The big steering wheel vibrated lithely in my hands, the great engine propelled the noble vehicle along at a whispering sixty miles an hour. I made a slight adjustment to the advance and retard lever on the steering column, checked the oil pressure and water temperature gauges and consulted the clock. The time was ten thirty on a glorious morning. The sun was so hot that we had moved the sliding roof forward over the front two seats.

'I still don't understand how we got away with it so easily,' Romy said.

I turned in my seat to admire her profile yet again. It was forty-two hours since we had fled from the Villa Celeste and I was still waiting for her to recover from the numbing shock of that terrible final scene. Her face was pale but I thought she had never looked more beautiful or more desirable.

'The green light was on from the moment Lionel checked with

the Foreign Office,' I explained. 'Ritchie and I are the blue-eyed boys of Interpol and the Customs Co-operation Council. Thanks to us they've made one of their biggest killings to date in the drug-smuggling and terrorist field. And it was a good thing I hadn't bothered to change my trousers. The key of the Rolls was still in the fob pocket.'

From the high seats of the Rolls we could see far more of the countryside than from a modern car. A field of brilliant sun-flowers, their brown faces framed in yellow petals, swam past on our left. Beyond, a long line of dark-green tapering cypresses marked the driveway to a farm.

I said: 'Do you feel ready to talk about it yet? There's two things I've been wanting very badly to ask you.'

Romy took her eyes off the road ahead and really smiled at me for the first time since that morning on the hills above Sedbergh.

'It's all right. I feel better now. But please don't go back to what we talked about at the Villa Celeste. What my mother told you was the truth.'

'I believe that. What I don't understand is, why did Ahmed do it?'

'You have not realized?' Romy exclaimed in surprise. 'He worshipped Madame de Sonis. After her death he grieved for days. When you spoke in French to Maman he understood, and when Aziz could not deny that it was he who had poisoned her – '

'I understand now. Ahmed was simple, but he had great in-tegrity. He would have found it hard to forgive Cheloui for using him as a pawn in his plans. And one more thing. What happened to the real Miss Favel?'

'She disappeared soon after Madame's death. Maman and I were sure Aziz had something to do with it but we never found out what happened to her.'

I nodded without great conviction. There were a dozen more questions in my mind but they would have to wait. Perhaps I would never know the answers to them all and I was not really sure that I wanted to. A great part of Romy's fascination lay in the mystery she held for me and if I ever learned all there was to know about her that fascination might vanish.

'No more questions?'

'Perhaps one. Romy. Is that your real name?'

'It is part of it. My name is Faromyl, with the stress on the O. But I've been called Romy since I was quite small.'

A Fiat full of young men went past us, all of them, including the driver, craning their necks and gesticulating at the Rolls. Romy laughed as they nearly lurched into a ditch before accelerating away towards the tawny village down the road ahead.

'You know, Patrick, you can be quite mysterious yourself. You have not told me where we are going.'

'I have not told you for the very good reason that I don't know. I'm just following where the Spirit of Ecstasy leads.'

'The Spirit of Ecstasy?' Romy bent forward, peering into my face to judge whether I was being serious or not.

I pointed to the emblem which has graced the bonnet of every Rolls-Royce ever made: the silver lady leaning eagerly forward into the wind, with flowing draperies shaped round her body by the speed of her flight.